Book 3 in the Amber Ridge Series

untouched

NYSSA KATHRYN

UNTOUCHED
Copyright © 2025 Nyssa Kathryn Sitarenos

All rights reserved.

An NW Partners Book
Cover by Deranged Doctor Design
Developmentally and Copy Edited by Kelli Collins
Line Edited by Jessica Snyder
Proofread by Amanda Cuff and Jen Katemi
Cover Photography by Briquelle Kayanne Photography

❀ Created with Vellum

He's scared to live and to love...she's scared not to.

Five years ago, Clara Hayes got the diagnosis no one wants: cancer. She fought it. And she won. But that diagnosis changed everything. Now, she has one goal...to live. Without fear. Without hesitation. Or at least without fear and hesitation when it comes to anything other than her brother's best friend, Holden. She's loved him for as long as she's known him. And now that he's moved to Amber Ridge, she knows needs to take a chance on him, even if ends in heartache.

Holden Forbes knows what loss feels like. It touched his life in a way that changed him. He's tried to move on. Joined the military. Became a member of a dangerous Ghost Ops team in the military. Now he lives in the small town of Amber Ridge with his best friend, Jesse. But Amber Ridge doesn't just have Jesse...it has his sister, Clara. Beautiful, resilient Clara. A woman who'd be easy to love. A woman he *wants* to love. A woman who could ruin him.

When questions start being raised about Clara's roommate, dangerous questions, Holden gets closer. He tells himself it's just to keep Clara safe, but every day that passes, makes that lie a little more obvious. It doesn't take long for the danger to heat up, and as it does, Holden realizes, that it's too late to run, and losing Clara, is no longer an option...or maybe it never was.

ACKNOWLEDGMENTS

As always, I have to thank my incredible team of editors and proofreaders—Kelli, Jessica, Amanda and Jen, you ensure my book gets out to the world in its best form. Thank you.

Thank you to my beautiful ARC team for reading, reviewing and filling me with confidence before I send my book baby into the world.

And thank you to my beautiful husband and two amazing daughters—every day I am reminded of how lucky I am to have you.

PROLOGUE

hree years ago

COOL AIR BRUSHED over Clara Hayes's cheeks as the music boomed around her.

She'd been to so many of these Amber Ridge street parties. One a year since she was born. Well, except for the ones she'd missed while she lived in New York.

"It still hasn't sunk in that Monday's my first shift at Amber Ridge Hospital. I've wanted this for so long."

She nodded absentmindedly at Malcolm's words. She'd needed a moment to sit and rest, because even though she hated to admit it, the chronic fatigue often weighed her down if she exerted herself. Malcolm had joined her, sitting at the small table beside her. They'd gone to high school together, and he'd just moved back to Amber Ridge to work at the local hospital as a doctor.

She should be paying more attention to him. But most of her focus was on something else...or *someone* else.

Holden. He stood beside a taco truck, beer in hand, talking to one of her older brothers, Jesse. They were both home on leave from the military. They were best friends. *Had been* best friends since joining the same dangerous Ghost Ops team. Now Holden was basically family.

At least, everyone else saw him as family. Not her. Not in the same capacity that she saw her brothers, anyway.

Suddenly, Holden's hazel eyes caught hers, making the breath freeze in her lungs.

One side of his mouth lifted, showing a signature dimple.

She gave him a small smile before quickly looking away. Did he see the pink of her cheeks? The widening of her eyes?

Probably.

God, she'd become so fearless in every other aspect of her life. Why not with him?

Sure, he was a gazillion feet of gorgeous, with the broadest shoulders she'd ever seen. And he was kind and funny, and whenever she heard his voice, every hair on her arms stood on end.

But she was a grown-ass woman, dammit. A grown-ass woman who'd gone through a lot in her nearly twenty-seven years. She shouldn't be blushing like a schoolgirl every time he glanced her way.

Twenty-seven. Man, she was getting closer to that big thirty, an age that once upon a time she hadn't known if she'd reach. She'd done a lot in the last couple years, but she definitely hadn't experienced everything she wanted to experience.

Sex. She hadn't had sex. *Argh.*

Why? Because she'd always been too busy building her career as a lawyer. Then she'd gotten her diagnosis and moved back home.

Was that pathetic? To be twenty-seven years old and still a virgin?

"Were you treated at the Amber Ridge Hospital?"

Her attention snapped back to Malcolm. "What?"

"Hodgkin's lymphoma, right? Were you treated here or in New York? I know there's an oncologist who splits his time between here and Bozeman, but I wasn't sure if you moved back before or after treatment."

People rarely mentioned her cancer, usually because they didn't know what to say beyond offering their sympathy and looking at her with pity. It was kind of refreshing that Malcolm had brought it up himself.

"I came back to do my chemotherapy here. I wanted to be close to Mom. I wanted to be home."

Once upon a time, the word cancer had felt big and scary. But now? Now it was just a part of her story.

Malcolm nodded. "Your hair looks nice."

Her hand twitched to reach up and touch her short blonde locks. A few years ago, she'd had long, thick hair. And even though it was growing back, it wasn't as thick or soft as it had been.

But she was alive. Not just alive—she'd kicked cancer's ass and become stronger for it. "Thanks."

"Can I ask you something personal?"

She frowned. Asking about her cancer had already been personal. "Depends on what it is."

"Did being diagnosed change your perspective on life?"

She could have laughed. "It changed my entire world—mind, body and soul. I don't think it's possible to hear a doctor tell you that you have stage four Hodgkin's lymphoma and remain the same person."

Malcolm leaned forward, seeming genuinely intrigued. "*How* did it change?"

"It made me realize that tomorrow isn't guaranteed. I was living like I had forever, working a job I didn't like because of the prestige. Living in a city that was too busy and loud. Always thinking I was building toward the life I wanted. Then the doctor told me I was sick and all I could think was—what am I doing? I could die tomorrow. I should be living the life I want *now*."

"So you came home."

"Yep. I'm studying acupuncture and I love it. I'm living on my terms."

"That's brave."

It *was* brave. *She* was brave. So why was she a twenty-seven-year-old virgin staring at her crush, too scared to tell him how she felt?

Her gaze shifted to her cousin Indie, who was wrapped in her husband's arms. They looked happy. Sure, they had issues, but they loved each other. She wanted that. She wanted to experience a love—*feel* a love—so fierce that it made her feel alive every day.

Well, she wouldn't get that by sitting over here watching Holden from beneath her lashes. She needed to put herself out there.

"Malcolm, I need to go talk to someone." She stood and moved to walk away, but Malcolm was suddenly on his feet.

"Wait—"

She turned back at the same moment he stepped forward, and his drink hit her in the chest, cool liquid immediately seeping into the thin material of her cropped sweater.

Malcolm's jaw dropped. "Oh, Jesus, Clara. I'm *so* sorry." He turned and grabbed a handful of napkins that had already been on the table when she'd sat down, and started dabbing her top.

She gasped. "Malcolm, stop. I'm okay."

He dabbed one more time before strong fingers suddenly wrapped around Malcolm's wrist. "What the hell are you doing?"

Her body locked at his deep, raspy voice.

Holden.

His familiar cedar scent tinged the air, making her belly give a little kick. And when she looked up, she saw his deep hazel eyes were narrowed on Malcolm.

Malcolm's mouth opened and closed. "I'm trying to dry her sweater."

"By pawing my sister's chest?" Jesse growled.

Oh God, now there were two of them.

The cool liquid began to slip down her belly, touching the top of her jeans. *Yuck.*

"Holden, Jesse, it's fine. I've got a spare sweater in the car. I'll go change."

She turned and walked through the crowd, the wet material getting more uncomfortable by the second.

As she passed Indie, her cousin grabbed her arm. "Hey. Are you okay?"

Her husband, Colt, shifted his gaze from her to Malcolm like he was a step away from joining Jesse and Holden.

"Yeah, I just need a new top." Not entirely true; she could also use a shower.

Indie stepped away from Colt. "I'll come with you."

Clara shook her head. "No, stay with Colt. He has to go back to California tomorrow. My car's just around the corner anyway."

Indie frowned but nodded.

She moved through the crowd again, the heels of her boots clicking against asphalt. When she reached her car, she searched her back seat for the spare she kept there.

Crap, where was it? She always kept a spare sweater in here. Hell, she usually had half her wardrobe in her back seat.

Then she remembered…the big cleanout last week.

Damn her spontaneous need to clean.

She straightened and turned—only to scream at the sudden sight of a large chest right in front of her.

"Whoa, Clara, it's me."

"Holden?" Air whooshed out of her. "Jesus freaking Christ, if hearts could jump out of bodies, mine would be on the ground."

His lips didn't so much as twitch. "Sorry. I didn't like you being out here by yourself."

"Unless a grizzly bear makes his way into town, I'd say I'm pretty safe in Amber Ridge."

"You can never be too safe."

Despite the cool evening air, warmth crept up her throat. He'd always been protective. From her brothers, she'd found it smothering, but with Holden, she felt a mixture of nervousness and comfort.

"I'm okay. Just sticky." Sticky? Jesus, she was always so awkward in front of him. "And unfortunately, I don't have a spare sweater, because clean Clara decided to take the spare out of the car."

"Here." He pulled his hooded sweatshirt over his head and handed it to her.

"No." No, no, no. She could not take that. It would smell like him, and then *she'd* smell like him, and she'd be so distracted when she finally drove home that she'd probably crash her car. "You'll be cold."

"I'll survive."

"I'm not—"

"Please." He held it out. "It will make me feel better. You'll be doing me a favor."

Her lips curved. "Well, if it's for you…"

"It is."

She took it from his hand, their fingers grazing and a tingle running up her arm. He turned to give her privacy.

Thoughtful. She could add that to the list of perfect things about him.

She switched the wet cropped sweater for his oversized hoodie…then he was everywhere. His scent. His warmth. It surrounded her.

"Thank you."

He turned back to her and frowned. "Where's your necklace?"

She absently touched her bare chest, where her amethyst necklace used to sit. It had been a gift to herself after chemo. The gem signified growth and transformation.

"I went bungee jumping in the Crooked River Gorge in Oregon last month. I forgot to take it off before I jumped." Stupid.

His brows flickered. He didn't say it but she could tell he didn't approve. No one did. Any time she did anything remotely dangerous, she had a million voices in her ear.

"I'm sorry."

She lifted a shoulder. "It's just a stone."

"Come on. I'll walk back with you."

She stepped beside him. "Tell me the truth—I look like a guy with my baggy hoodie and short hair, don't I?"

He looked at her, and even in the darkness, the way he scanned her body made electricity shoot through her system.

"You look beautiful."

Butterflies—they took off in her belly. Hundreds of them.

The nerves suddenly sped up her heart, making her tongue-tied and her head feel heavy and completely empty of any smart or witty comebacks.

Her gaze moved to the street party, then to Holden again.

Now, the voice whispered in her head. *Tell him now.*

"Wait. Before we go back…" She touched his arm. He stopped. And the second his entire focus hit her, those dang nerves crawled around inside her, making her throat feel too tight to squeeze words out.

This man had supported her through chemo as much as her brothers. A million calls and texts checking in. Using all his leave to visit her between missions.

What if she told him and she lost him for it?

It's worth the risk. The voice inside her was loud and so sure.

Holden tilted his head. "Clara. You can tell me anything. We're family."

"That's actually the thing. You *are* family, but you're also not."
He frowned.

And she shook her head. "That isn't what I meant. I mean...I care about you."

"I care about you too."

"No. This is different. I..." One big breath. "I love you."

Silence. It hung in the air—thick, almost suffocating.

Holden's frown deepened.

"And not like a brother," Clara hurried to add. "I love you like count-down-the-days-until-you're-back-in-town kind of love. Get-nervous-when-you're-around kind of love." She glanced at his lips and lowered her voice. "Want-to-kiss-you-whenever-I-see-you kind of love."

There. She'd said it. The truth was out there in the world, and it was up to Holden to decide what to do with it.

* * *

CLARA'S WORDS hit Holden Forbes like a physical blow. They stole his breath and tipped him off-balance, as if the world had shifted beneath his feet.

"Clara..."

She inched closer, her soft palms pressing to his chest. "You don't have to say anything. I just needed you to know."

She needed him to know that she loved him...*love*. She said it like it was the easiest thing in the world. But it wasn't. Nothing about love was easy. It was messy and complicated and could bring a man to his knees.

Not much scared Holden, but love...it terrified him.

How was he supposed to vocalize all of that to Clara when she looked at him with those big indigo eyes though? Eyes he'd been hopelessly chained to for so damn long.

His chest rose and fell faster, and before he could stop

himself, words were slipping from his lips into the air. "You'd be so easy to love, Clara."

So easy that he could lose himself. And then what? What happened if she got hurt and sick or decided she just didn't love him anymore? Would his world be ripped from beneath his feet for the second time in his life?

"Holden—"

"That's why"—he forced himself to step back, letting her hands drop even though he craved her touch—"I should stay away from you. I'm sorry."

She frowned, confusion marring her features. A hint of tears began to glimmer in her eyes.

Fuck. Now he'd made her cry. He was hurting her just by being there. "I'm—"

"Don't. Don't say you're sorry for not loving me. You were honest. I appreciate that. Thank you for your sweatshirt. I'll wash it and get it back to you. But I should go." Then she spun and walked away, almost running from him back to her car.

A voice in his head told him to go after her. It was loud, a fucking shout in his ears.

But he couldn't. He physically couldn't get his feet to move.

So he just stood there—a damn coward, too scared to love her, and too weak to move on from his past.

CHAPTER 1

 *resent day*

CLARA TIPPED BACK HER HEAD, the warm shower soaking her waist-length blonde hair.

God, those post-run endorphins were good. How it had taken her almost thirty years to get into running, she had no idea. She should have started earlier. Of course, she wouldn't be winning any awards for her speed or endurance, but heck, she had no one to impress.

Plus, it was a good way to start her week.

For most people, Monday meant the first day of the work week. Not her. Not anymore, anyway. She had one thing on her to-do list today—buy pink peonies from Sassy Stems, the local florist.

Okay, two things, because she also needed an almond croissant from The Tea House as urgently as she needed air. God, even thinking about Mrs. Gerald's croissants made her stomach rumble.

When the water suddenly turned cold, she groaned.

Guess Scarlett's shower time had started, and Clara's was over.

Every time her roommate turned the water on in the other bathroom, *her* shower went cold. It was like the woman knew when she was in the shower and scheduled her own at the same freaking time.

They weren't friends by any means, but Scarlett was quiet and rarely home—two things that worked well for Clara, considering she had acupuncture clients coming in and out of her converted garage all day.

She stepped out of the shower and grabbed a towel. In her bedroom, she put on some loose, high-waisted beige pants and a tight white tee. Younger Clara had been all about tight, uncomfortable high fashion. Twenty-nine-year-old Clara? She was definitely a comfort-with-a-side-of-more-comfort girl.

Heck, even the fact that she used tinted moisturizer instead of applying a full face of makeup showed what a different person she was.

She was about to pull her long hair up into a messy bun when she stopped.

It had finally reached the pre-chemo length, and she loved it.

Down...definitely down.

In the kitchen, she grabbed a bottle of water from the fridge.

A printed article on the corner of the island caught her attention. Strange. Scarlett rarely left her stuff lying around. She lived and breathed her work as an investigative reporter, and when she wasn't out chasing a story, the woman was on her laptop or phone ninety percent of the time.

Clara lifted the piece of paper and scanned the title.

Thirty-Two-Year-Old Masseuse, Lauren Tabs, Suffers Fatal Heart Failure.

Thirty-two...it was so young for heart failure.

She scanned the article. The woman hadn't smoked. Hadn't

drunk alcohol. In the photo, she looked fit and healthy. She'd had no reported underlying medical conditions. She'd gone in for rotator cuff surgery.

How did a patient die of heart failure after rotator cuff surgery?

"What are you doing?"

Clara jumped and dropped the stapled pages to the island. "Scarlett. Hey."

Her roommate wore jeans and a blue tee. Her cute brown pixie cut and whimsical red-framed glasses did nothing to take away from the annoyed pinch of her brows.

"I just saw the article." She glanced at the papers, then back at Scarlett. "It's so sad."

"Did you know her?" Scarlett asked, lifting the papers and pushing them into her laptop bag.

"No, I never met her."

Scarlett kind of looked disappointed.

Clara cleared her throat. "Working today?"

"Researching."

Clara nodded, but she knew better than to ask *what* she was researching. She'd done that once and received a spiel about how investigative journalists don't share until their work is published.

"There's still that big crack in the floorboard in my room," Scarlett said, looking down at her phone. "I feel like I'm going to trip on it every time I move. And it squeaks. If you could fix it, that would be great. I'll see you later."

Scarlett turned and started toward the door.

Clara almost laughed. If there was a word for someone addicted to a job *and* devices, there would be a photo of Scarlett next to it in the dictionary.

"Bye," Clara called as she cracked open her bottle of water and lifted it to her lips.

Scarlett was halfway across the living room when she stopped and turned back. "Actually, before I go, I noticed that you run."

Clara lifted her brows. "I do…kind of. It's new." And this was the first time Scarlett had ever taken any interest in her life.

"Would you be interested in joining a running club with me?"

Clara could have choked on her water. "You want to join a running club together?"

Scarlett nodded. "Yeah. We're roommates, and we haven't spent a lot of time together. It could be fun."

True. They hadn't spent a lot of time together. But that was Scarlett's doing. Clara had *tried* to get to know her. "I didn't know there was a running club in Amber Ridge."

"Some people from the hospital just started it. They're called the Pulse Pounders." Then Scarlett did something Clara had never seen her do before. She smiled.

"Um…okay, sure. I love trying new things." And hanging out with Scarlett would most definitely be a new thing.

Scarlett straightened. "Great. It's Thursday morning at six. We'll drive in together."

Wait, what? Six?

She opened her mouth to take it back or ask if the start time was in any way negotiable, but Scarlett was already gone.

Six. Okay. She could do that. She might be half asleep during the run, but she'd survive.

She grabbed her phone and keys before heading out to her red Volkswagen Beetle.

As she pulled out of her driveway, her gaze caught on the cute bungalow across the road. It belonged to Mildred, the owner of Sassy Stems. It was actually how she'd developed her flower obsession. Live across the road from a florist and see her bringing home beautiful flowers long enough and an addiction would begin.

When she reached the florist's shop, she stepped in to see another lady already talking to Mildred, who was behind the counter.

"No, this is not what I ordered," the woman with short

bleached-blonde hair said. She wore a sleek pencil skirt and heels. "I asked for *deep blue* irises. These are light blue at best."

Mildred straightened, a lock of black hair falling into her eyes. "Ma'am, this is all that was available, and they look deep blue to me."

"Are you saying I'm lying?"

Clara peeked around the woman to see the most beautiful bouquet of irises she'd ever seen. And yes, they were most definitely a deep blue color.

The customer crossed her arms. "I'm not buying those."

Annoyance flared in Mildred's eyes. "Ma'am, I ordered these for you."

"Well, you should have ordered the right ones." Then the woman turned and stormed out, her shoulder brushing against Clara's.

Jesus. Someone woke up on the wrong side of the bed.

Mildred sighed and slid the bunch behind the counter. It was the first time Clara had seen the woman without a smile on her face.

"I'll take them."

Mildred's brows rose. "Oh, Clara, you don't need to do that. You like peonies."

"No, I like beautiful flowers that smell nice, and that bouquet fits the bill."

The smile returned to Mildred's face. "I'll discount them for you."

"You absolutely will not. They look like they're worth a lot. I'll pay whatever she was going to pay."

Mildred chuckled. "I won't let you do that. But I will wrap them up for you."

Clara looked over to the board to see Mildred's flower joke of the week.

Why did the tulip refuse to speak to the daisy? It was a little stalk-y.

Clara grinned. *This* was why she loved her town. Because

ninety-nine percent of locals were Mildreds and not whoever that rude customer had been.

Mildred turned. "Here you go. Oh, and Jesse came in the other day to buy your mom some flowers."

"He's always showing me and Becket up." She was half joking, of course. She reached across with her credit card to pay.

Mildred leaned forward and lowered her voice, even though there was no one else in the store. "He was with that cute friend of his."

Her skin tingled. She was talking about Holden.

Holden, who now lived in Amber Ridge.

Holden, the man she'd once declared her love and in front of whom she now became a nervous wreck.

"Really?" That was good. She kind of sounded unaffected.

"Mm-hmm. I would mention that your brother's cute too, but—"

"Nope. Don't do that. As their sister, it is my duty to profusely deny either of my big brothers being even mildly hot."

"Well, they're both madly in love and off the market now anyway."

It was true. In the last few months, Jesse had found Aspen, and Becket had found both Sky and Bella. Bella being the Chinese Crested dog they'd adopted. Which was a surprise in itself, seeing as Becket hated dogs.

"Here you go."

Clara grinned as she took the bouquet. "Thanks, Mildred. Have a lovely day. And I hope you don't get any more customers like the last one."

"Me too, Clara. Me too."

Clara stepped outside and smelled the flowers. Holy flaming God, they smelled good. Maybe irises would be her new peonies?

She was about to climb into the car to go get her croissant but stopped. It was a nice day. Why would she drive?

Flowers in hand, she walked, still smiling when she reached

16

The Tea House. That smile widened when she stepped inside because there, in the display case, was one almond croissant left…and it had her name on it.

She was halfway to the counter when Mrs. Gerald took out the croissant.

"*No.*" She'd meant to say that in her head, but the word just slipped out of her, along with any hope she had of eating the croissant.

Mrs. Gerald looked up and cringed. "Sorry, dear, I didn't know you were coming in. I just sold it."

She stopped at the counter. "To who?" Maybe she could bribe them into selling it to her. She probably had a twenty, or at least a ten, in her purse. Or maybe some coins, but hey, some people would do anything for free cash. Or maybe she could Venmo them?

"To me."

She gasped at the deep voice.

Before she could turn, a large figure came to stand beside her.

Then she looked way up into Holden's hazel eyes. "Hey." Her voice was breathy and nervous…everything she *didn't* want.

"Hey, Clara." That familiar smile stretched across his lips.

Had he gotten even prettier today? Because he looked prettier.

"I see you bought the last almond croissant." That was better. Less breathy and minimal heat to her cheeks.

"I did."

She nibbled her bottom lip. "You know, I *love* almond croissants."

"Really?"

"They've kind of become an obsession of mine." She eyed the cake display. "The rhubarb pie looks good."

"It does."

God, he was really going to make her ask? "What do you want for it?"

One side of his mouth lifted. "You're bribing me for my croissant?"

"Ten bucks."

"You really think I can be bought off so easily?"

"Fifteen." Did she have fifteen dollars? In her bank account, she did.

He chuckled before turning to Mrs. Gerald. "I'll change my order to pie. Clara can have the croissant."

"Just like that?"

"Just like that." He studied the flowers in her hands, a frown forming between his brows. "Are they from someone?"

"Yeah. Me."

For a moment she thought she saw relief in his eyes, but that couldn't be right.

He tilted his head. "I thought you liked peonies."

Her heart thumped. He knew her favorite flower? "I do. But there was a rude lady and Mildred looked sad, so I bought these."

"I have no idea how that led to you being the owner of those irises, but they look good in your hands."

"Thank you."

"Here you go," Mrs. Gerald said, setting pie and coffee in front of Holden and a sweet tea and almond croissant to go in front of her.

Clara grinned at the older café owner. "This is why I love you, Mrs. Gerald. You know me too well."

"Next Monday, I'll save you an almond croissant."

"You are my favorite person."

She paid and turned to see Holden still looking at her. And geez Louise, his gaze was intense.

"You look happy," he said quietly.

Why did that little comment make heat creep up her neck? "I am. I've got my flowers and thanks to you, my almond croissant. Heck, Scarlett even asked me to join a running club with her. It's a good day."

The smile dropped from his face. Shit. She'd forgotten about his reaction to her newfound hobby. Which was ridiculous, by the way.

"A running club? Is that a smart idea?"

Her back straightened, the nerves turning into something far more defensive. "Why wouldn't it be?"

"A running club will have seasoned runners in it. You'll feel pressured to keep up with them. You still get fatigued after being sick."

Okay. Butterflies in the belly had officially ceased. "I *know* what I went through, and I know my body. I'm very capable of monitoring my limits and stopping when I need to. I'll see you later, Holden." She turned to go but he gently gripped her arm, stopping her.

"Clara. I didn't mean to offend you. I'm just worried."

She swallowed. "I don't need you to worry. I can look after myself, Holden."

His brows twitched, but he released her arm and she walked out, wondering if she would always be the girl who'd had cancer to him. Whether that would forever be the lens through which he saw her.

CHAPTER 2

*H*olden's fingers were tight around the wheel of his truck.

A running club. She was joining a fucking running club. Why? She wasn't a runner. Sure, she'd started jogging about a month ago, but that was different. That was her going at her own pace and her own distance.

He should mind his own business. But he couldn't. Clara was his best friend's little sister. He cared about her. And yeah, he saw it as his responsibility to make sure she was okay.

He pulled up in front of his first appointment of the day—quoting cabinetry for a new kitchen install. He needed to get his fucking head on straight.

Not that he was desperate for the job. Since moving to Amber Ridge, he'd had plenty of work. So much that he'd had to turn jobs down. He did everything from built-in cabinetry to wooden tray tables, and it seemed that stuff was in high demand in Amber Ridge.

Which was great for him. Because working with wood was what he was good at. And he fucking loved it.

He was about to get out when his phone rang, Jesse's name flashing on the screen.

He answered on the second ring. "Hey, Jess."

"Holden. I haven't seen you in a few weeks. Just checking in."

"Sorry about that. I just finished a big job for Jonny Miller on Fifth. New closets for his bedroom."

"My best friend's too busy for me?"

He chuckled. "Says the town sheriff."

"Yeah, well, things have been quiet since the fire in the mountains, and I'm holding out for everything staying that way."

Holden's fingers tightened on the cell. Jesse's brother Becket's woman had almost died in that fire. And Becket had almost died trying to save her. Thank God, the person responsible was locked away now.

"It's always quiet until it's not. I'm sure you're ready for anything to come though." He tapped his fingers on the wheel, his mind going back to Clara. He shouldn't say anything, but when did he do anything he was supposed to do? "Did you know your sister's joining a running club?"

There was a short pause. "Since when?"

"Since her roommate asked her this morning."

"Her roommate? They're not friends. They don't even talk."

"Well, that changed this morning." He paused, watching the trees outside the car without really focusing on them. "She'll be okay, right?"

"Unfortunately, even if I thought she wouldn't be, she wouldn't listen to me."

She wouldn't listen to Holden either. The only people she seemed to listen to were her mother and cousin. All the men in her life had been labeled as overprotective…and yeah, that was usually accurate.

"Do you know when and where it is?" Jesse asked.

"No. I could ask." But he was almost certain he knew what response he'd get…and it wasn't what he wanted.

Jesse laughed, because yeah, he was thinking the same thing. "Let me know how that goes."

He undid his seat belt. "I should get on to this quote. I'll catch you later."

"Have a good one, Holden."

He climbed out of his truck, his fingers twitching to send the text. She wouldn't like it, and he was ninety-nine percent certain she wouldn't give him the information.

He sent the text anyway.

Holden: When and where is this running club?

The three dots popped up immediately.

Clara: No.

Holden: No what?

Clara: I am not telling you the details so you can show up and babysit me.

Holden: I wouldn't be babysitting you. I'd be running with you.

Clara: No.

Goddammit. Why did she have to be so stubborn?

Most of the time she was sweet and calm and, hell, she even got nervous around him. But the second she thought he was being overprotective, she got her back up.

He grabbed his toolbox from the back of his truck and crossed to the front door of the modern home. It had clean lines and a minimalistic design in contrast to the rustic charm of the surrounding homes. An exterior of smooth concrete and dark steel accents with large panels of glass.

He knocked on the wood and a second later, a woman opened the door. She had big blonde curls and wore a tight pencil skirt.

A smile immediately crossed her face. "Hi. Holden?"

"Yes, ma'am. I'm here to quote your kitchen cabinetry."

"Just Briar. Ma'am makes me feel old. Come in. I'm sorry if I look surprised. I was expecting to see some old guy with a potbelly."

He stepped into the house. There was a staircase with frame-less glass railings in front of him and molding on the walls. "Nice place."

"Thank you. I got it in my recent divorce." She led him down the hall to a sleek kitchen. The counters were topped with cool concrete, and the cabinets were painted black.

"This is the kitchen you want to renovate?" He ran his fingers over the countertop. Who the hell would rip this out?

"Yep. New divorce, new me."

It would be a crime to remove this.

Briar crossed her arms over her chest. "I really hope you're not going to tell me you can't do it. I've already had a dreadful morning at Sassy Stems. God, even the name of the store annoys me."

It seemed everyone had been to the florist that morning. "It's your kitchen, so you can do what you want with it."

"Good. Floor plan can stay the same. I just want white shaker cabinetry with rose gold hardware and the marble countertops."

"I can do the cabinetry, the demolition, and installation. You'll need to be the one to order in countertops though. I don't deal in marble or quartz."

Annoyance flickered on her face. "Fine."

Holden got out his tape measure and phone to start taking measurements.

Briar watched him move around her kitchen. "So...you're new in town?"

"Kind of. Moved here less than a year ago."

"Why'd you move here?"

"Jesse, the town sheriff, is my best friend. We served together. And his family's like my family." He sure as hell had no one else.

"Friends in high places. I like it. I've seen your friend a bit at the hospital when he comes in for sheriff stuff."

"You work at the hospital?"

"I do. I'm a nurse."

He nodded as he measured. "That would be a busy job."

"It is. Stressful too. Exactly why I wanted those irises for my work desk. Damn Mildred."

Holden frowned. "Irises?"

"Yeah. The woman ordered me the wrong color, then had the gall to tell me they were deep blue when they clearly weren't."

Okay, that couldn't be a coincidence. "So you left them."

"Of course I did. I told Mildred what I thought too."

And then Clara had bought them. Of course she had. She was the most empathetic person he knew, and she'd probably felt bad for Mildred, not just because Briar hadn't bought the flowers, but because of the way the woman had no doubt spoken to the older shop owner.

Briar's phone rang and she huffed before answering it. "Yes?"

Jesus, this woman wasn't exactly sunshine and roses.

"No," she said firmly. "The run starts at six sharp. If he's late, he misses it."

Holden's ears perked up.

She hung up and shook her head. "It's wild to me that one person thinks they can inconvenience an entire group of people. Consideration is well and truly dead."

She couldn't be talking about the same running club Clara had just told him about? Of course she could. That's how small Amber Ridge was.

"Was that about a running club?"

Her frown shifted into a smile. "Yes. We're called Pulse Pounders. My idea. A few of us from the hospital started the initiative. Mostly me."

"Are there other running clubs in Amber Ridge?"

"Nope. Exactly why we—I—started the club. I like to help. It's just who I am."

Surprising. This woman didn't have a do-gooder vibe, but then, he didn't really know her. "Can anyone join?"

"Of course. It's for the community." Her brows lifted. "Wait, you want to join?"

"When and where is it?"

"Thursday and Sunday mornings at six a.m. sharp. We meet in the center of town on the grassy area."

Clara would hate it if he showed up. But it would put his mind at ease. And if she needed to rest, he could rest with her. Hell, he could carry her back to her car if needed.

Chronic fatigue was something she'd suffered from since the chemo. When she pushed herself too hard, she was susceptible to passing out. Just a few weeks ago, she'd just about passed out at Jesse's house.

"Yeah, I think I'll join," he finally said.

Briar's smile widened. "Great. Well, I guess I'll see you there."

"I guess you will."

Over the next twenty minutes, he took the last of the measurements and finished his sketch. He also took some photos and asked Briar a couple more questions about what she wanted. He still wasn't sure about this whole ripping-out-a-perfectly-good-kitchen thing, but if there was anything he'd learned about woodworking, it was that people often requested jobs that weren't to his taste, and that was okay, because it wasn't for him.

He lifted his tools. "All right. I've got everything I need. I'll go home, draw up some plans, and send you a quote within the next week."

She nodded. "Sounds good."

He'd just gotten into his truck when his phone dinged with a text.

Jesse: My sister will hate me for this, but I think you're right. One of us should join this running club...just to be safe.

Holden: I'm a step ahead of you, brother. I've got the details. I'll let you know how it goes.

Jesse: This is why I like you.

He put his phone in the middle console and started the truck.

He was probably overthinking this entire thing. But maybe Briar having the information about the run was a sign. Like the universe was agreeing that he should go...even if it was the last thing Clara wanted.

CHAPTER 3

"*H*e asked you if that was a smart idea?"

Clara cupped her mug of dandelion root tea, angry all over again just hearing Indie repeat the words Holden had said to her yesterday. "Yep. And *then* he texted me asking for the time and place of the run."

Indie's expressive green eyes widened. "No...you don't think—"

"He'd better not. I didn't give him any details, but this town is the size of a thumb. It wouldn't be hard to get the details."

"It's just a running club though. It's not like you said you were joining a biker gang."

"I know. He's out of his mind, just like my brothers." They sat in her acupuncture studio, which was actually just a converted garage attached to her house. Tea and a chat before Indie's appointment was a long-standing tradition.

"I told Mom, and do you know what she said?" Clara asked.

"I can hazard a guess."

"She said that it was sweet. That he was just looking out for me." She loved her mother, but the woman could never say a bad word about any of her family members.

"Well, lucky for you, you have one sane family member," Indie said as she sipped her tea.

"Who?"

Indie jokingly shoved her shoulder.

Clara chuckled. "You know what I need? A date. Holden takes up far too much of my brain space."

Indie grinned. "Oh yeah? And who, pray tell, will this date be with?"

"I don't know. Maybe someone who can fix my problem before I turn thirty next month."

Indie tilted her head. "Being a virgin is not a problem."

"It is when you're my age. But it's okay, because you know what I realized yesterday?"

"That for all of history, societal structures have been designed to oppress women when really we're the more intellectual and emotionally intelligent gender, so independence is actually a good thing?"

Anyone else probably would have been shocked by that response. Not Clara. Indie was still recovering from separating from her husband and in her "I hate men" stage of grief.

"No," Clara said firmly. "But close. I realized I've been sleeping on the masculine side of the bed."

"The what?"

"The masculine side."

"The masculine side according to who?"

"According to Feng Shui. So last night I slept on the feminine side."

"Which is the feminine side?"

"The left. And now the masculine side is open and available."

"You're crazy."

"And pretty." She grinned as she sipped her tea one last time before setting it on the desk. "All right, your turn. How are you doing?"

Indie's chest rose and fell, any hint of a smile slipping off her face. "Honestly?"

"Always."

"Lost."

Clara swallowed hard. "Tell me about it."

"It's been almost a year since Colt and I separated, and there are still days where it hits me so hard. I had this life all planned out. Colt and I were going to have kids. I had a thriving photography business. And now everything's a mess."

Clara leaned forward and squeezed her best friend's hand. "Going through IVF for years would take a toll on the strongest couple."

Indie had completed round after round of IVF for five years, often struggling alone while Colt was away on missions. She'd also split her time between living in Amber Ridge and California, where Colt was stationed. To say Indie's life had been hard these last couple years would be an understatement. And her mental health had taken a battering.

Indie ran her finger over the mug handle. "I run into his mother around town sometimes. And her fake niceness makes me so angry. She made a comment about how she didn't think I was the type to be so independent, and it was good to see I was managing so well."

Another stress on their marriage...his mother. She'd been nice at the start, but by the end, something had changed. She'd become so unkind, but not in an overly obvious way. She was the queen of passive-aggressive comments and doing anything to get Colt to herself, including faking illness when needed. "I so wish you'd spoken to Colt about his mother."

"Honestly, IVF and him being away for missions so much was putting such a strain on our relationship that I didn't want to add anything else."

"But *she* was a strain on your relationship."

Indie lifted a shoulder. "Colt loves her. And she never said

NYSSA KATHRYN

anything obviously unkind. It was all underhanded." She shook her head. "It's not really her though."

"What is it?"

"I still have these moments where I feel this suffocating 'life isn't fair' weight on my chest. I see these mothers walking around with babies and children, and I wonder why they get to be mothers and I don't."

"There's still time."

"I'm thirty-four, separated from my husband, and with a history of infertility. Time is not on my side."

No. Clara was not going to let her best friend and cousin spiral. She stood. "Come on. Let's get you on the bed. I know just the points to put in today."

The focus would be circulation, hormonal balance, and relaxation. Definitely relaxation.

As Indie climbed onto the bed, Clara got her needles ready. Her passion for acupuncture had started when she'd looked for natural ways to bring the body into alignment during chemotherapy. She'd found acupuncture, and she hadn't looked back.

Acupuncture worked by balancing the body's energy, also known as *Qi* or *Chi*. It could basically be used as a holistic approach to help the body feel better.

Unfortunately, she hadn't been able to help Indie get pregnant.

Once Indie was comfortable, Clara lifted her wrist and felt her pulse. The quality, strength, and rhythm of the pulse allowed her to get a sense of her patient's overall energy and balance. As suspected, Indie's wasn't as strong as Clara would like it to be.

The first needle she put in was at the Yin Tang point, also known as the Third Eye point between the brows, just above the bridge of the nose. It was her favorite for calm and relaxation, and the second it was in, Clara saw Indie's body relax.

Magic. Acupuncture was pure magic—exactly why she loved it so much.

30

She systematically moved around Indie's body, inserting the thin needles into all the points she needed. When Clara was done, she dimmed the lights, turned up the calming music, and set a small buzzer by Indie's hand. "Press the buzzer if you need anything."

She usually left the needles in for half an hour. Today, she might leave Indie's in for a bit longer, not just for the benefit of the needles but also the rest, something her cousin needed right now.

Clara stepped out of her studio and into the house, closing the door quietly before moving into the kitchen.

Scarlett, of course, wasn't home. No surprise. Exactly why Clara liked having her as a roommate. She helped Clara pay her mortgage while rarely being home.

Something on the kitchen counter caught her attention—a pile of printed pieces of paper on a laptop. But something was poking out.

She frowned as she slid out an ID card. It had Scarlett's photo, but the name was different.

She lifted it. "Rosie Thorpe."

"*Hey.*"

Clara jumped and dropped the ID. "Scarlett...I didn't know you were home. I'm sorry, it was sticking out and I was curious—"

"Curious? You were looking at my private stuff because you were curious?" She snatched up her things. "Here's an idea—how about you mind your own business?"

Then she turned and stormed out.

Okay, maybe Clara needed to rethink the whole keeping Scarlett around just because she was quiet, because Jesus Christ, that was rude. After all, this was her freaking house, and Scarlett had left her "private stuff" sitting out on the kitchen counter. It was ridiculous to be angry at that.

Well, the run-club-bonding thing was probably off the table.

* * *

BRANCHES SNAPPED beneath Holden's feet as he ran, cool air slapping him in the face. Jesse ran beside him, his best friend matching him step for step.

It was later than they normally ran. The sun was already up and the temperature slightly warmer than usual. It was still damn cold though, something he appreciated about Montana. Because who the hell wanted the heat when they ran?

He sucked in a lungful of air, the smell of pine and forest filling his nose.

Fuck, he loved these mountains. He'd spent his entire adult life in the military. The transition out had been hard, but this big open space beside his house made it easier. So did living in the same town as his best friend.

What didn't make it easier? Clara.

Dammit, why couldn't he get her out of his head? The sheer fucking fact that she'd been angry at him yesterday was toying with him. Making him want to call her. Hear her voice or that sweet laugh of hers.

He shouldn't be thinking about her this much. She was a friend. That was all.

He ran faster, Jesse once again upping his pace to match him.

Exhaustion weighed on his limbs, and he loved it. Exhausting his body was what drowned out everything else. It allowed his brain to stop working and focusing on everything he *shouldn't* be focusing on.

When they finally reached his place, his chest was moving quickly, sweat dripping down his bare chest.

The house he'd bought was old and on four acres of land, but the reason he'd bought it was for the attached workshop. It fit all his woodworking tools and boasted large doors so that when he opened them, he could work with just the sound of the wind in his ears. The mountains as his backdrop.

They stepped inside his house, and he felt Jesse's gaze on him before either of them spoke.

"Something on your mind?" Jesse finally asked.

Usually, he told his best friend everything. They'd been to hell and back in the military, assigned to the same Ghost Ops team. But anything to do with Jesse's sister felt too strange.

"Just thinking about work." A damn lie. And the look Jesse gave him said he saw right through it.

"How'd your quote go yesterday?"

"It was fine, although the woman had her quirks." He crossed to the kitchen and grabbed two bottles of water from the fridge. "You know, if you stay long enough, you'll see your mom. She's dropping by to pick up a key holder."

"A key holder?"

"Apparently she keeps losing her keys."

Jesse scoffed. "That isn't a new thing. She's been losing her keys for as long as I can remember. I lost count of the number of times I had to walk to school because she couldn't find the car keys. They usually turned up a day later under some Pop-Tart wrappers between the couch cushions."

Holden chuckled. "Becket's Pop-Tart wrappers?"

"Who else. That guy used to eat Mom out of house and home."

Holden laughed. Jesse had grown up with two siblings. With noise and laughter. While Holden had grown up with his mother. They'd been best friends. It was great...until she'd gotten her diagnosis.

He swallowed the acid in his throat as his phone rang, Briar's name flashing on the screen. "Hi, Briar."

"Hi. Just wondering if you had that quote for me?"

Holden moved into the living room. "Not yet. I'll probably take a couple more days." He'd told the woman up to a week but shouldn't be surprised that she expected it earlier.

"Oh. Okay."

"I'll—"

"Actually, I wanted to ask you something else. Would you like to drive together to the run on Thursday? I can show you where we start, and I can introduce you to some of my coworkers in the group."

He ran his fingers through his hair. Honestly, being around the woman for that much time wasn't exactly how he wanted to spend his morning. "That's a nice offer, but I might be going straight to a job after, so I'll need my truck." Not true. He'd be checking on Clara before going home for a shower. But Briar didn't need to know that.

"Really?" He could almost hear her nose wrinkling. "Won't you be all sweaty?"

"Depends how fast everyone runs."

"Hm. Okay. Um, well, I guess I'll see you there then."

"You will. And I'll have the quotes to you ASAP."

"Okay. Thanks." Her voice was flatter now.

Holden hung up to see Jesse staring at him.

"Who was that?" he asked.

"The woman I quoted yesterday."

"What did she want?"

"Offered to drive us to the run. She's the organizer."

"Uh...so she's into you."

"She's newly divorced."

"Looking for a rebound?"

"Even if she was, I wouldn't be interested."

Jesse nodded slowly. "Okay. Good."

"Good?"

"Yeah. Good. You don't want to date someone like that."

"Who do I want to date?"

Jesse gave him a strange look, but before Holden could ask him about it, the doorbell rang.

Jesse moved toward it before Holden could and opened the door to Pam Hayes. Jesse's mother was tall, with chocolate eyes that matched her sons', and a kind smile.

"Jesse, what a nice surprise." She pulled her son into a hug, and when she looked up at Holden, her smile softened further. "Holden."

He met her halfway and they hugged. And God, there was something that always kicked in his chest when Pam Hayes hugged him. Something that reminded him so infinitely of his own mother's hugs. A warmth. A gentleness.

Hell, every time the older woman smiled at him or even spoke to him, he felt like he was a fifteen-year-old kid again.

Pam moved back, hands going to his arms. "How are you, honey?"

"I'm good."

"Great."

"I'll go get your key holder."

"We'll come," she said.

Jesse grinned. "Guess we're all going."

They stepped outside and headed to his workshop. He opened the heavy, weathered barn doors and the scent of sanded wood hit him hard. He loved it.

The floor was littered with sawdust, a testament to the hours he spent working in this space. There were tools stored along the walls and a workbench in the center, which still held Mr. Bruno's half-finished coffee table.

He turned on the lights and lifted the piece he'd made for Pam. It still smelled of the polish he'd used on it the previous night.

Pam took it from his fingers, a gasp slipping from her lips. "Oh, Holden. This is spectacular."

He grinned. It was just a key holder, but Pam had been his biggest supporter since the day they'd met. "Thank you."

She looked back to him. "You, my boy, are marvelous, you know that?"

"Careful, you'll give him a big head." Jesse chuckled under his breath.

"No," she corrected. "I'll cement to him just how talented he is." She ran her fingers over the key organizer like it was a rare piece of art. "Beautiful."

He always thought that if this was the sort of praise Jesse had grown up with, it was a wonder *his* head fit through doorways. "It's nothing."

Pam gave him a look. "It's not nothing." She drew Holden into another of those big hugs. "You're so very talented. Your mother would be proud."

His limbs froze, something heavy suddenly sitting on his chest.

Another thing he loved about Pam—she wasn't scared to talk about his mother, even though she'd never known the woman. And yeah, it felt kind of good to have her remembered by someone other than him.

CHAPTER 4

*T*he bang of Clara's bedroom door opening was loud, closely followed by a gasp and an angry shout. *"Clara."*

Clara scrunched her eyes. She'd been having the best dream. It involved croissants and sweet teas and Holden without a shirt on.

Something hit her head. A pillow?

"Clara…can you hear me? Why are you still in bed?"

She cracked one eye open. The light immediately made her want to snap it closed again. She didn't. She forced herself to focus on the figure in front of her. Scarlett. And boy, she looked mad.

"Because I don't like to sleep on the floor," she finally mumbled.

The wrong thing to say, if the flaring of Scarlett's eyes was anything to go by. "It's five forty-five."

"Yeah, sleep time." Was the sun even up?

"We need to *go*."

"Go where?"

"Have you got amnesia? The running club."

Okay, sleep time was well and truly over.

She pushed up and rubbed her eyes. "You still want to do that after you yelled at me in the kitchen two days ago?"

"I didn't yell at you. I was just mad."

Clara barely held in the snort.

"You have three minutes." The words had barely left Scarlett's lips before the bedroom door slammed behind her.

Jesus freaking Christ. Who did the woman think she was?

Well, she wasn't going now. What she *was* doing was going back to sleep. And getting a lock for her bedroom door. In that order.

She rolled to her side, but before closing her eyes, she tapped her phone screen, only to frown at a text. It had been sent last night, but she'd gone to bed early and missed it.

Becket: Hey, Jesse told me about some running club tomorrow morning. I think you should sit it out, C. You get tired too easily and you almost passed out in my kitchen a month ago. Be smart.

Be smart? Her brother was telling her to be freaking *smart*, as if she was a child who needed to be told what smart and dumb decisions were?

Screw it.

She was going to this running club. No, she didn't need to prove herself to anyone, but if she didn't go, her family would think it was because they didn't want her to.

She quickly typed out a response.

Clara: I'm okay, Becket. You don't always need to worry about me.

Yes, she still suffered from chronic fatigue, but it was something she'd learned to live with over the years. Something she was capable of managing on her own. Something she wished the men in her family would understand.

After slipping on some running shorts, a sports bra, and a T-shirt, she grabbed her hoodie and stepped out into the hall to see her roommate by the door.

"I grabbed us waters. Is it okay if I ride with you?"

Scarlett was talking like she hadn't just barged into her room and thrown a pillow at her head. Did this woman have a personality disorder? Or was she just used to her moods giving people whiplash?

At this point, Clara was too tired to care. "Sure."

The second they started driving, Scarlett started typing on her cell.

"Texting someone?"

Scarlett didn't even look up. "No. I'm working."

"You work a lot."

"Because there is *always* a story to report on. Too many people think they can do bad shit and get away with it. It's my job to make sure the public knows who lives in their community."

Clara frowned. "You think there are people in Amber Ridge doing bad things?"

"Absolutely. Small towns are worse than big cities."

"They are?"

"Lower population, so tighter social circles, which means power and influence are concentrated in a few people. Those people can then control the narrative and manipulate others around them to get what they want. There's also limited law enforcement and resources. Hell, some people in small towns fear outsiders, which makes them act like idiots. Others have a strange need to protect the town's reputation."

Jesus, Scarlett made small towns sound like hotbeds of crime.

Clara cleared her throat. "You're really passionate about what you do, aren't you?"

"I'm passionate about freedom of information and the bad guys being identified for the world to see."

Clara shot her a look. This was more than Scarlett had ever told her about herself. It was good. It kind of felt like she was seeing the real Scarlett.

When they reached the park, it was to see a group of people in running gear already waiting.

She climbed out of her Volkswagen and frowned when she

39

saw someone she recognized. Malcolm. She saw him around town every so often. Not much, but he always made a point to say hi.

His gaze met hers, his shaggy brown hair tipping into his eyes. He ran his fingers through it before leaving the group he was talking to and heading her way.

"You know him?" Scarlett asked.

"Not well. We went to high school together. He's a doctor."

Malcolm stopped in front of them. "Clara, it's good to see you."

"You too. You're in the running group?"

"I am. As a doctor at the hospital, it would have been frowned upon to miss it. You're here to run?"

"Probably not well, but my legs will be moving."

He laughed.

Scarlett cleared her throat.

"Oh, sorry." Clara turned toward her roommate. "Scarlett, this is Malcolm Trundle. Malcolm, this is my roommate, Scarlett Calloway."

The widest smile Clara had ever seen spread across Scarlett's face as she reached out a hand. "Hi, Dr. Trundle. It's nice to meet you."

And her voice. What was *that*? Soft and friendly and completely unfamiliar.

Malcolm returned the smile, obviously not realizing he was talking to a Scarlett Clara didn't recognize. "Just Malcolm. And you too. Are you an acupuncturist like Clara?"

"Oh no. I dabble in writing."

So Scarlett wasn't revealing that she was an investigative reporter. Was that the norm in their industry?

Two other women stopped beside Malcolm, and he turned to them. "Clara, Scarlett, this is Helen and Deb, nurses at the hospital."

Helen looked to be in her thirties, with bright red hair, while

Deb was older, maybe sixty, with a few grays woven throughout her long brown locks. Both women had large smiles on their faces and looked fit. In fact, everyone here looked fit.

Scarlett cocked her head, eyes still on Malcolm. "I feel like I've seen you before."

Helen slipped an arm around Malcolm's shoulders. "That's probably because Malcolm here is the face of a new, revolutionary early detection and rapid response protocol for sepsis."

Deb nodded. "It's pretty great. It reduces mortality rates from septic shock."

Scarlett nodded. "Yeah, I remember now. You were in papers all over the country."

Clara didn't know that. "Congratulations."

Malcolm lifted a shoulder. "I was just doing my job."

The four of them continued talking about the protocol, but Clara got distracted by the sight of some very broad shoulders a few feet away.

She straightened.

Wait…she knew those shoulders. And that hair. Hair that had been in her freaking dream this morning.

No…

The man turned and—yep. Holden, in the flesh, standing only a few feet away, wearing running shorts and a T-shirt.

Really? She'd told him no and he'd *still* come? She shouldn't be surprised—it was a Holden move. The man had made his intentions to come today pretty clear, but dammit, she'd made her desire for him *not* to come clear, too. She was actually surprised her brothers hadn't joined him. But, man oh man, she was angry.

She was a microsecond away from storming straight over to him when suddenly, his gaze caught hers.

And a part of her—the part she absolutely did not like in this moment—felt something other than anger. Something warmer that sat low in her belly and made her cheeks grow hot.

Then he was moving toward her. And every stride he took

41

made that anger shrivel up a little more. Maybe it was because he was wearing a tight white shirt that stretched across his thick biceps. Or maybe it was because the power in his legs was evident even in his shorts.

He stopped beside her. "Hey, Clara."

"What are you doing here?"

"Running."

Well, of course he was running, but that wasn't *why* he was here and they both knew it.

She opened her mouth to tell him just that, but Malcolm got in first.

"Hey. Holden, right?"

Holden frowned at Malcolm. "Yeah. Do I know you?"

Oh, hell no, they were *not* going to bring up *that* night.

"We went to high school together," Clara said before Malcolm could answer. "This is Malcolm, Helen, and Deb, who work at the hospital, and my roommate, Scarlett."

"I take it you don't work at the hospital?" Scarlett asked.

"No. I'm a woodworker."

"Really? You any good at fixing cracked floorboards?"

Clara's chest rose on a sharp inhale. "He doesn't need—"

"You've got a cracked floorboard?" Holden interrupted.

Clara started shaking her head as Scarlett answered. "Yeah, and it's a tripping hazard. Can you help?"

"Sure."

Clara shook her head more vigorously. "You don't need to do that."

"Of course he does," Scarlett said with a frown. "It's been an issue since I moved in, and he's your friend. What's the problem?"

The *problem* was that if this tall, dark, and too-sexy-for-his-own-good man entered her house, the entire place would smell of peppermint and pine, and he'd take up too much space with his broad shoulders and look far too good while he fixed things.

"Clara, I'm happy to do it," Holden said gently, his voice like velvet.

"I—"

"Holden, you made it."

They all turned to see a woman in mini running shorts and a sports bra walking toward them.

Clara frowned. Wait...she knew her. Well, she didn't know her. But she'd seen her before. She was the rude iris lady.

They knew each other?

Briar touched Holden's arm, and even though the touch was innocent, Clara had the sudden violent urge to tear the woman's hand off.

Holden offered her a small smile. "Hi, Briar."

How did he know her?

"Come. Run with me." Miss Short Shorts tugged him away.

Clara should be happy. She hadn't wanted him here anyway. So why was that violent urgency just intensifying at the woman's hand on him?

* * *

"And she just complained for her entire stay. You'd think she was dying, but no, just a burst appendix."

Briar hadn't stopped talking the entire run. Actually, it was less talking and more complaining. Mostly about her patients at work, but also about every single person she came into contact with in Amber Ridge. Her ex-husband had received a few special mentions.

Deb had run with them for a bit. He liked her. She was funny. Good at countering Briar's negativity. But the woman had obviously grown sick of Briar's moaning and was now running with someone else.

His gaze shifted to Clara. She was running with Malcolm and

Scarlett a few feet ahead. He was intentionally jogging slowly to remain behind her so he could keep his eyes on her. So far, she looked to be doing okay. Although, the farther they got, the more sluggish her movements became.

Suddenly, Clara glanced over her shoulder and looked at him. Her eyes flared when she saw him staring back. Then she quickly looked forward again. She'd done that a few times. And every time, Malcolm glanced back too, looking at him and Briar, before focusing on the road in front of him.

It had hit Holden two seconds into the run who Malcolm was...the jerk from the street party three years ago who'd pawed Clara's chest after spilling beer on her.

A tightness clutched at his lungs at the memory of that night. Of the words she'd spoken to him. And the words he'd said back.

Fuck, he wanted to kick his own ass at how he'd handled that. *You'd be so easy to love.*

He'd been drinking, and the sight of Clara in his sweatshirt had made something deep and primal spring to life inside him. But even if he hadn't been drinking and the sun had been up and emotions weren't heightened, he wasn't sure what the hell he would have said. That fear of loving someone completely, of needing and relying on them, still lived inside him, and shit, it was burrowed deep.

"Don't you think?"

He looked down at Briar. Dammit. What had she said? "Yeah, I agree."

"*Thank you,*" she huffed.

Surely, they were almost done. "How long is this run?"

"Five miles. So we're about halfway."

"That's more of an intermediate run. Wasn't this designed so anyone in the community could join?"

"It was designed to help people get and remain fit. That won't happen if we only run a mile or two."

Suddenly, Clara stumbled, her knees hitting the ground hard.

Shit.

Holden sped up, but Malcolm was already crouched beside her, setting a hand on her shoulder. "Are you okay?"

Holden lowered on her other side and scanned her body, his gaze stopping on her knees. "You're bleeding."

"I'm fine. They're just grazes."

She was breathing quickly. Too quickly.

Scarlett huffed. "I'm going to jog with Helen and Deb." She started moving again.

Briar continued to jog in place. "Come on, we're going to be left behind. She said she's fine."

"I'll stay with her."

Holden's eyes narrowed on Malcolm at his words. "No, *I'll* stay with her."

Malcolm frowned. "I'm a doctor—"

"I don't think it takes a doctor to clean a scraped knee."

He opened his mouth, presumably to argue, but Clara touched his shoulder. "I'm fine, Malcolm. Go rejoin the run."

His brows flickered. He clearly didn't like it, but he rose and started running, Briar taking off beside him.

Clara looked back at Holden, head tilted. "You didn't need to stay."

"I know." He started to slide his hands beneath her knees and back, but she gasped and pushed at his chest.

"What are you doing?"

"I'm carrying you back to my truck. I have a first aid kit in there."

Her eyes widened. "Like hell you are. I'll walk."

"Clara—"

"Don't *Clara* me." She went to push up, and he growled and took her arm to help her. "You showed up when I asked you not to. You stayed with me when I told you I was fine. You are *not* carrying me back against my wishes as well."

"I'm trying to look out for you."

"Because you think I can't look after myself?"

He took a second longer than he should have to answer, and that was all it took for hurt to cut across Clara's features. She started walking back the way they'd come.

He took several long strides to catch up. "Because I care about you."

Some of the anger slipped from her features. "You don't play fair."

"Never said I did."

As they walked back, they cut through the side streets. The entire way, he itched to slip his arm around her waist and shoulder some of her weight. But he already knew he'd get an elbow to the gut.

"Do you carry a first aid kit everywhere?" she asked.

"Yep. Never know when I might hammer my finger instead of a nail."

She snorted, and immediately her cheeks went a pretty pink shade.

He grinned. "What? You don't think I can hammer my finger instead of a nail?"

"I think if you're coordinated enough to be one of the deadliest, best-trained soldiers in the world, then you wouldn't be taken down by a meager hammer."

"Uh-huh, but you see, a lot of damage can be done with a hammer."

"Is that right?"

"Oh yeah. Swing it with enough impact and some serious harm occurs, especially aimed at soft tissue."

Her brows dipped. "I'll remember that."

"If you ever need to use a weapon like that for self-defense, attack joints like knees and elbows, or pressure points like wrists, to immobilize or disarm an attacker."

"I won't—"

"You might. Everyone should know at least basic self-defense."

She looked away from him.

When they finally reached his truck, she sat on the grass while he got his first aid kit.

"So," she started, sounding almost nervous, "how do you know the woman you were running with?"

He squatted beside her and poured some water over her knees to clean the wounds, biting back a grin at the way she said it. "I'm quoting Briar's kitchen cabinetry."

"Hm."

He dabbed her knees with antiseptic wipes. "Do *you* know her?"

"Those were her irises I bought."

"She mentioned something about that."

"She seems fit." Clara plucked at a blade of grass. "She didn't lose her breath like the rest of us."

He grabbed a bandage from the kit and applied it to her knee. "She organized the event, so I'm sure she's a runner."

"She doesn't strike me as a do-gooder type."

"Clara Hayes. It's not like you to say something unkind about someone."

She rolled her eyes. "I bet you were thinking it. Does she really seem like someone who would organize a community event out of the kindness of her heart?"

"I don't really know her well enough to make that judgment." He closed his first aid kit.

"Maybe you can get to know her while you renovate her kitchen."

"Maybe." He sat back. "All done."

"Thank you." She wet her lips. "And even though I didn't want you to come today...thank you for looking out for me."

His lips stretched into a smile. "That was hard for you, wasn't it?"

Another roll of her eyes. "I'm going now."

She stood and took a step away from him, but he rose and gripped her arm, tugging her back. "Hey."

She turned, eyes wide.

"You don't need to thank me. I'll always look out for you, Clara." Even though it was a dangerous fucking game to be around her.

CHAPTER 5

*C*lara gasped as the scraper slipped from her fingers and her hand slid against the wood, a splinter cutting into her palm.

Holy godfather, that hurt. And why was this her third injury in the span of an hour? Surely she should be able to follow a simple YouTube clip without a dozen injuries. They made scraping flakes off wood look so easy. It *should* be easy, shouldn't it?

She went to the bathroom to grab tweezers from the drawer. It'd been years since she'd had to remove a splinter, but it shouldn't be too hard.

She tried to grab the end of the splinter, only to cringe at the sting of pain.

Well, apparently, nothing was easy for her.

She tried again, her nose wrinkling at the pain. Good Lord, she could go through chemo, but she couldn't deal with a splinter?

The doorbell rang.

And that was the universe telling her to give up.

She went to the front door, not bothering to look through the peephole before opening it.

Her jaw dropped. "Holden."

The man was here...at her house...and she was a mess. Like, *mess*-mess. Had she even done her hair? No. Well, technically yes —she'd pulled it up into a messy bun, but she was pretty sure she hadn't looked at her reflection once.

His gaze ran down her body, something dark and primal flashing through his eyes. And that's when she realized what she was wearing...

The sweatshirt. *His* sweatshirt. The one he'd given her to wear that night at the street party all those years ago. The one she'd told herself a million times to return, but as time passed and she'd continued to wear it, it'd started to feel too late. Not to mention, it had become worn and faded after so many washes.

"I can explain—" she began quietly.

"Don't. It looks good on you. Better than on me."

And it probably appeared to be *all* she was wearing. She had tiny workout shorts underneath, but the sweatshirt drowned her.

She cleared her throat. "What—what are you doing here?"

He lifted a toolbox. "Here to fix that floorboard."

"I told you that you don't need to do that."

"And I told *you* that I would."

Man, this guy was frustrating. Cute, and made her flushed and nervous, but frustrating. "Well, you're too late."

His brows rose. "You fixed it?"

"I'm in the *process* of fixing it."

He glanced down at her hand. "With tweezers?"

"No, smart guy. These are for my splinter. But that's a battle I am not winning." She held her hand up as if to prove the splinter's existence.

He stepped forward and gently gripped her wrist. His touch made all the fine hairs on her arms stand on end and her heartbeat go fast and loud.

"Lucky for you," he said quietly, voice deep and raspy, "I'm an expert at removing splinters."

That didn't sound safe. What *did* sound safe was about ten miles of distance between them. "You don't need—"

"Come on." He stepped around her and walked straight into her house like he'd been here a million times.

Almost on autopilot, she closed the door and turned. And holy mother of hell, he made her hallway look small. Although, he only remained there for a second before setting a hand on the small of her back and guiding her toward the kitchen.

"I can't believe we've known each other for so many years and I've never seen your house," he said, almost to himself.

Seven. They'd known each other seven years, and he hadn't seen her house because, after a person declared their love and the recipient didn't reciprocate, distance was best. "Well, this is it."

He went to the sink and turned on the warm water before gently grasping her wrist again and guiding her hand under the stream.

"A little trick my mother showed me," he said, face close to hers now. Far, *far* too close. "Warm water softens the skin around the splinter and can loosen it, making it easier to get out."

She frowned. He never spoke about his mother. She'd always assumed it was too painful. His mother had passed away from cancer when he was a teenager, and he'd had to go into foster care until he turned eighteen. "Sounds like she was a wise woman."

"Either that or she was desperate for a quick way to remove a splinter from a kid who didn't sit still." He smiled at her before taking her hand out of the water and slipping the tweezers from her fingers. Then, as if he'd done it a hundred times, he easily slid the splinter from her palm.

No pain. None. In fact, she hadn't even felt it.

"I take it back," Clara said softly. "Your mother wasn't wise. She was magic."

His gaze met hers, and there was something in his eyes she couldn't name. An emotion that ran deeper than the usual ones Holden let people around him see.

But then he blinked and stepped back. "Why don't you show me this floorboard?"

She swallowed hard. "This way."

She led him down the hall. When they stepped into Scarlett's bedroom, Holden crouched near her tools. Although, she used the term "tools" very loosely. There was a scraper, a piece of sandpaper, and a bottle of wood filler. Holden's tool kit looked a bit more extensive.

He ran his finger over the large split in the floorboard before glancing at her stuff again. "You were going to use wood filler?"

"No, I'm *going* to use wood filler, as per YouTube telling me to."

He gave her an "I don't think so" smile. "This crack is too deep for wood filler. You need epoxy resin."

"Oh. Um, okay. I'll need to go back to the hardware store and—"

"I've got it in my toolbox." And without another word, he lifted her scraper and just started working, beginning where she'd left off but making it look a heck of a lot easier.

* * *

HOLDEN COULD FEEL Clara's eyes on him as he worked. She'd left the room a couple of times in the last hour but always returned after a few minutes, sometimes just standing in the doorway. Other times sitting on Scarlett's bed and chatting.

He cleared his throat and glanced up. "So, this is Scarlett's room?"

"Yeah. She's been asking me to get the floorboard fixed for a while. It squeaks whenever she steps on it."

"Doesn't sound like a huge problem."

Clara lifted a shoulder. "I like to think she doesn't want to wake me when she gets home late, but I'm not really sure if she cares about me that much."

"Does she get home late a lot?"

"A lot a lot. She's barely here. Her job is her life."

"What does she do?"

"Investigative reporter. You'll never see her without her phone or laptop in hand."

He nodded, needing to physically stop himself from glancing at her for the hundredth damn time. But fuck, she looked good in his sweatshirt. There was something about her wearing his clothing that made him want to be possessive as hell.

But she wasn't his, so that was a stupid thought.

"Can I ask you something?"

He nodded. "Anything."

"Do you think it's suspicious for someone to have a fake ID?"

He stopped, his biceps contracting before he looked up. "Yes." A big fucking yes. "Who has a fake ID?"

"No one. It's just a general question."

She was lying. He'd worked out over the years that when she lied, she fidgeted. And right now, she was messing with a thread at the bottom of the sweatshirt.

"A fake ID means someone's trying to do something without their identity being revealed," Holden pushed.

She nodded quickly. "I thought so too."

What was she not telling him?

"We had to use fake IDs during missions sometimes," he said, as he started applying the epoxy. "It was always to do something so dangerous that being caught meant putting our lives and the lives of our loved ones in jeopardy."

Clara's brows furrowed. "I don't like the idea of you being in danger."

"Hazard of the job when you're in the military."

"Do you miss it?"

"Every damn day. I miss the brotherhood and the purpose it gave me. I miss the team environment. The military gave me a family when I had no one. But nothing lasts forever."

"I disagree."

He looked up. "Name one thing that can last forever."

"*Love.*"

His hand paused, that single word kicking him in the gut.

She shook her head. "Sorry, I didn't mean—"

A faint click sounded, so quiet he almost didn't hear it. What was that? The back door opening?

Clara heard it too, because she stopped and looked at the bedroom door.

He rose. "Does Scarlett usually enter the house from the back?"

"No. And she usually isn't back until later." Clara stood. "But I can—"

"No. Stay here. I'll check." Because who the fuck was entering her house through the back door?

Clara frowned but nodded.

He grabbed the wrench from his toolbox and quietly slipped out of the bedroom and into the hall. The faint sound of footsteps reached his ears—someone walking on kitchen tiles.

He stepped into the kitchen—only to stop at the sight of Clara's roommate, wearing a black cap on her head. Her head was down, gaze on her phone as she typed something.

Then she looked up at him and gasped. "What the hell?"

He pushed the wrench into his back pocket. "What are you doing coming through the back door?"

"Excuse me? I *live* here. I can come in through whichever door I want. What are *you* doing holding a wrench like a machete?"

Except, what she was doing wasn't normal.

Before he could respond, footsteps sounded behind him. Then Clara's soft voice. "Scarlett. It's just you."

"Your boyfriend seemed to be about to whack me with a wrench, Clara."

She frowned and opened her mouth, but Holden got in first.

"You never answered my question," he said quietly, not letting her off the hook so easily. "Why'd you come through the back door?"

"That's none of your damn business." Scarlett's eyes flashed between them. "I'm going to my room."

"Holden's just fixing the floorboard," Clara said quickly.

"It's fixed," Holden said, not taking his eyes off Scarlett. "Just needs sanding."

"I'll do that later," Scarlett muttered, as she skirted around them.

Why the hell was this woman so rude?

The second she was gone, Clara's nose wrinkled. "I'm sorry. She's moody. But nice and quiet for my acupuncture clients."

"I'll get my stuff."

By the time he reached the hall, Scarlett had already dumped it all outside her door.

Thank you, Scarlett.

When he got to the front door, Clara was already there.

She stepped outside and closed the door behind them. "I really am sorry about her."

He waited until they reached his truck and he'd put his supplies in the back before responding. "It's overcast."

"What?"

"She was wearing a cap when it's overcast outside. Does she do that often?"

"Um...I don't think so. But maybe I just haven't seen her do it. A lot of women do. She usually doesn't get home in the middle of the day, though."

His gaze shifted to the house, then up and down the street before looking back at her. "It was her with the fake ID, wasn't it?"

"No. Well...yes, but don't tell my brothers."

"Why not?"

"Because they overreact—exactly like you're doing right now in your head."

"You're not concerned that the woman you live with has an illegal fake ID?"

"It's not my business."

The fuck it wasn't. "It sure as hell is. She's living in your house. If she's in trouble, *you're* in trouble."

"She's not in trouble."

He could have laughed. "You don't know that."

"She's an investigative reporter. I bet she uses it for that."

"Doesn't matter. She shouldn't be putting herself in situations where she needs to use it ever." He stepped closer, his hand twitching to touch her. "Just...be careful."

"I'm always careful."

She was also trusting...too trusting.

Then, because he couldn't stop himself, he reached up and cupped her cheek, his voice lowering. "I don't want anything happening to you."

Her gasp was soft and airy, and did she lean into his touch? "It won't."

It had better not. "Call if you need anything."

She nodded, and he forced himself to lower his hand. To step back and walk away even though each step felt as unnatural as the last.

CHAPTER 6

*H*olden pulled his truck into the Amber Ridge sheriff's station. The parking lot was half empty. Good. Hopefully that meant Jesse wasn't too busy.

The chill of the air hit him in the face as he stepped out of his truck. He moved to the back and lifted out the carved wooden sign for the sheriff's office. Jesse had requested an emblem of an eagle with the words *Freedom and Protection* underneath. Apparently, it would go above the reception desk.

He carried it across the parking lot, the scent of redwood drifting from the sign. He'd used a Danish oil to finish it. He liked Danish oil because it penetrated the wood, made it look great and kept the item durable.

Most people found oils and woodwork boring as hell, but he'd always been fascinated with the stuff. Pair that with the fact that he worked with the mountains on his doorstep and he had the best job in the world.

Inside the station, an older woman smiled up at him from behind the front desk. "Hi there. What can I do for you?"

"I'm here to see—"

"Holden." Jesse stepped out of the hall, a wide smile on his face. "Right on time."

"Hey. Got your sign." He held it up.

"Great. But you forgot the big-ass photo of me."

Holden laughed. "You can always add it later."

Jesse chuckled as he took the sign. "Maybe I will. It's great though. Mom was right. You're talented as fuck."

"Not sure that's exactly what she said."

"I paraphrased." He tilted his head toward his office. "Come in."

Holden stepped into the room. "I still can't believe you're the town sheriff. They do realize you once got so drunk you couldn't remember your way back to base, right?"

Jesse leaned the sign against the wall behind his desk. "That was after a long-ass mission. I earned my night off, and you guys were there to steer me back."

Holden sat in the seat opposite the desk. "You know Lock wanted to leave you to fend for yourself?"

"Not surprising. That asshole was angry at the world until he got Callie back."

It was true. Lock lost the woman he loved, which made him a nightmare to be around until he returned to Misty Peak, Tennessee, and made things right.

"Have you got time for a coffee?" Jesse lowered into his seat.

"Nah, I've got to get a quote to someone, unfortunately."

"The woman who called you the other day?"

"Yeah, she's been on my ass about it. How'd you know?"

"She sounded the type."

He ran his fingers through his hair. "She asked me to meet her at the hospital on her lunch break."

"You hate hospitals."

He fucking loathed them. He hated the smells. The sounds. Even the sight of the building turned his stomach. It all reminded him of the worst part of his childhood. "Yeah. This woman's pushy. I felt like if I said no, she'd show up at my house in the middle of the night when her shift finished."

"Does she know where you live?"

"No. But in this town, she'd find out." He frowned at the newspaper article on Jesse's desk. "A thirty-two-year-old died of heart failure?"

Jesse frowned. "Yeah. Sad story. Went in for what should have been a routine surgery and died in recovery."

"What the fuck happened?"

"That's what her family wants to know. Blood tests were sent off, but they weren't stored properly, so all we can assume is that she reacted badly to the medication."

"Shit."

"Yeah, shit. A fucking mess, and hospital administration hasn't been much help."

"This is why you're in the job and I'm not. I don't have your patience." Holden rose. "I should get going."

"Sure." Jesse stood too, but slower. "Hey, how'd the run go?"

"Clara stopped halfway, and I walked back with her."

Jesse's features hardened. "Was she okay?"

"Yeah. Just tired."

"Okay. Good. I'm glad you were there for her."

Holden chuckled. "*She* wasn't."

"She says that, but I'm sure a part of her appreciates it."

Her soft thank you after he'd helped her with the graze on her knees flickered back to him.

He'd never told Jesse about the night Clara had said she loved him. He'd never told anyone. It felt too personal to share with even his best friend and Clara's brother.

Or maybe he was just ashamed of his response.

He was about to go, when he remembered her questions about the fake ID. "Hey, you're not able to do a background check on someone, are you?"

"Not without cause."

"That's what I thought."

"Anything wrong?"

He scrubbed a hand over his face. Clara would hate him for sharing, but fuck...he needed the town sheriff to know. "Scarlett, her roommate, has a fake ID."

"Have you seen it?"

"No. But Clara has."

Jesse's frown deepened. "You think she's involved in something she shouldn't be?"

"Not yet. But I don't like that she's so close to Clara."

"I can talk to—"

"No. And you shouldn't even tell Clara I brought it up. But I think we should keep an eye on them."

Jesse nodded. "I tend to keep as close an eye on my sister as I can, anyway."

"Good." Holden cleared his throat. "I'll see you later."

On the way to the hospital, his chest started to grow tight. Then he saw the building. And even though this was a different hospital than the one his mother had died in, it looked almost the same. He parked out front but didn't get out right away. He wanted to stay exactly where he was. Not go inside but just leave instead.

But that was fucking stupid. He was an adult. He should be able to walk into a damn hospital without anxiety closing his throat.

He texted Briar.

Holden: Hey. I just got here.

He didn't have to wait more than a few seconds for a response.

Briar: Great. Meet me in the cafeteria. Be there in ten.

He climbed out of his truck and grabbed his laptop and the printed quote from the passenger seat. He always offered his clients both a digital and printed version.

The second he stepped inside the building, that familiar

burning flared in his gut. Some people described the smell of a hospital as a mix of antiseptic and bodily fluids. To him, it was a sterile, metallic scent that, no matter what part of the hospital he entered, he couldn't escape. It was a clinical smell. And he fucking hated it.

He strode down the hall, following the directions to the cafeteria.

A man in a white coat rounded a corner, almost walking into him. "Holden!"

He frowned. "Malcolm."

"Yeah. Hey. Everything okay?"

"Just meeting Briar in the cafeteria."

His brows rose. "Briar. Okay."

Why the hell did he say it that way? Was he surprised?

Malcolm cleared his throat. "You need help—"

A loud, piercing beep suddenly rang out from one of the rooms beside them.

Malcolm cursed and ran into the room, others following him, while Holden just stood there like a fucking statue, thrown back to when he was sixteen years old and that same beeping had pierced the air—all coming from the machines attached to his mother.

Panic crawled up his throat. The same panic he'd felt that day, knowing without anyone saying the words that his mother was gone. That he'd just lost the last person in the world who was family. The only person who loved him.

A hand suddenly touched his arm, making him flinch. He turned to see Clara and Pam standing in front of him, concern on their faces.

* * *

SOME PEOPLE DIDN'T LIKE hospitals. A lot of people who'd gone through chemo actually hated them.

Not Clara. To her, the hospital was the place she'd faced the biggest obstacle of her life and won. The place that had saved her.

Twelve weeks she'd spent in this hospital, receiving chemotherapy. Originally, she'd been told she'd need four months, but she'd responded well to the drugs. Even that had been a victory.

It was *after* chemo that things had gotten hard. That's when she'd lost her hair and her hormones had been all over the place. During chemo, she'd had a plan. Something to work toward— kicking cancer's butt. But after, she'd kind of felt lost, like she didn't fit into the world she'd created in New York anymore, but she also wasn't sure if she fit anywhere else.

"Are you okay, darling?"

Clara glanced at her mother. Pam Hayes sat in a hospital chair, a Band-Aid on the inside of her elbow. "You're finished."

"Blood's all taken, just need to wait for the results."

Her mother got routine blood tests, and today Clara had offered to take her.

"The nurse was telling me about this doctor who's basically famous for his new sepsis protocol," her mom continued.

"Malcolm. We actually went to high school together."

"Really? Is he cute?"

She laughed. "I suppose some women would find him attractive. But he's not really my type."

"I see."

Why did her mother say it like that? Like she knew some big secret Clara was keeping. "Should we go?"

"Sure." Her mother tilted her head. "Are you okay being here?"

"Of course. I told you, Mom. I don't mind the hospital."

"You're so strong, darling."

Compliments were not hard to come by around her mother. "For coming to a hospital?"

"Yes. After everything you've been through here, absolutely. How are you doing?"

Her mother checked in regularly. Sometimes Clara wondered

if the cancer had hit her family harder than it'd hit her. "I'm doing really well."

"You *look* really good. When's your next annual check with Dr. Farmer?"

Her oncologist split his time between their hospital and the one in Bozeman. "In about a month."

Her mother nodded, and even though she pretended she was fine, Clara knew her mother got nervous around the time of her checks. "Well, I'd like to be at that appointment with you if that's okay."

"Of course. I wouldn't know what to do without you at those things." Her mother had come with her to every appointment. Every. Single. One. Indie had joined them for a few as well. Another reason she loved the women in her life. "Should we go straight home?"

"I was thinking we could stop by—"

"The Tea House? Get some sweet tea?"

Her mother grinned. "You read my mind."

"No. I'm just as hopelessly addicted as you."

They stepped into the hall, and Clara almost ran into a woman wearing a cap and carrying a laptop.

Wait...she knew that black cap. "Scarlett?"

The other woman looked up, and sure enough, it was her roommate. "Clara. What are you doing here?"

"Just keeping my mother company. Mom, this is my roommate, Scarlett. Scarlett, this is my mom."

Her mother smiled. "Hi. It's nice to finally meet you."

"Yeah, you too. I've got to go. I'm having lunch with Malcolm."

Clara's brows rose. "You are?" With her laptop? That should be fun.

"Yeah, and I'm running late. I'll see you later." Scarlett stepped around them.

"Hm."

Clara looked at her mother. "What's your 'hm' mean?"

"She just seems...busy."

"She's always busy. It makes her a bit rude."

Her mother chuckled. "I've met worse people." Her mother linked their arms as they continued down the hall.

"Trust me," Clara said under her breath. "Scarlett can be worse. Especially when you don't wake up in time for things you've planned to do with her. Then you get pillows thrown at your head."

"So why'd you join a running club with her?"

"Who told you that?"

"Becket."

So Holden had probably told Jesse, who'd told Becket, who'd told her mother. Man, her family had big mouths. "I joined because it sounded fun and I didn't think anything bad could come from doing some bonding with my roommate. Plus, so many people told me I shouldn't that I suddenly really wanted to."

Her mother chuckled. "The men in your life mean well."

"Yeah, well, they can mean well and trust me to make my own good decisions at the same time."

They rounded a corner to see Holden standing in the middle of the hall.

Clara frowned. He was pale, and he was looking at a patient room that had machines beeping loudly as if it held someone important to him.

She rushed forward and touched his arm, only for him to flinch before looking down at her.

Her frown deepened. "Holden. Are you okay?"

"Clara." He shifted his gaze to her mother. "Pam."

Clara's attention moved to the room, which held half a dozen hospital staff, before one of the nurses closed the door.

"Do you know the person in there?" Clara asked gently.

He shook his head. "No, I—" Then he stopped, the fear from

moments ago intensifying as he seemed to focus on her. "What are *you* doing here? Are you okay?"

"I'm fine. Mom needed some routine blood tests."

Relief washed over his features.

"Holden...why are you here?" Clara asked.

He cleared his throat. "I'm meeting Briar to give her the quote for her kitchen."

Something stabbed at her chest. Something she absolutely did not like and would not admit to. She shouldn't care that he was meeting Briar, a beautiful, ridiculously fit nurse. It had nothing to do with her.

He ran fingers through his hair. "I should get to her."

"Okay." Clara's single word came out quietly.

Holden gave them each a small smile before rounding the corner. She looked at her mother, who appeared deep in thought.

"He wasn't okay," Clara said softly.

"No, he wasn't. I suspect he spent a lot of time in hospitals with his mother and now they're not his favorite places."

Was that true? His face had gone white because he remembered his mother?

How much of his life did her loss really affect? Something told her it was more than he ever let on.

CHAPTER 7

*C*lara's legs hurt. Was it embarrassing if she limped across the parking lot to the bar? It *felt* embarrassing.

"Are you okay?"

Man, even Indie noticed. "Why do you ask?"

"You're walking...funny."

It was *that* obvious. "Sunday's run is still killing me. I forced myself to finish the five miles."

It was Wednesday. Three days had passed since the run and her legs were still hurting. In fact, there'd been three more running club sessions since the first, and at each one, she'd pushed herself to finish, so she'd just been in a permanent state of pain.

When did it start getting easier?

"You know, you don't have to finish," Indie said, always the smart one.

"I absolutely do. Holden just watches, waiting for me to pull out. I'm determined not to prove him or my brothers right."

"Clara...they're—"

"Don't say they're just looking out for me. I don't need a shadow at a community run. He's the fastest and fittest there.

He should be leading the group, not lagging behind watching me."

A soft smile curved Indie's lips. "It's kind of sweet."

"You sound like my mother."

They were about to step inside when Indie touched her arm. "Clara, I know you don't like it when Holden and your brothers get overprotective. But they care about you. We *all* care about you."

She ran her finger over the seam of her high-waisted jeans. She'd gone casual, tucking in a T-shirt and pairing it with heels.

"I know they care about me," she said softly. "It's just...I fought the cancer."

"No, you kicked cancer's butt."

"I did. And that made me feel strong and resilient, and when the guys hover, they make me feel a bit *less* strong."

"Oh, Clara, I can understand that." Indie slipped some hair behind Clara's ear. "But they know how strong you are. They just have protector in their DNA."

"You're probably right."

"Of course, I am." Indie tilted her head toward the door. "But we can still drink some huckleberry martinis while thinking violent thoughts about them."

Clara laughed. Huckleberry martinis were Indie's favorite. Clara didn't really have a favorite because she didn't drink very often, but she'd have at least one glass tonight.

They stepped inside, immediately hit by loud, booming music, and the competing noise of voices and clinking glasses. The bar was warm, filled with so many people there was barely room to move.

Indie took her hand. "Let's get a pitcher."

That was something locals loved about CJ's—almost any cocktail could be bought by the pitcher.

Five minutes later, they were standing at a table, two glasses filled with martinis and a jug in the middle.

Clara looked at her cousin. "Okay, your turn. How are you doing?"

Indie ran her finger around the rim of the glass. "Actually, I did something."

"A good something?"

"I sent Colt the divorce papers."

Clara straightened. "You did?"

They'd been separated for almost a year, but neither of them had started the divorce process. In fact, they hadn't really spoken in the last twelve months...well, Indie hadn't spoken. Colt had texted. Called. Emailed. And Indie had always said the same thing. That nothing had changed. That it hadn't worked between them.

Indie nodded. "Yeah. I decided it was time."

The pain in Indie's voice was hard to hear. "How do you feel?"

"I was hoping I'd feel good. The end of a chapter. I thought maybe it would give me some closure. But that was probably naive of me. It will probably always hurt."

Clara swallowed. "You'll always love him."

"But love wasn't enough. Not for us, anyway. And I can't go back to that dark place I was in a year ago." Indie shook her head. "Let's talk about something happier—like the budding love between you and Holden."

Clara scoffed. "Trust me, there is *no* budding love." Although a part of her, a really big part, wished there was. Would probably always wish he loved her the way she loved him.

Indie gave her a look. "That's because you haven't told him how you feel. Tell him. Take a chance."

Clara wet her lips before scrunching her eyes and blurting the words out. "I did tell him."

"*What?* When?"

Clara looked at her cousin. "Three years ago. I never told you because...I don't know. I was embarrassed."

"Okay, I need more details."

"It was the night of the annual street party. Holden and Jesse were home. Even Colt was there."

Indie's brows creased. "I remember that night. You got a drink spilled on you, so you went to get a clean shirt from your car, but you never came back."

"Holden followed me. He gave me his sweatshirt and I...I told him I loved him." She wrinkled her nose and hurried the next words out. "I told him it was the kind of love that made me want to kiss him and count down the days until I saw him again."

Indie was silent for a moment before uttering one word. "Wow."

"Yeah, wow."

"What did he say?"

She looked back at her drink, his response burned into her brain. "That I'd be easy to love. And that's why he has to stay away from me."

"What does *that* mean? Why can't he love you?"

Clara lifted a shoulder. "I don't know. But the next time we saw each other, it was Thanksgiving at Mom's, and he just acted like it had never happened, so I did the same...and neither of us ever mentioned it again."

"Oh, Clara—"

"It's okay." Well, it wasn't, but what was she supposed to do? Dwell on the fact that she loved someone who didn't love her back? "He cares about me like a sister. I need to get over this little infatuation and move on." Little? Huh. She'd loved the guy as long as she'd known him. She sipped her drink before looking at her cousin. "Maybe I just need to find a random guy and have sex with him."

Indie choked on her cocktail. "What?"

"I'm going to be thirty in the next month. *Thirty*."

"I know. I wanted to throw you a party and you said no."

"And it's still a no. But I shouldn't go into my thirties a virgin. That's weird, right?"

"No. There's no right or wrong time."

"I think it's weird." She looked around the bar. "I should just pick a guy and do it. Rip off the Band-Aid."

"You absolutely should *not*."

She looked back at Indie. "Malcolm's nice."

"Who's Malcolm?"

"Hey!"

They both looked up to see Helen Monroe, from the running group. "Helen...hi."

The other woman's eyes were wide and her smile big. Before Clara knew what was happening, Helen drew her into a hug, and all Clara smelled was sweet alcohol.

She was drunk. Probably too many of CJ's famous cocktails.

Clara chuckled. "You seem happy."

She pulled back. "Because it's *so* good to see you."

"You too. Helen, this is my cousin Indie."

Helen released Clara's shoulders and wrapped Indie in the next hug. "Hey, Cousin Indie!"

Indie's brows shot up. "Um, hi."

"Are you here with anyone?" Clara asked.

"Only a *ton* of people from work. Deb. Malcolm. Briar. Come join us!"

Clara started shaking her head. "Oh, I don't—"

"I *insist*." Helen yanked her hand, and Clara almost stumbled as she was dragged through the crowd. She glanced behind her to see Indie following, their drinks in her hands.

Helen stopped at the pool table, where half a dozen people stood, some with pool sticks, others with drinks. All people she recognized from the running club. "Look who I found. Clara and Cousin Indie."

A few people said hi. Most of them seemed sober.

When Helen grabbed Indie's arm and went around to introduce her to everyone, Malcolm came to stand beside Clara. "Hey. I have a feeling it wasn't your choice to come over here?"

"No. But I don't mind. How much has she had to drink?"

"Too much."

Clara chuckled. "Have you been here long?"

"About an hour. You?"

"Maybe ten minutes." She scanned the group of people. "You run with your colleagues *and* you drink with them? You must really like each other."

He grinned. "Either that or no one else likes how much we talk medical speak, so we only have each other."

Clara laughed. "Hey, I'm here."

"You are. You must enjoy being bored to death with talk of sepsis and catheters."

Briar joined them. "Hi. Karen, was it?"

The smile slipped from Clara's face. "Clara."

The other woman just nodded, no apology. "Did you hear? I hired Holden to do my kitchen."

Her heart gave a little jerk, but she was careful to keep any emotion off her face. "That's great. He does amazing work."

"I know he does. It's why I hired him."

Was it? Or was it because Holden was cute and funny and kind and a million other things?

Helen suddenly stepped between Briar and Malcolm and threw her arms over their shoulders. "Why does this little subgroup seem so docile?"

"Helen, how much have you had to drink?" Briar asked, annoyance in her voice.

Helen held up two fingers, showing the smallest gap. "A teeny, tiny bit."

Briar rolled her eyes while Malcolm chuckled.

While the three of them continued to talk, Clara's phone beeped with a text.

Scarlett: Are you at the bar? Is everyone from the hospital there?

Clara frowned. Firstly, how did Scarlett know she was at the bar? Secondly, how did she know people from the hospital might be here? Thirdly, why did she care?

Clara: Yeah, I'm at the bar with Indie. And yes, Malcolm and a few others from the hospital and running group are here.

She waited a moment for a response, but none ever came.

Thanks, Clara. I really appreciate the information. You're such a lovely roommate.

All things Scarlett *should* have said.

Malcolm bumped her hip. "Hey. You okay?"

She looked up and nodded. "Yeah, just messaging Scarlett."

"We keep trying to arrange a lunch at the hospital, but every time, I get caught up with an emergency." A shadow passed across Malcolm's face.

Clara frowned. "Everything okay?"

He opened his mouth to respond, but then Deb's loud voice cut through the noise of the bar.

"Holy crack on a cracker. It's that sex-on-a-stick Holden—and he brought his hot friends. Someone get me a fan."

Clara's head whipped around, and sure enough, Holden and her two brothers stepped into the bar, Aspen and Sky with them.

Her throat snapped closed at the way the tight fabric of Holden's black T-shirt traced the muscles in his chest and arms. At the sharp edge of his jaw and his warm sun-kissed skin.

Holy Hannah, he was all strength and power and sex.

Butterflies were still fluttering in her lower belly when Briar suddenly pushed past her. The shove was so rough she almost spilled her drink all over her shirt.

Then the nurse walked straight up to Holden. She didn't hear what they said, but Briar stood so close it looked intimate.

It felt like a punch to the stomach. One where the freaking air was forced out of her.

And she hated that *that* was her reaction. She knew he didn't love her the way she loved him. And he was eventually going to date.

But it still hurt.

"Here." Indie filled her glass with more martini.

Without a word, Clara took a big gulp. She'd probably be needing a few of these tonight.

CHAPTER 8

*H*olden lifted the beer to his mouth, his gaze returning to Clara for what had to be the fiftieth damn time. She stood with Indie and Malcolm, and every time she smiled or laughed at something he said, there was this strong fucking urge to go over there and rip her away from the jerk.

Okay, maybe he wasn't a jerk. He was a doctor. He helped people. Didn't mean Holden wanted the guy getting close to Clara.

Briar had joined Holden for a while, but she'd obviously gotten bored of the little attention she'd received from him and returned to her friends.

"Careful, brother, you almost look jealous."

He dragged his gaze from Clara to Becket, who stood beside him. Jesse was at the bar while the women were on the dance floor. "I don't know what you're talking about." A damn lie. And by the look of Becket's smile, he knew it.

Becket swished his drink. "Is it Jesse?"

"Is what Jesse?"

"The reason you two aren't dating."

The worst part of this? Jesse hadn't even been a consideration. Jesus, he was an asshole.

"Because," Becket continued, "I think my brother would be honored to have his best friend date his sister. And so would I. You're a great guy."

His fingers tightened around his glass. "Thanks. But there's nothing going on between me and Clara. She's like a sister to me."

Another fucking lie. They were just rolling off his tongue now.

Becket threw back his head and laughed. "You forget, Clara *is* my sister, and neither Jesse nor I look at her like that."

Suddenly, Malcolm took Clara's hand and led her to the dance floor.

Holden straightened. The fuck? They were dancing now? They barely knew each other.

"Hm," Becket said softly, "that looks romantic."

Becket was a shit stirrer, and he was damn good at it. But his words didn't affect Holden. What *did* affect him was the way Malcolm's hands touched Clara's waist. The way the doctor held her close to his body like there was slow music playing when there wasn't.

Gritting his teeth, he turned away. He needed to ignore it. Clara wasn't his. She could dance with whoever the hell she wanted.

Jesse returned to the table, his brows lifting at the dance floor. "Who's our sister dancing with?"

"His name's Malcolm," Holden said.

Jesse nodded. "And he's with the hospital crew, so...nurse?"

"Doctor," Holden corrected.

Becket cringed. "Ouch. That's not good. For you, I mean. For Clara, it's great. She always wanted to marry a doctor."

Jesse frowned. "Since when?"

"Freshman year, she had to write about her dream guy. Hers was a doctor. Brown hair. Six feet tall."

"And you remember it so specifically?" Holden just about growled.

"I'm good with details."

He was tempted to tell the guy to fuck off, but the music suddenly changed to something slower.

Becket set his drink on the table. "That's my cue to find my woman before someone else does." He crossed to the dance floor and slipped an arm around Sky's waist. She turned, her smile wide as she pressed her hands to his chest.

Jesse straightened as Aspen began to move through the crowd toward him. The second she reached him, they wrapped their arms around each other.

Holden told himself not to look at the dance floor. He fucking yelled it in his head.

But he looked. And Malcolm was even closer to Clara now, his arms still around her waist, and they were so close there was basically no space between them.

Screw it.

He set his beer on the table and strode to the dance floor.

Clara's gaze shot up. "Holden."

"Can I have this dance, Clara?"

Her mouth dropped open.

Malcolm frowned at him. "Actually, we're just—"

"Thanks." He took her hand from Malcolm's and tugged her away, not caring about the open-mouthed doctor. Then he pulled her so close that her body was flush with his. And *fuck*, she was soft and warm.

Malcolm made a loud, exaggerated huff before walking away.

"What are you doing?" she asked quietly, shock weaved into her words.

"Dancing with you."

She cocked her head. "Okay, but why?"

Her floral scent lingered in the air, surrounding him. And the feel of her sweet curves beneath his palm and her warm hand in his other...it made him want to hold her tighter.

"Because I want to." It was all he had in the way of answers. That, and the fact that he didn't want Malcolm anywhere near her.

She frowned, then she looked at something over his shoulder. He followed her gaze to Malcolm and Briar, now on the dance floor.

He almost scowled. "Do you like him?"

Her gaze shot back to him. "That's none of your business."

He knew that. And it just made him even more frustrated. He *wanted* it to be his business. He wanted to know exactly what she was feeling, and for who, even though he had no right to the information.

"I didn't know you had a thing for doctors."

"I don't. I have a thing for nice guys."

Holden laughed, but there was no humor in the sound. "He's not a nice guy."

"How do you know?"

"The way he goes on about the protocol every week at running club. Like he wants every fucking person to tell him how brilliant he is. That's not *nice*. That's arrogant."

"Well, I find him nice."

A muscle ticked in Holden's jaw.

A couple bumped into them. One of the women from the run, Helen maybe, looked up. "Whoops, sorry!"

A guy with a goatee didn't even look up. He wore a leather jacket and had tattoos down his neck.

Clara watched them closely as they stepped away. "She drank a lot."

"Are you worried about her?"

"Well, yeah, kind of. She just met that guy tonight. And he has a friend somewhere. People don't make the best decisions when drunk." She shook her head. "Her friends will step in if needed."

That was the thing about Clara; she cared.

As if his thumb had a mind of its own, it stroked her waist.

Her chest rose on an audible inhale, and her gaze shot up. "Holden, what are you doing?"

"I told you, I'm dancing with you. Beyond that, I have no idea."

Her head tilted slightly, and she looked like she wanted to ask him something, when yet again, something caught her gaze. "Scarlett's here. What is going on with her?"

"Why do you think something's going on?"

"She's just really fixated on everyone who works at the hospital." She shook her head. "It's none of my business."

"It is your business because she lives with you."

"You don't need to worry about me."

"I will *always* worry about you, Clara."

Her focus shot back to him, eyes wide, emotions he couldn't name flickering through them.

Another song started, this one slightly faster in tempo, but Clara didn't stop or change the slow sway of her hips, and neither did he. He couldn't. Because standing here, with Clara in his arms...it was the most at peace he'd felt for a while.

Throughout the dance, she softened against him, her body melding into his and her head almost touching his chest.

"Can I tell you something?" Her soft words cut through the quiet between them, catching him off guard.

"Anything."

"Sometimes I get caught up in the memory of the moment the doctor told me I had stage four cancer."

Something wrapped around his lungs at the mention of Clara having cancer...clenching, digging its nails into him. Every time he heard that word, he forgot how to breathe.

But he was careful to mask it. To watch the expressions play over her face. To wait, because damn, he wanted to hear what she had to say.

"It felt like my entire future disappeared in the span of a few seconds," she continued. "Everything felt so infinitely unfair. I would have given anything to go back to before those words had left his mouth, to where my life didn't feel like it was over."

"But it wasn't over."

"No. It wasn't. But I didn't know that. I still remember him saying to me that if you're going to get cancer, Hodgkin's lymphoma is the 'better' kind of cancer. He said it like I was lucky, and his words just felt so absurd. Because no one's lucky to get cancer."

"Some people think they know what to say to make you feel better."

"*Nothing* in that moment could have made me feel better. I had to feel it before I was ready to fight it."

He tightened his arm around her. "You're the strongest woman I've ever met. You know that, right?"

"Just woman?"

He chuckled. "Person."

"That's better." She smiled up at him, but he couldn't even lift the corners of his lips. Because, fuck, she was beautiful. The kind of beauty that made the world quiet. The kind of beauty that was impossible to look away from.

Her smile shifted into a frown. "When you look at me like that, I can almost convince myself that you..." She stopped, and even though she didn't finish her sentence, he knew exactly what would have come next. Because she saw everything he tried to hide.

He stepped back, forcing his hands to drop. And the look on Clara's face, the disappointment...it gutted him.

"Thank you for the dance, Clara."

"Anytime." The single word was quiet, almost a whisper, and laced with hurt.

Yeah, he was an asshole. An asshole she was better off without.

CHAPTER 9

*C*lara's heart beat fast as she walked off the dance floor, every step away from him heavy and wrong. How she could feel hot and needy but also hurt and frustrated all at the same time, she had no idea. But she did. She felt all of it.

He didn't want to be anything more than friends, but then he danced with her, held her, like she was all that existed in the world. He looked at her like...God, she couldn't even explain how. Like he *wanted* her. Really wanted her, and not in a friendship or sisterly way.

She stopped beside Indie, grabbed the martini from her cousin's fingers, and downed half the glass in one go.

Indie turned away from Deb and Briar and gave her a sympathetic look. "Hey. You okay?" She kept her voice low so it only reached Clara's ears.

"I don't know. He makes me feel like this thing between us isn't one-sided, but then he just shuts down and walks away."

Indie stepped closer, slipping a strand of Clara's hair behind her ear. "If he's too scared to love you the way you deserve to be loved, that's his loss."

"Then why does it feel like mine too?"

"Because you love him."

"More than I should."

"Who's to tell us how much we should love someone?"

There should be a rule. If the feelings were unrequited, then the love faded or died or something equally conclusive. She needed to move on.

She opened her mouth to tell Indie exactly that, but Helen passed their table, bumping Clara's shoulder and looking so unbalanced, Clara wouldn't be surprised if she toppled over.

She watched the other woman head for the back door, which led to the alley, probably to be sick.

Clara handed the glass back to Indie. "I'm just going to check on Helen."

"I'll come."

"No, it's okay. Stay. Drink. I won't be long."

She wove through the crowd, only stopping when she stepped outside to see Helen throwing up behind a dumpster.

The poor thing. Clara jogged over, which wasn't an easy task in her heels, and held Helen's hair back. "It's okay. I'm here." She used her other hand to rub Helen's back.

When Helen finally stopped throwing up, she looked behind her, cheeks red and eyes teary. "Clara?"

"Yeah, it's me."

"I'm so embarrassed. You should go back inside."

"You don't need to be embarrassed. Everyone's been here at one point or another. And I'm not leaving you here by yourself."

Helen's brows furrowed but before she could respond, she groaned and looked away, her stomach heaving once again.

Clara went back to rubbing her back.

During chemo, there'd been days where she'd been so sick she hadn't been able to keep any food down. Her mother and Indie had taken turns rubbing her back, and God, it was the only thing that had even slightly made her feel better.

Finally, Helen straightened once again.

"Are you okay?" Clara asked.

"No." She hiccupped. "I'm so silly. I shouldn't have drunk so much. But things are so stressful." She stood but wobbled on her feet.

Clara wrapped an arm around her waist. "Is there anything I can do?"

"Can you reverse time to when the hospital wasn't in chaos?"

"What do you mean?"

"A dead patient...other patients going into heart failure and respiratory depression..."

Clara frowned. "Really?"

Helen opened her mouth to respond, but the door opened and two guys wearing leather jackets stepped out, one of them being the guy Helen had been dancing with.

Immediately, dread trickled through Clara's body, settling in her belly when they looked straight at Helen before starting toward her.

Clara forced herself to straighten. "We're just going back inside."

The taller guy smiled, but it seemed...off, and made the pit in Clara's belly deepen. "I'll take her home."

Hell no. "No need. I'm already taking her home." She pulled Helen closer.

The taller guy stepped forward, his height suddenly feeling threatening. "She and I were having a great chat inside. Really getting to know each other. She's happy to go with me."

The jerk said that so confidently.

He took another step forward, and Clara instinctively inched in front of Helen. "*No.* We're going back inside now."

The second guy lifted a brow. "I don't think so, honey." Then he stepped forward, and before Clara realized what he was doing, he slid a strong arm around her waist.

"Hey! Get your hands off me."

She shoved at his chest, but he just laughed as he tightened his arm and tugged her away from Helen.

Helen stumbled, and the taller guy caught her. "I've got you, honey."

"No…" Helen tried to push him away.

"Shh. It's okay. I've got you."

Clara's pulse took off, and she was a second away from kneeing the guy in the balls when the back door flew open and a very tall, very angry-looking Holden stepped out, closely followed by Jesse.

* * *

HOLDEN TIPPED BACK HIS BEER, the cold liquid doing nothing to cool the burning frustration running through his body.

She'd seen it. She'd seen everything he was trying to hide. His want for her. His need. Hell, he told himself he'd moved here for Jesse. To be closer to his best friend and his found family, but he wasn't even sure if that was true anymore.

Jesse came to stand beside him. "Hey. You okay?"

"No. I might head home."

"Why don't you have a beer with me first?"

"I—"

Indie suddenly ran up to their table, panic in her eyes. "You both need to go check on Clara—*now*."

Holden's back straightened as he scanned the bar. "Where is she?"

"She followed one of the women from the hospital outside," Indie said in a rush. "I was watching the door, waiting for them to come back in but they didn't, and two guys in leather jackets followed them out there. I didn't get a good feeling from them."

Holden was moving before Indie had finished speaking, dread burning through his gut.

When he reached the back door, he pushed outside—and

what he saw made him see black. One guy with his arms around Helen, and the other holding Clara, who struggled against him.

He was a fucking dead man.

Jesse cursed from behind him. Holden shot forward.

Suddenly, the guy holding Clara threw her to the side and withdrew a gun, but before he could even aim, Holden grabbed the man's wrist and squeezed. He cried out and dropped the pistol. Then Holden spun and threw him against the dumpster.

Noise sounded behind him, a grunt followed by a hiss—Jesse detaining the other guy. Holden ignored it, because this dumb fuck was getting up.

The second the asshole was on his feet, he growled and ran, body low as he sprinted toward Holden.

He stepped to the side at the last second and grabbed the guy around the middle before spinning—this time throwing him headfirst into the brick wall.

A crack sounded, followed by the guy's body hitting the ground.

Then he was still.

Holden turned back to see Jesse's guy down too, and Becket crashing outside, fury on his face. "What the hell is going on?"

Jesse lifted his phone, probably calling the station, while Holden ran to Clara. "Are you okay?"

"I'm fine." She was breathless and her eyes were wide. Shock.

He cupped her cheek. "Did he hurt you?" Because if he did, Holden was turning back to the fucker and murdering his ass.

"No," Clara said softly. "He didn't hurt me. They wanted to take Helen, and I said no."

Holden followed her gaze to Helen. Jesse was by her side, hand on her back.

Suddenly, Becket and Indie were beside them, pulling Clara up and into their arms.

Holden's hands twitched to bring her back to him. He wanted

her as close as fucking possible. He fisted his hands to stop himself.

It didn't take long for Jesse's deputies to arrive. By that time, the guys were starting to wake up and there were even more people in the alley. Briar, Deb, and Malcolm all huddled around Helen, who was looking paler by the second. Even Clara's roommate was there, but she seemed to be more of an observer than anything else.

"Are you okay?" Becket asked, as he came to stand beside Holden.

Holden watched as Clara told her version of events to the deputies. Then he looked at the back of the sheriff's car, where the two men sat in handcuffs. "No. He had his hands on her, and I can just imagine what would have happened if Jesse and I hadn't come out here when we did. I want to murder them both."

"Me too, brother. Me too." Rage coated Becket's words. Rage that matched Holden's.

When Clara was done talking to the deputies, Indie slipped an arm around her waist. "Come on. I'll take you home."

Holden stepped forward. "I'll take her."

Clara shook her head. "You don't need—"

"I do." He needed to see that she got home safely the same as he needed air to breathe.

Indie looked at Clara. "What do *you* want?"

Clara looked up at Holden, and she must have seen something in his eyes, maybe the sheer desperation to be close to her, because her features softened as she turned to Indie. "I'll go with Holden."

The two women hugged, then Holden slipped an arm around Clara's waist and led her to his truck. He felt her questioning gaze on him as they walked, but he put all his energy into tamping down the fury, especially as he passed the assholes in the car.

They remained silent the entire drive to her place. But he shot her plenty of glances. Her face was always too pale. Her brows knitted too tightly together.

It wasn't until her door was unlocked and opened that she finally turned and spoke to him. "Holden...I'm okay."

"That could have played out very differently."

"But it didn't." She touched his arm. "Thank you for keeping Helen and me safe."

He inched closer, barely leaving a breath of space between them. "Don't do that again."

"Do what?"

"Walk into a deserted alley behind a bar late at night."

This time a flash of annoyance shaded her indigo eyes. "I was checking on a friend. I didn't ask those jerks to follow us."

"No one ever asks for trouble, but it happens. That's why you need to be smart."

"You don't think I was smart?"

"Not tonight."

Her lips thinned, voice harder now. "Okay, well. I should get inside."

She took a step into the house, but he grabbed her arm to stop her. "Clara. Promise me."

"What?"

"Promise me you'll keep yourself better protected next time."

She frowned. "Why?"

"Because I *can't* lose you."

The annoyance shifted into something else. Confusion maybe, like she was trying to figure him out.

"Holden, you're not going to lose me." When he didn't respond, she reached up and cupped his cheek. "I'm right here."

That floral scent hit him so hard that it was all he could smell. Paired with the feel of her palm against his cheek...she was everywhere. Yet still not close enough.

"Tell me you know that," she whispered. "Tell me you know that I'm here to stay."

Her thumb moved over his cheek, leaving a trail of heat on his skin.

He couldn't stop himself. With a small growl, he dipped his head and kissed her.

At first, she was still beneath him. So still that he wasn't even sure she was breathing. Then she melted into him, her lips softening and moving against his.

It was an instant rush of need. A complete obliteration of the world around him.

He wrapped his arms around her and drew her closer, needing her entirely against him. She was soft and warm and everything he craved.

A feminine sigh slipped from her lips, puncturing his chest. When her lips parted, he took advantage, sliding inside. Then he was tasting her. Curving his tongue around hers and making her a part of him.

Gently, he pushed her against the wall beside the door, crowding her. Surrounding her. Memorizing every little sound she made.

She felt like she was *his*. And fuck, he wanted that.

He was on the brink of losing his goddamn mind when she moaned. And there was something about the sound cutting through the silence that brought a whisper of reality back. And with it came the familiar fear. Fear of needing Clara. Fear of loving her.

It crawled around his chest, wrapping around his lungs and making his next breath feel impossible.

Quickly, he stepped away, and the second that connection broke, he felt cold. The kind of cold that crept beneath the surface of his skin, settling into places that had been on fire moments ago.

"I'm sorry."

She blinked once. Twice. Three times. Like she was trying to chase away the haze. "You're sorry? I'm not."

He took another step back. Right now, distance was his only protection. "You should go inside."

"Is that what you want?"

No. A voice inside him screamed the word. It was so fucking loud it was deafening. But there was also this other voice, one that told him to run. Get away. To not look back. And that voice was more familiar.

"Yes. I'll wait until I hear the click of the lock."

Disappointment darkened her expression, and maybe a bit of hurt. But she nodded. "Okay. I'll see you tomorrow, Holden."

She stepped inside, and the click of the lock was loud and so fucking final.

He didn't move right away. He just stood there, his feet feeling heavy as he wondered what the hell he'd just done.

CHAPTER 10

*C*lara dropped onto the couch and died...*literally died.*

Okay, maybe not literally. But wasn't that fitness thing supposed to be kicking in by now? She'd joined the running club weeks ago.

If her fitness had improved, she was *not* reaping the benefits. Her lungs were ready to collapse just finishing the five miles. It didn't help that she was distracted by *him*. Every time she turned her head, *he* was all she saw. His beautiful hazel eyes. His sharp jaw.

But even though the man was pretty, he was giving her whiplash. Why the heck was he giving her the best kiss of her life last night, then today not saying a word to her?

Yeah, that's right—he hadn't said anything. In fact, he'd arrived just late enough that he didn't talk to anyone before the run. She'd almost thought he wasn't going to show up.

Whereas she'd arrived early. She'd wanted to see if Helen showed up, to check on her. She hadn't. Not a surprise. And when Clara had asked Briar if her friend was okay, the other woman had barely looked at her, just mumbled a, "She's resting," and walked away.

Clara's eyes were still closed when the front door opened and shut. She cracked one eye open to see Scarlett walk in and head straight down the hall.

How was she so in shape and Clara wasn't? The woman sat on her phone and laptop all day but somehow didn't seem affected by the five miles at all.

Maybe this was a Clara thing. Maybe her chronic fatigue meant that she'd never run five miles and feel okay?

That was a depressing thought.

Her phone rang in her leggings pocket, and she blindly pulled it out. "Hello?"

"Clara, are you okay?"

She scrunched her eyes closed. She hadn't spoken to her mother about what happened last night, because she hadn't had a chance yet. And maybe she knew her mother wouldn't be happy. "Who told you?"

"Jesse."

Of course it was her sheriff brother. "I'm fine, Mom. Holden and Jesse made sure of it."

"Why didn't you call?"

"I didn't have a chance. It was late last night and this morning I went for a run."

"You still went for a run?"

She wrinkled her nose. "I'm okay, Mom."

"I want to stop by with some soup. You can rest while I take care of you."

God, she loved her mom. She'd really hit the jackpot with her. "Thank you, but I've got a client in an hour so will eventually peel myself off the couch and shower."

"You didn't take today off either?"

"I couldn't. I have clients. But I told you, I'm okay."

"Darling, I hope you're not overworking yourself?"

"Never." It was true. She only worked part time, exactly why she had a roommate in the first place. "Mom, can I ask you something?"

"Sure."

She picked at a loose thread on the couch. The thing about her mother was that she gave great advice. And man, she needed advice right now. "There's this guy. I like him. A lot. And a few years ago, I told him how much I like him, but he didn't reciprocate my feelings. After that, I told myself to leave it. That he wasn't interested. But then he kissed me."

"He kissed you?"

She wrinkled her nose. "Yeah. And it was a good kiss. I could feel how much he cared about me in this kiss. But right after, he pulled away from me again."

"Oh, sweetheart. That sounds tough. And it sounds like he's been hurt. People don't build walls like that unless they've felt them crumble before."

She frowned. What had hurt him? Losing his mother? "I don't know what to do."

"What do you *want* to do?"

"I want to break down those walls." The response was instant, not a flicker of doubt.

"Well, darling, there's your answer. Listen to your heart."

Her heart screamed to fight for him. "Thank you."

"I'm always here for anything you need, honey."

"I know." A part of Clara expected her mother to ask who he was. Or at least ask when she'd reveal his name.

She didn't. "Are you sure you don't need me to come by with soup?"

She forced her tired body up from the couch. "I'm okay. I'm going to make a big smoothie and have a long, hot shower." The longest shower of her life. As long as Scarlett wasn't in the other one, that was.

She might also put some needles in before her first client. She could use some acupuncture right now.

"Okay. I love you."

Clara smiled. "I love you too, Mom."

She hung up, her mind immediately on Holden again. On the kiss. The way he'd held her.

She wasn't going to give up on him. She couldn't.

Every muscle groaned as she walked to the kitchen.

Pain...Too. Much. Pain.

In the kitchen, she plugged in her Vitamix and had just started peeling a banana when her roommate walked in, already dressed in slacks and a T-shirt.

Clara cleared her throat. "You were fast today."

"Thanks. I've got a lot on my to-do list."

Clara nodded. "That's great."

"I noticed Helen wasn't there," Scarlett said. "I wonder if she's feeling worse from the alcohol or the attack."

"Probably both." Clara dropped the banana into the blender. "Maybe even the stress of work too."

Scarlett grabbed an apple and stopped. "She's stressed at work?"

"Apparently. I don't think things are great at the moment."

"What do you mean?"

Clara lifted a shoulder as she grabbed the blueberries from the freezer. "She just mentioned something about the hospital being in chaos."

She closed the freezer and turned, only to find Scarlett right there.

Clara gasped. "What are you—"

"What did she say? Exactly."

Clara's mouth opened and closed. "Um...not much. Something about a dead patient—"

"Lauren?"

"Maybe. She didn't say a name."

"What else?"

"Um...other patients going into heart failure and respiratory depression."

"How many? Has anyone else died? Who were the doctors?"

"I don't know. She didn't say. The guys came outside and interrupted her." Clara frowned. "What's going on? Why do you care so much?"

Frustration filled Scarlett's eyes and she stepped back. "I have to go." Then she turned and left before Clara could say anything else.

* * *

HOLDEN PULLED up outside The Tea House and ran his fingers through his hair. He hadn't said one word to Clara all morning. He'd smiled at her. Gave her a nod. But not one fucking word after their kiss.

Shit, he was a coward.

He leaned back against the headrest. A lot of people lost family members. So why had the loss of his mother scarred him so much? Because she'd been sick for so many years? Because by the end of it, he'd just been waiting for her to die? Or because once she *had* died, he'd been left with no one?

Whatever the hell it was, it taught him that loving another person, *needing* another person, could hurt you. No, not just hurt. Rip apart the very foundation of your world.

He climbed out of the truck and crossed the parking lot to The Tea House. He needed coffee. Hell, he needed more than coffee, but it was nine in the damn morning.

Inside, he scanned the space. An old military habit. No matter what room he walked into, it was ingrained in him to identify possible threats. To be aware of his exits at all times.

The first people he noticed were Malcolm and Helen. They sat in a booth by the window. Malcolm's back was toward him, and they both leaned forward and spoke in hushed voices.

Holden went to the counter. Mrs. Gerald had hired some

employees in the last few months, but it was still the lady herself who made most of the coffee.

She turned her head and smiled at him. "Holden, honey. Hi. Your usual?"

"Can we make it a double shot today?"

"Absolutely. Is everything okay?"

"Mostly." Which was true. Most of his life was great. He had a great job. A great best friend who came with an amazing family. It was just Clara who sat heavy on his chest and took up too much space in his mind.

"It seems to be a tough morning for a lot of people today." Mrs. Gerald's gaze shifted behind him, presumably to Malcolm and Helen, before returning to the coffee machine.

He lowered his voice. "Yeah, she had a rough night last night."

"She did? Oh, I thought they were talking about the hospital." Mrs. Gerald shook her head. "I should mind my own business. Although, it's not always easy to do that with Dr. Trundle here. He's almost famous these days."

"Is he?"

"Oh, yes, he was all over the news and in the papers for some treatment he created."

That should probably make Holden like the guy more than he did.

"I'll get that coffee." Mrs. Gerald turned back to the machine.

Someone suddenly tapped him on the shoulder. He turned to see Helen behind him, her face pale.

He frowned. "Hey. How are you doing today?"

"Um...not too good." She sniffed. "I didn't really get a chance to thank you last night. Thank you. You really saved me and Clara."

"I'm glad I was there. Next time, be careful who you befriend, especially while drinking."

"Oh, don't worry. I don't plan to drink for a very long time."

Helen went to turn away, but he grabbed her arm. "Is there

something other than last night that's upsetting you?" He glanced behind her at Malcolm, who was already crossing toward them. "You looked like you were arguing over there."

Her eyes flared, and she opened her mouth, but then Malcolm stepped up to them and put a hand on her shoulder. "We should get going, Helen."

She nodded and turned. Malcolm gave Holden a tight smile before they both walked out of The Tea House.

What was going on with them?

He shifted his attention back as Mrs. Gerald set his coffee on the counter. "Here you go."

He paid and thanked the tea house owner. He was just stepping outside when he ran into Pam Hayes.

The older woman smiled at him. The same wide, welcoming smile she always offered. "Holden."

"Hi, Pam."

She welcomed him into one of those tight, familiar hugs.

When she moved back, her features were harder. She gripped his upper arms. "Thank you."

"You don't need to—"

"*I do.* Jesse told me everything that happened last night. If it wasn't for you..."

Holden was glad she didn't finish her sentence. He didn't want to think about what those assholes would have done either.

"You know I'd do anything to protect Clara," he said, voice lower now...harder.

"I know. It's just one of the reasons I love you." Then she tilted her head and studied him, something he couldn't place flickering over her features.

He wanted to squirm. She was the only person in the world who could make him feel uncomfortable with a single look. And he only felt like that because she saw too much.

"You're coming to dinner Sunday night, aren't you?" Pam finally asked.

Family dinner. Shit. He'd forgotten about that. It had been hard enough to be around Clara this morning. How could he go to a dinner with her family?

"I actually—"

"Don't you tell me you're busy, Holden Forbes. It's called family dinner for a reason, and you're family, which means you're required every week."

His gut gave a hard kick. Because before he'd met Jesse, he hadn't had a family. "I'll be there."

She squeezed his arm. "Good. I'll see you later, honey."

Then she walked into The Tea House, and he was left wondering what the hell he was going to do about Clara.

CHAPTER 11

"*I*'m going to tell him."

Indie's glass paused halfway to her mouth before she looked at Clara. "You're going to tell who what?"

Clara glanced at Holden across her mother's yard. He was drinking beer with her brothers, and it was taking everything in her not to stare.

She looked back at Indie and lowered her voice. "I'm going to tell Holden I'm a virgin."

An almost thirty-year-old virgin. God, she could already feel the heat crawling up her neck.

Indie grabbed Clara's arm and dragged her to a corner of the yard. "Why?"

"Because I turn thirty in two weeks, and I don't want to go into my thirties a virgin. It's not just about sex. It's about being close and intimate with another person. I want that. I want to experience it. And I'd like it to be with him."

"Clara—"

"He kissed me. *He* kissed *me*. When he did, it was like every nerve in my body woke up, and I felt alive and electric. It was raw and real, and he felt it too. I know he did. I saw and felt it in him.

And now I just need to give him all the information and he can do with that what he wants. He can decide if the kiss changed anything."

"And if it didn't?"

Her stomach did a sad roll. "Then I'll live with that. I'll put space between us. I'll try to get over this thing between him and me. And I'll explore other options. I think I've really closed myself off to those other options because I've always hoped he'd love me." It sounded pathetic.

Indie tilted her head. "You know I love you. But I don't want to see you get hurt."

"It would hurt more for me to give up after that kiss." She swallowed, catching sight of him across the yard again, a deep yearning stirring in her belly. "I've been on this journey the last few years to chase everything I want. And I need to give this one last chance."

Indie sighed. "Come on. You're going to need a drink then."

Clara glanced at her friend as they made their way across the yard. There was something almost off about her today. "Are you okay?"

"Colt sent back the divorce papers."

Clara stopped. "Oh my gosh. And you let me go on about my little issues?"

"They're not little."

She rolled her eyes. "So he signed them?"

"I don't know. I can't bring myself to open the envelope yet, but I assume so."

"Why haven't you opened it?"

Indie lifted a shoulder, a thin film of tears building in her eyes. "I just saw his handwriting on the envelope and it did something to me. It threw me back to this time when we were together and happy, and the strain of him being away all the time and us trying to have a baby hadn't taken a toll on us."

"Oh, Indie..."

"I thought I was ready for this. I did everything—engaged a lawyer, got the papers written up, signed and sent them. But I know the second I open it..."

"It becomes official," Clara finished for her.

"Yep." Indie's chest rose and fell. "It's going to hurt."

Clara touched her friend's arm. "I'm here if you want me by your side. Heck, I can open it for you. You don't even have to look at the papers."

Indie leaned her head on Clara's shoulder. "I love you."

"I love you more."

"Dinner's ready, everyone," her mother called.

Clara's tummy rumbled so loudly that Indie laughed. "Let's get some food into us."

With the sun shining, they ate outside—grilled barbecue ribs, corn on the cob, potato salad, coleslaw, and green vegetables.

As she ate, her gaze kept inadvertently shifting to Holden. Sometimes he looked up and caught her gaze, and every so often she thought she caught a glimmer of something on his face. Emotion that she could have sworn matched the ones inside her.

She'd just finished eating when her phone rang. She frowned when she saw Malcolm's name on the screen. They'd exchanged numbers at one of the runs, and he'd messaged a couple times just to check in since the bar incident, but he'd never called.

She set her plate down and moved around to the side of her mother's house to answer the call. "Malcolm, hey. Is everything okay?"

"Yeah. I, um, need to ask you something. I actually asked Helen to ask, but she said the night was such a haze that she can't remember."

That sounded ominous. "What is it?"

"Did Helen say anything to you while you were outside? Did she mention anything about work?"

"She didn't say much," Clara said carefully, not sure why

Malcolm sounded so nervous. "She just mentioned the woman who died."

She wasn't sure why she left out the other part. Maybe because it felt kind of like ratting Helen out?

There was a small pause before Malcolm spoke. "Okay. Sure."

"Malcolm, is there anything going on at the hospital? Anything the community should be worried about?"

"No." Malcolm's answer came quickly. Almost too quickly. "Absolutely not. I need to go. Talk soon?"

"Yeah. Talk soon."

She hung up. That was...strange. After the attack, she hadn't really given a lot of thought to what Helen had told her. But if people were going to the hospital and getting worse rather than better, the public should be made aware, shouldn't they?

"Hey."

She jumped and spun to see Holden behind her, beer in hand. "Holden, I didn't hear you."

"Sorry." His gaze shifted to her phone, then back to her. "Is everything okay?"

"Yeah. That was Malcolm. He just had a quick question."

"About what?"

"It's not important." Or at least, she hoped it wasn't.

He stepped closer. "Clara, is something going on?"

"With Malcolm? No, of course not."

Holden watched her closely, as if trying to spot a lie, and she tried not to squirm. Finally, he nodded. "Okay. Come on, I'll walk back with you."

He stepped away, and her feet just started moving with him.

Was this it? Was this the moment to tell him?

Of course it was. She just needed to spit the words out.

He frowned down at her hands, which were wringing together. "Are you all right?"

"Actually, there's something I want to tell you."

"Shoot." He sipped his beer.

"I'm a virgin."

He choked and stopped in his tracks. *"What?"*

"I'm a virgin. And I'm turning thirty in a couple of weeks, and I don't want to go into my thirties *still* being a virgin."

His jaw was open and the expression on his face was almost comical. The man who was always so guarded and steady now looked at her with wide unblinking eyes and had a death grip on his beer.

She sucked in a breath. "You don't need to say anything right now. I just needed to tell you. Because when you kissed me, I felt something. I felt a lot of things actually, and they all make me think the same thing—that it's supposed to be you."

That familiar fear crept into his eyes, so she hurried to get the last words out.

"I know you're scared. But I would have kicked myself if I hadn't at least told you. I'm putting the ball in your court. If you say no, that I'm still not what you want, then that's okay." It would hurt, but she'd accept it. She'd have to. "But a part of me will always love you. And I want it to be you."

* * *

HOLDEN COULD BARELY STOMACH the huckleberry pie. Clara's words repeated in his head, toying with him.

A virgin. Clara was a virgin.

How was that even possible? She was gorgeous and smart and the kind of person people gravitated toward. And she was almost thirty.

He looked at her. She was eating her pie while talking to Aspen and Sky as though she hadn't just dropped the biggest bomb on his head.

"This pie is damn good," Jesse said as he sat beside him on the log.

"Has Clara dated over the years?"

Jesse's fork paused midway to his mouth. "Uh, not that I'm aware of. She's never brought anyone home to meet the family, but maybe while she was in New York. Why?"

"Just wondering." He downed half his beer.

"Uh-huh." Jesse glanced over at his sister, then back at Holden. "Clara's always known what she wants. First, it was to be a corporate lawyer in New York. She was twelve when she made that decision and she was laser focused. It took up almost all of her time and energy. Then she got sick, and she wanted to be home. She wanted family and a more relaxed life. So she put the same energy into making *that* happen."

"You have the same tenacity," Holden mumbled. "It must be a Hayes thing."

Jesse shook his head. "No. Clara's better than me. Remember when she was diagnosed and everyone was freaking out, including you and me?"

Holden had only known Clara for a couple of years when she'd been diagnosed with cancer, but it hadn't mattered. The diagnosis had felt fucking heavy. He'd called and messaged to check in as much as he could. And any time he got any leave, it was spent here, in Amber Ridge.

"Clara *didn't* freak out," Jesse continued. "She gave herself one week to grieve, then her entire focus went into beating the cancer. She didn't let it break her. She just did what she needed to do."

"She's focused."

"She is."

"But how does that relate to her not dating anyone?"

"She fights for what she wants. So, if she hasn't dated anyone, she either hasn't met the person she wants yet or she's still fighting for them." Jesse squeezed his leg before rising. "I need more whipped cream for my pie."

Holden frowned at Jesse as he walked away. Did he know? Holden hadn't told him about the kiss because he hadn't known what the hell to say. And it would have brought up questions that he didn't have the answers to.

His gaze shifted back to Clara, but she was no longer with the women. She was holding an empty jug and walking toward the back door of the house.

Like his feet had a mind of their own, he stood and started in the same direction.

He stepped in just as Clara was moving away from the sink, full jug in hand.

"Holden, what are you—"

He slipped the jug from her fingers and led her into the walk-in pantry before closing the door with a thud. Why, exactly, he wasn't sure. Because he'd lost his goddamn mind at the exact moment this woman had told him she was a virgin?

Clara gasped. "What the heck are you doing?"

"You can't do that." He was shout-whispering, but he didn't care.

"Do what? Refill the water at my mother's house?"

"Tell me you're a *virgin* at your mother's house."

Pink tinged her cheeks. "I wanted you to know."

"Not here."

"Then where? At our Thursday or Sunday running club? You've barely looked at me the last few sessions."

It was true. But even if it wasn't, *that* wasn't the right place to do it either. *Nowhere* felt right. "What am I supposed to do with that information?"

She tilted her head. "You *know* what. Decide whether you want me like I want you."

"Before your thirtieth birthday? It sounds like an ultimatum."

"It's not an ultimatum."

"Have sex with you in the next two weeks or you'll have sex with someone else?" Fuck, even saying it out loud sounded wrong.

She squirmed where she stood. "Okay. I guess saying it like

that sounds like an ultimatum. But if you're really not interested in me, then you can give me a simple no and move on."

He growled. "Nothing about this is simple."

She stepped closer and lowered her voice. "Holden, look, I'm sorry. Maybe I shouldn't have said anything. I just...I wanted you to know."

She stood so close that he could see the specks of gold in her blue eyes. Could smell that floral scent right under his nose. "Why?"

"Why did I want you to know?"

"No. Why haven't you...slept with anyone?"

Her throat bobbed and the smallest line creased her brow. "Because I was always busy. Busy studying. Busy being a lawyer. Then busy trying to live."

"You haven't been busy these last few years."

"You're right. I haven't." Her voice was softer now, her gaze shifting between his eyes. And the way she looked at him, as if she were unraveling all of the unspoken fears inside him, made his heart beat faster. It was like she saw the weakest parts that he tried to keep hidden, but she didn't run from them.

"We shouldn't have kissed the other day." The words felt wrong on his tongue.

"Says who?" A beat of silence passed before she tilted her head. "It's okay to be scared, Holden. But do you really want that fear to dictate your life forever?"

The quiet in her voice spoke to him, like a fucking lullaby. He reached for her hip, letting the gentle curve of her body calm that storm in his chest. He stepped closer so that her front pressed to his.

Then a question whispered in his head...one that had no business being there. Would one more taste be so terrible?

Her palms smoothed over his chest, and suddenly his head was lowering. He could almost feel her lips against his...

When the pantry door swung open and Pam stood there.

Clara's mother's mouth opened in an 'O' but that was quickly replaced by a small smile. "Sorry."

She closed the door, and he and Clara were left alone once again. But the moment was broken.

Holden stepped away. "We should get back."

She nodded, but disappointment shone in her eyes.

He seemed to be disappointing her a lot lately. And yeah, he hated himself for it.

CHAPTER 12

*A*ir whooshed in and out of Clara's chest as her feet hit the asphalt.

Still not easier. Not even a little bit. Her body felt heavy, her legs begging her to stop or cave.

She glanced beside her to see Scarlett and Malcolm holding a conversation and not even breaking a sweat. Heck, even Deb, who was a good thirty years older than her, seemed to barely be pushing herself.

Helen didn't look great. But it didn't seem like a physical thing. She just seemed…off. She'd seemed off since the bar. Was the attack still affecting her?

Clara snuck a peek at Holden behind her. Same as always, he looked straight at her, like he could feel her eyes on him. Her skin tingled and she faced front again.

She shouldn't have told him she was a virgin on Sunday. What had she expected? For him to admit his undying love, take her into his arms and sweep her off to a bedroom in her mother's house?

Ha. That didn't happen.

Although, she was sure he'd been about to kiss her in that

pantry. If her mother hadn't opened the door, she was almost certain he would have.

Her hand twitched to run a finger over her lips, as if she could feel his kiss right there.

She stumbled, and Malcolm grabbed her arm. "Hey. Are you okay?"

"Yeah. Just distracted." Her words were as choppy as her short breaths, while Malcolm's voice was completely even.

One side of his mouth lifted. "We're almost at the diner."

Yes, because today they were having coffee at the diner after the run.

Argh. The drinks at the diner sucked. She would have chosen The Tea House, but Briar had organized it, so Clara would be getting a big cup of ice with soda water. Maybe two.

"Hey, are things still okay at the hospital?"

There was a small flaring of his eyes. "Of course. I'm focusing on the new sepsis treatment protocol. I'm doing a couple of speaking gigs later this week."

"Good. That's great."

It really was. The last thing the small town of Amber Ridge needed was for the safety of the only hospital to be brought into question.

She shot a glance at Scarlett from beneath her lashes. Clara needed to talk to her. She'd been piecing things together since her behavior in the kitchen, about what Helen had said about the hospital. First there'd been the article about Lauren Tabs. Then Scarlett's obsession with everyone who worked at the hospital, paired with her basically lying to Malcolm about what she did for a living.

She was researching the woman who'd died...maybe even linking that incident with anyone getting sick while in the hospital's care.

Clara swallowed the lump in her throat.

Maybe she was an undercover agent. That would explain the fake ID. Maybe Scarlett wasn't even her real name.

An uncomfortable pit formed in her belly. Yes, undercover agents were important to reveal horrible stuff that happened all over the country, but the idea that Clara didn't know who she was really living with didn't feel great.

When they finally reached the diner, Clara found a stool and dropped her head to the counter, trying to catch her breath. Not the most graceful and the cool counter might leave a mark on her cheek, but she had zero cares. She was tired.

The stool beside her moved, and for a moment she thought it might be Holden. It wasn't. Scarlett sat there, looking at the menu. Clara snuck a peek behind her to see Holden at a table beside Briar.

A vein throbbed in her temple. They were together a lot at these runs, not to mention they had to be spending a bit of time on the kitchen renovation.

Could there be more there than a friendship? Her stomach rolled, and she looked away from them.

"Jesus, there's only one person serving." Scarlett scowled, shaking her head. "Should have gone to The Tea House."

So it wasn't just her.

Clara glanced around. No one was in listening distance. Good. She shuffled her stool closer. "Scarlett. We need to talk."

"Shoot." Scarlett lifted her phone, not even giving Clara eye contact.

"Can we go somewhere else?"

"I'm a little busy. My editor needs an answer on something, and I can't leave her hanging."

Fine. If she wanted to do it here, they'd do it here. "Are you investigating the woman who died and linking it to the recent heart failures and respiratory depressions at the hospital? Are you trying to put the hospital at fault?"

Scarlett's head flashed up, shock widening her eyes. "What?"

"That's why you joined this group, isn't it? To get close to everyone who works there."

Scarlett leaned in close to Clara and hissed, "First of all, what I do is none of your business. Second, if you tell anyone your little theory, you'll regret it." Then she got up and stormed off.

She'd regret it? Was that a threat? Was that even allowed in the world of journalism?

At the feel of eyes on her, she looked at Holden's table to see him staring straight at her, questions and concern in his gaze.

The stool beside her scraped once again as Malcolm sat down. "Hey. Is everything okay?"

Should she tell him? If she did, what would Scarlett do?

She opened her mouth, not sure what words were about to come out, when she noticed Helen down at the other end of the counter, drinking a coffee alone. "Is Helen okay? She hasn't seemed herself since that night at the bar."

He glanced at Helen, then back to her. "You don't need to worry about Helen."

"I *do* worry about her. I worry about you too, and everyone else. I know stuff's going on at the hospital. Patients are getting sick. It has to be weighing on you."

He blanched before grabbing her wrist and leading her to the hall beside the counter.

"Malcolm, what are you—"

He turned. "Did Helen tell you that?"

"Um…maybe. Why?"

"You can't talk about it in public."

"But if it's okay now, why does it matter?"

"Because we're all trying to leave it in the past. It's *over*. Helen's fine. I'm fine. Everything's okay."

"You don't pull someone into a hall to tell them to stop talking about something if everything's okay."

His lips thinned, and little lines formed beside his eyes. It was the first time she'd seen him visibly frustrated. "Clara—"

"Everything okay here?"

Clara looked up to see a very annoyed-looking Holden.

* * *

HOLDEN FISTED HIS HANDS, trying like hell to remain exactly where he was and not break up whatever little chat Clara and Malcolm were having. It was none of his business, so he shouldn't care how close they sat or how intimate their conversation looked.

Briar had sat next to him and was talking about some doctor at work and something the guy had done to piss her off. Holden could barely pay attention.

Suddenly, Malcolm grabbed Clara and dragged her into the hall.

Fuck no.

Holden shot to his feet and crossed the diner, weaving through the customers and ignoring Briar calling him from behind.

He stepped into the hall to see Malcolm's fingers still closed around Clara's wrist, and his face too damn close to hers.

"Clara—"

"Everything okay here?" Holden asked, interrupting Malcolm and putting every ounce of effort into using his words, rather than his hands like he wanted to.

Malcolm stepped back, eyes wide, as if Holden had caught him doing something he wasn't supposed to.

Clara frowned. "We were just talking. You don't need—"

"It's okay," Malcolm said quickly. "I should get back to the group."

The doctor slipped around Holden, but he barely spared him a glance, his entire attention on Clara. "Him?"

The frown on Clara's face deepened. "Him what?"

"You're gonna have sex with *him*?"

Her chest rose on a sharp inhale. "Shh." She pushed Holden deeper into the hall before whispering, "First of all, that's rude. There's nothing wrong with Malcolm. Second, it wouldn't be your business if he and I *did* decide to sleep together."

She started to slip past him, but he gripped her wrist and stopped her. "You *made* it my business by starting this conversation."

"You're right. I'm sorry about that. You've made your feelings for me perfectly clear. I don't know what I was thinking." She swallowed and stepped back. "I respect the fact that you see me as a sister, so *you* need to respect the fact that I can talk to whoever I want, whenever I want."

He could have laughed. Hell, he almost did. "You think I see you as a sister?"

"Of course. You call me family. Other than looking out for me at running club and protecting me from scary doctors, you don't seem to want anything more to do with me. Now, if you'll excuse me."

"I don't want you dating him."

She stopped, frustration all over her face. And something else. Disbelief?

Not a surprise. He had no fucking right to dictate who she dated, and they both knew that.

"Excuse me?" she whispered.

He said it again, slower this time as he inched closer. "I don't want you dating him."

"You're unbelievable. You know that?"

"Clara—"

"No. Don't *Clara* me. I put myself out there for you—more than once. I took risks and allowed my heart to be trampled on. You've turned me down, and yet you stand there and tell me that you don't want me to date someone? And not just anyone. A great guy. A great *doctor*. A man who's kind and friendly and—"

"He's not for you."

"Who the hell are *you* to tell me who is and isn't for me?"

"I know you."

"No. You don't. You know parts of me. But not that part."

"I *know* you."

She stepped closer. "Don't ever tell me who I can and can't date again." She stepped away, only to stop and face him once more. "You know, I think a part of me has been waiting for you since the day we met, thinking that it was supposed to be us. But I'm done waiting."

She turned again but for the second time, he gripped her arm and tugged her back—and this time he kissed her.

And there was no hesitation in this kiss. He dove straight into her mouth and tasted her. Drank her in.

She groaned, and the sound was becoming so achingly familiar that it felt like it was his. Like the sound of her passion was *designed* for him. For *them*.

He turned her and pressed her to the wall, caging her in. Needing her to feel exactly how much of a lie he'd been spinning all these years.

* * *

CLARA COULDN'T BREATHE. She couldn't think. Holden was everywhere. Locking her to the wall. Touching her. Tasting her.

Every time he kissed her, it just cemented the fact that he was supposed to be hers and she was supposed to be his. It made the risk of waiting for him feel worth it.

She ran her hands down his chest, as though she needed to feel and memorize his body. To know him as well as she knew herself.

His tongue swiped against hers, making a shudder roll down her spine. And those strong hands of his enclosed around her waist, his fingers so long, they almost encircled her.

She leaned her hips into him, groaning when his hardness pressed into her.

This was it...this was what she'd been waiting for. She'd kissed men before but nothing like this. Nothing that even touched this.

She slipped a leg around his waist and nudged him closer. Immediately, his palm went to her thigh, holding her there, before sliding up and cupping her ass.

She was seconds from losing the thin hold she still had on her sanity when her phone rang, its tone loud in the otherwise quiet hall.

Suddenly, he stepped back, his finger slipping into his hair and a pained expression crossing over his face.

"Shit. I'm sorry, Clara."

She frowned, ignoring her phone, focusing on Holden. "Why are you sorry?"

"Because I can't keep doing this to you."

"You wanted to kiss me. You wanted *me*. I could feel it."

When he just stood there, holding the weight of the world on his shoulders, she stepped closer and placed a gentle hand on his chest, right over his heart. "Holden. It's okay to want me. It's okay for us to embrace this."

The pain shifted into something else. Panic? It looked so out of place on such a strong, powerful man.

"I have to go," he whispered.

She frowned, hurt cutting into her belly. But she didn't stop him. She watched him walk away. Because she couldn't keep fighting if he wasn't going to fight too.

CHAPTER 13

"*H*e kissed you *again?*" Indie gasped.

Clara poured hot water into two mugs. "Yep. And it was better than the first."

"You're kidding?"

"Nope." She stirred dandelion tea into the water. "But *then* he did the same thing he always does. He put this distance between us and acted like it was a mistake. Like touching me was the worst thing he could have done."

"Oh no. Why's he so scared to explore this thing between you? It's so clear there's something there."

"Mom thinks it's something about him being hurt. Not that I told her it was Holden I was talking about. It's confusing and frustrating and…it hurts me, Indie."

"Of course it does. He makes you think there's hope, then he rips it away from you."

That's exactly what it was. "You know what I need? Some space from him. I'm going to text him and let him know that I'm not going on any runs for the next couple of weeks, and then I'm just going to keep my distance."

"You know that won't be easy. Not in this town, which is the size of a shoebox, and not when he's basically part of the family."

She lifted her mug. "Well, lucky for me, I'm great at being a hermit." She wasn't even kidding—she loved being home. Seeing her acupuncture clients and drinking tea was what she lived for. She absolutely could stay away from him...at least, she was pretty sure. "How are *you*?"

"Well, I have a photography client this morning. An engagement couple."

Didn't really answer her question. "So business is picking back up?"

Indie scoffed. "No. It's one of two bookings this week. I really don't know what's going on this past year. I used to be *so* busy."

"You're the only family photographer in town. If people aren't going to you, where are they going?"

"I don't know. I ran into Betty Hopper, who used to get yearly photos of her and her husband with me, and she was so strange."

"Strange how?"

"Cold and distant, and when I mentioned that she missed her yearly photo, she just mumbled something about forgetting to book it, then left."

Clara frowned. "Betty Hopper never forgets anything."

"Exactly. She's sixty years old with the best memory around."

"You don't think Colt's mother has anything to do with it, do you?"

There was a small pause. "I mean...it's crossed my mind. But no, Sylvia wouldn't do that. She says things that annoy me a lot, but she wouldn't directly try to sabotage my business...would she?"

"I'm not sure." She nibbled her bottom lip before asking the next question. "If you're not getting many bookings, money must be tight. Do you need—"

"Don't say it."

"Indie, you're family and you're my best friend. If you need help—"

"I don't need help. Things will pick up. I know they will." She cleared her throat. "Do you have your first client soon?"

Clara sighed and lifted her cell from the counter to check the time. "Yeah, in ten minutes. It's actually Helen, from our running club. I was really surprised when she booked it."

"She didn't tell you she was?"

"No. She made the booking online yesterday."

"Is that strange?"

"No. I think she needs it. From what I can see, she hasn't been herself since the incident at the bar."

"Well, lucky you're the magic needle lady."

Clara chuckled. "I feel far from magic at the moment."

Indie checked her watch. "All right. I need to go to the shoot."

"You haven't drunk your tea."

Indie cringed. "Sorry." Then she leaned over and kissed Clara's cheek. "Chat soon."

The second her cousin stepped out, Clara glanced at her phone. Should she text Holden now? But what would she write?

Her fingers tapped across the screen.

Clara: Hey. Just letting you know I won't be at running club for the next week.

Send. Done.

The three dots popped up immediately, and her dang heart gave a little thump when his text came through.

Holden: Is everything okay?

Did he really need to ask that?

Clara: I'm not injured or sick, if that's what you mean. Have a great week.

The three dots popped up again, then disappeared. A second later, his text came through.

Holden: You too, Clara. Call if you need anything.

She absolutely would not be doing that. She'd made herself

vulnerable twice with him, and both times he'd basically run from her. Kissed her and run, that was.

She lifted her tea and moved to her acupuncture studio, where she turned on the music before setting up her diffuser. Lavender, bergamot, and ylang-ylang. The perfect essential oil blend to turn her morning around. The moment the scents hit the air, Clara's nerves calmed.

This was why she did what she did...to create peace and alignment. It was more powerful than a lot of people realized. A person's nervous system could wreak such havoc on health.

A knock came at the door to the studio, and Clara opened it with a smile to see Helen on the other side. "Hi."

Helen returned her smile. "Hi, Clara."

"Come in."

Clara stepped back and indicated the seat. "Please, sit. How are you today?"

"I'm okay."

Not at all convincing. "I noticed on your form that this is your first time trying acupuncture?"

"Yeah. It's supposed to be good for stress, right?"

"*Great* for stress. You didn't write much else on your form though."

Helen lifted a shoulder. "That's all I'm really here for."

Clara nodded slowly. "Okay. So what my clients usually do is—"

"Could I use your bathroom first?"

"Oh, um...sure. It's just inside the house. I'll take you through."

Helen followed her into the living room and down the hall, where they stopped at the bathroom door. "Here you go. Would you like me to wait here?"

"It's okay. I can make my way back."

"Okay. See you back in the room."

Clara returned to her studio. Luckily, Scarlett had left early

NYSSA KATHRYN

that morning, something Clara only knew because her car was gone. It wouldn't matter a whole lot if the two women bumped into each other, but Clara preferred to keep her clients separate from her home life during appointments.

She got the needles ready, then waited. When five minutes passed and Helen still wasn't back, Clara frowned and looked at the door.

Should she check on her?

She waited another minute, and when Helen still didn't return, she moved back into the house. In the hall, she stopped at the bathroom door. It was open.

She poked her head in to see an empty bathroom.

What the heck?

Suddenly, Helen stepped out of Scarlett's room.

Clara straightened. "Helen, what are you—"

"I'm *so* sorry. I noticed the records in this room and I'm a sucker for a good Bob Marley record."

Clara crossed over to Scarlett's room and ducked her head in. Nothing looked out of place.

She closed the door. "Come on. Let's get back." But the entire walk, she kept flicking her gaze toward Helen, wondering what she'd really been doing in Scarlett's bedroom.

* * *

HOLDEN CUT a piece of foam weather stripping to fit the length of Deb's new doorframe. The adhesive back was sticky, but he worked quickly, pressing it firmly into place along the bottom of the door, just where the frame met the threshold.

He'd been here all morning. Deb was home and had popped out a dozen times to offer him water and coffee and cookies. She'd also spent a fair chunk of the morning talking to him about anything and everything. He was pretty sure he knew her entire life story, had the name of every family member, and was up to date on the full schedule of her week.

It was a good distraction from Clara and their kiss. *Second* kiss. And the second damn time he'd run afterward.

He tried to focus on what he was doing. On making sure the weather stripping was flush, tight, and clean. After this, he'd apply the doorknobs, then he'd go home and work on Briar's kitchen cabinetry.

Maybe if he could exhaust his body enough, he could get Clara out of his head.

When the weather stripping was done, he went to his truck and got the knobs and the tools to install them. The door had already been pre-drilled, so it wouldn't take long.

He'd just returned to the door when footsteps sounded in the hall, then Deb's voice.

"Oh my, look at that door. You, Holden Forbes, are *so* good with your hands."

His lips twitched. The woman had been complimenting him on anything and everything all morning. His ego certainly enjoyed being here. "Thanks. I'm almost done."

"And so efficient. Amber Ridge really hit the jackpot when you decided to move to town."

"Thank you, ma'am."

Deb threw back her head and laughed. "Oh God, please, no ma'am. I already feel old being around all these young-gun doctors and nurses. Even Malcolm's a good couple decades younger than me, and look at all he's achieved."

His fingers tightened around the baseplate as he aligned it with the holes, making sure it sat level and straight. "Do you know him well?"

"He's been at our hospital for three years. He's humble, but also proud of his work. And he should be after this whole sepsis treatment plan. Although..."

Holden stopped before putting the screws into place. "Although what?"

"I mean…he had a lot of help on the treatment plan and didn't really give anyone else any recognition. But he's young."

So the doctor was selfish. Good. Another reason to dislike him. "Is there anything else going on at the hospital?"

Deb's eyes widened, and she probably didn't realize it, but she'd just given away the answer—there *was*.

"There's always stuff going on," she rushed out with a nervous laugh. "I think you get that at every workplace."

He wasn't sure that was true.

He used his screwdriver to insert the screws into place, making sure the knobs were secure. Deb watched as he finished the last bit of the door installation.

"All finished," he said at the end.

"Oh, you are an angel." Her phone rang, and she withdrew it from her pocket and frowned. "Sorry. I have to answer this."

"All good. I'll pack up my tools."

She moved down the hall to answer the call, and he began taking things back to his truck. He was just packing the back of his truck when his phone vibrated with a text.

Clara: Hey. Just letting you know I won't be at running club for the next week.

What the hell? Why? Because of *him*? Or was it her health?

An uncomfortable pit formed in his stomach.

Holden: Is everything okay?

Clara: I'm not injured or sick, if that's what you mean. Have a great week.

It *was* him. He started writing that she didn't need to miss it on his account but stopped. If she was going, so was he…and she was clearly trying to avoid him.

And he couldn't blame her for that. He'd kissed her twice, then pushed her away.

He didn't know what the hell to write, so he went with something simple that didn't even begin to fix anything.

Holden: You too, Clara. Call if you need anything.

He cursed and shoved the cell into his pocket.

Once everything was clean and his tools were in the truck, he stepped back into the house. Deb still wasn't back. He started down the hall, only to stop when he heard a shouted whisper.

"Stop! You're blowing everything out of proportion. You need to let it go. I need to go."

Holden was just turning when a door swung open.

Deb's brows rose. "Holden."

He cleared his throat. "Hey. Just came to find you to tell you that I've finished."

"Good. Great. Thank you."

"Is everything okay?"

Her gaze flicked to her phone, then back to him. "Yeah. Like I said, every workplace is complicated."

So, she'd been talking to someone from work.

"Thank you again for your help," Deb hurried to add. "I'll pay the rest of the invoice today."

"Call if you have any issues."

He turned and headed back to his truck. Once inside, he didn't leave right away but kept his eyes on the house.

What was going on at that hospital? And why did it feel like a bigger deal than everyone was letting on?

CHAPTER 14

*C*lara stared at the text message as she leaned on the kitchen island, the cool evening breeze running over her skin from the open window. It was the third in the last three days from Holden. How was she supposed to get space from him when he kept contacting her? Did he *want* her to never get over him? Because that was how it felt.

She'd ignored the first text. Responded with a short "I'm fine" text yesterday. And just now, he'd texted to ask if they could talk.

About what? About how they kept doing this thing where she told him she loved him, he kissed her, then he pulled away and they were back where they'd started?

That wasn't healthy.

At the click of a door opening, she set her phone down as Scarlett stepped into the kitchen.

She wore a pretty red blouse with black slacks. It was nothing like how she usually dressed.

Clara straightened. "You look nice."

"Thanks," Scarlett said as she opened the fridge door.

"Got a date?"

"No. Just hanging out with some people from the running club."

Clara frowned. "Who?"

"Malcolm. Deb. A few others." She lifted out a plate of brownies that she'd made earlier and started placing them into a container.

Clara had been wondering why Scarlett made them. It was the first time she'd baked since moving in.

Should Clara be offended that she wasn't invited to this little catch-up? She felt like she should be offended. And hanging out with people and eating brownies sounded a heck of a lot better than stewing at home about the Holden stuff.

Clara cleared her throat. "You know, I have no plans tonight. I could—"

"Sorry, Clara. If it was at a public venue, I'd invite you, but it's at Deb's house." Scarlett popped another few brownies into the container before putting the plate back in the fridge. "I'll see you later."

Then she left. Just walked out. God, this was the same as high school when everyone she hung out with got invited to a party and she didn't.

Now she really was offended.

Maybe that wasn't rational. Scarlett wasn't her friend, just a roommate. And sure, Clara saw everyone from the running club a couple times a week, but they weren't really friends, either.

She shouldn't be offended. She wasn't. Absolutely not...well, kind of not.

What she *was*, was hungry. And if Scarlett wasn't going to invite her to their little hangout, well, she could at least share her brownies.

She opened the fridge door, spotting the two remaining brownies on the plate.

They had her name on them.

And you know what? She didn't drink often, but a vodka

seltzer would go great with the brownies. Yes, those were Scarlett's too, but right now, Clara didn't care.

She grabbed the brownies and drink from the fridge and took them to the living room.

Maybe it was time to look for a new roommate. She really hadn't wanted to, in case the new person was loud or messy or intrusive, but after the whole "are you investigating the hospital" conversation, she wasn't as willing to have the other woman in her life.

She flicked through Netflix. Nothing. There was nothing that she hadn't seen before that looked good.

Screw it. She was watching *Notting Hill*. She'd watched it a gazillion times and could probably recite the film scene by scene, but it was a comfort.

The second it was on, she grabbed a brownie and drink and leaned back on the couch.

How many times had she watched this movie while going through chemo? So many times she'd lost count. Usually, it helped the world make sense again. But today? Today she was distracted.

She was halfway through the movie, two thirds of her way through her vodka seltzer and one and a half brownies down, when her phone vibrated with another text.

She reached for the phone on the coffee table—only to almost tip right off the sofa.

She froze, and suddenly the room swayed.

What the heck?

She squinted at her cell, as if that could somehow keep it from moving.

What was going on? She couldn't already be tipsy, she hadn't even finished the whole bottle.

Maybe she'd drunk it too fast?

The doorbell rang, and she jumped. Who could that be? She wasn't expecting anyone and Scarlett used her key.

She pushed to her feet, only to waver.

Okay, the liquor had absolutely gone straight to her head.

Slowly, she moved to the door. When she opened it, her jaw dropped.

Holden.

She felt like she should be annoyed that he was there. But all she could feel was this fuzzy warmth in her belly. It had to be the alcohol.

Her lips stretched into a wide smile. "Hey. What are *you* doing here?"

"I need to talk to you." He ran his fingers through his hair.

Her gaze caught on those fingers. On the thickness of his knuckles. The veins in his hands. "You have sexy fingers."

He frowned. "Thanks."

"You're welcome."

"Can I come in?"

"Sure. It's nice that *someone* wants to spend the evening with me." See, she didn't need Deb's little gathering.

Holden stepped inside, watching her closely now. "Are you okay?"

"Depends on what you mean by okay. I almost fell over when I reached for my phone and I'm blaming the vodka seltzer."

He inched closer. "How many did you drink?"

"Zero-point-seven-five of a bottle...but that's an estimation." She turned, only to immediately kick her foot into the wall. "Sweet baby carrots, that hurt!"

Holden's reflexes were like lightning as he grabbed her arm. "Clara, what's going on?"

"I think I drank it too fast." She massaged her temple. "I need to lie down."

The room began to spin again.

Without hesitation, Holden slipped an arm around her waist and behind her legs and lifted her up against him.

She gasped and touched his chest...his very sculpted chest. "Oh...this is nice."

It was a two-second walk to the couch, but in that time, she managed to feel many muscular ridges.

"This is probably the best chest I've felt in my life," she said, speaking her thoughts out loud. "Not that I've felt many chests. Most men's chests don't appeal to me, but yours is like a fine wine."

He set her on the couch.

Her gaze zeroed in on the TV screen. "Want to watch *Notting Hill* with me? I haven't gotten to the, 'I'm just a girl, standing in front of a boy, asking him to love her' part. It's my favorite. Although, it might not be *your* favorite, if our past conversations are anything to go by."

Holden lowered in front of her and studied her eyes. "Are you sure you drank only half a bottle of vodka seltzer?"

"I'm as sure as a dog in a bone factory."

Not even a twitch of his lips. Well, *she* thought she was funny.

Holden scanned the room, as if it held answers to all his questions. His gaze landed on the half-eaten brownie. "Where did you get that?"

She scoffed and little bits of spit flew out of her mouth, and she quickly covered it with her hand. Whoops. "Sorry."

"Clara—where did you get the brownie?"

"The fridge."

A muscle in his jaw ticked. "Who made them?"

"Scarlett, for her private little gathering tonight that I didn't get invited to. Pretty silly, if you ask me. I'm great company."

He lifted what was left and smelled it, then he sat on the couch and studied her eyes some more.

The feeling of euphoria while having Holden's eyes on her was actually kind of nice. Screw Scarlett's gathering. This was better.

She reached out and smoothed the line between his brows. "You frown too much."

"It's what you do when you're angry."

She cringed. "Is it because I started *Notting Hill* without you?"

"Because your roommate laced those brownies."

Her eyes widened. "With what?"

"Marijuana."

Clara gasped. "She did not!"

"Then explain what's going on."

She closed her eyes and leaned back. "Can't. Too tired."

"I'm getting you water. And when your roommate gets home, we're having a conversation with her."

Holden's footsteps sounded, and she cracked one eye open to watch his back as he opened a cupboard door and grabbed a glass. Even though the world was foggy and moving in circles, Holden was crystal clear. The strength in his back through his shirt. The way he moved with such power and purpose.

He looked good in her house. Exactly why she hadn't wanted him in it.

"I need to ask you something," she said softly.

Those muscles in his back visibly tightened as he filled the glass with water. "Okay."

"Why does loving me scare you so much?"

* * *

EVERY MUSCLE in Holden's body tightened, and for a second, he didn't move.

Slowly, he forced himself to turn, glass of water in hand. "Now's probably not the best time for that conversation."

She snorted. "If it were up to you, there would never be a best time."

It was true. He was a damn coward.

He returned to the couch and handed the water to Clara. Her

eyes were half hooded, her lips stretched into a small smile. "Thank you."

Fury coursed through his veins that her roommate had laced the brownies. He didn't fucking care if they weren't meant for Clara, they were in *her* house. Why had she done it?

Clara sipped some water, then looked at the glass, her brows pulled together and, despite the drugs, she suddenly looked focused...almost sad.

"What are you thinking about?" he asked softly.

"This book that I read while I was going through chemotherapy."

Holden wasn't sure he wanted to know. Still, he asked, "What book?"

"It was called *The Slight Edge*. And there was one part that hit me so hard. Olson wrote that on average, only ten people cry at a funeral." She looked up at him. "You live an entire freaking life and only *ten people* are sad enough that you're gone to cry."

His voice softened. "People will cry at your funeral, Clara." Although, that wouldn't be happening for a long fucking time.

"*Then,*" she continued like she hadn't heard him, "he wrote that the number one factor that determines whether people will go from your funeral to your burial is the weather. So if it rains, half of those non-crying, pretend-to-love-me fakers won't be there for my final moment before I'm put into the ground."

"You're not going to be put into the ground."

"One day I will."

His back teeth ground together. He hated that thought. "Not for a long fucking time."

"But when that day does come—"

"People will go to your burial."

She tilted her head. "Will you go to my burial, even if it rains?"

"You're not—"

"I know. I'm not going to die for a *long fucking time*." His lips twitched. "But when I do...will you go to my burial if it rains?"

"I'd go to your burial in a hurricane."

A slow smile curved her lips. "You would not."

"I would. But I won't have to. Because I'm dying first."

She laughed, and the sound hit him in the fucking chest. "I don't think so. You know too many ways to defend yourself, and you won't let sickness take you down. I'm definitely going first. And when I do, I'll be watching from the sky to make sure you cry at my burial."

He squeezed her thigh. "I believe you."

"Good." She yawned and closed her eyes. "Do laced brownies make you tired?"

"Yeah, they do."

"Good. This is good. A new life experience. I like adding those to the list. I'm not even mad at Scarlett anymore."

He was.

Clara suddenly lay down and pillowed her head on his lap.

For a moment, he was still. So still that he didn't move a single muscle. Because she felt good against him. Really damn good.

Then she reached behind her for his wrist and placed his hand on her waist. "Mm. It feels good to have your arm around me."

"Yeah, it does." He hadn't meant for that drop of truth to come out, but it had.

He caressed her hip with his thumb, neither of them watching the movie.

"Holden?"

"Yeah, honey?"

"Is it because I was sick?"

Something hard and uncomfortable lodged in his gut. "Is what because you were sick?"

"Is that why you're scared to love me? Because you think I'm damaged or less than...or I'm more at risk of getting sick again?"

He cursed before gently tugging her up so he could see her face. "No. You're *perfect*. Everything about you is perfect. And I never want to hear you say anything to contradict that again."

She swallowed, her gaze shifting between his eyes. "Then what is it?"

"It's me. It's *all* me." His chest rose and fell, and the words just tumbled out. "I'm scared to love because I can't allow a person to become my entire world. I never want that power to be put into another person's hands again."

"Why?" she whispered.

"Because when they leave, my whole world crumbles."

Her frown was deep as she studied him. "Because of your mom?"

"Yeah. She was my only family. My best friend. And when she got sick, she told me—*promised me*—that she was going to be okay. And then I watched her become sicker and sicker, year by year, and I was helpless to do anything about it. I watched her die, and I couldn't protect her from that."

"You can't protect everyone."

"Exactly."

Tears gathered in her eyes. "So you learned that love hurts."

"I learned that love leaves you vulnerable and is inherently painful and doomed to end."

Pain cut across Clara's features. "Maybe." She reached out and cupped his cheek. "But love is also the most magical and powerful emotion in the world. It can make you feel things, good things, that nothing else can ever make you feel. I believe that to have loved, even if it ended in loss, is better than never to have loved at all."

He tried to swallow, but his throat felt fucking dry. "What if when you lose the person you love, you also lose yourself?"

"I lost myself the day the doctor told me I had cancer. But then I became someone else. A more authentic, more resilient version of who I was. Losing yourself doesn't have to be bad."

"I didn't notice a change in you. You were always authentic and resilient to me."

One side of her mouth lifted. "Are you just saying that because I'm high?"

A soft laugh slipped from his lips. "I'm saying that because it's true."

There was a small pause, and the slight smile fell from Clara's mouth. "I wish things were different."

He wished *he* was different. Stronger. More willing to risk his heart.

She yawned again before leaning her head against his shoulder.

Instinctively, his arm went around her. He leaned his head against hers and closed his eyes. It felt good to hold her. For a second, he could almost convince himself she was his.

He wasn't sure how long they sat that way. At some point, the movie ended and the room fell into silence, with Clara's soft breathing the only sound in the room.

Even when he knew she was asleep, he didn't move. He wanted to stay exactly where he was and just hold her for as long as he could.

But eventually, he knew he had to get up.

Gently, he slipped one arm around her back and the other behind her legs and stood. She sighed and snuggled into him.

When he reached her bedroom, he gently slid her into bed and tucked the sheet and blanket around her. He was about to leave when she spoke.

"Holden?"

"Yeah, honey?"

"Can I tell you what I think?"

"You always do."

Her eyes opened, her indigo eyes beaming into him. "There's a future version of you who's standing in the clouds watching, screaming down at you that you're stronger than you think. You should listen to him. He's very wise."

Her words hit him hard in the gut, knocking the air right out of him.

He slipped a lock of hair from her cheek. "You make me want to be stronger."

"Then do it."

CHAPTER 15

*C*lara groaned as she rolled from her belly to her back. She felt hungover. Her head was groggy, she was tired even though she was pretty sure she'd slept all night, and *God*, her mouth was dry.

Water. She needed a big, gigantic glass of water.

She opened one eye. Light streamed into her room from the crack between the curtains. Definitely morning.

She was about to climb out of bed when water on her bedside table caught her attention. Interesting. She didn't usually sleep with water beside her bed.

She pushed up and lifted the glass, then drank half of it before noticing the note. A tingly sensation ran over her skin.

Slowly, she reached for it.

Morning, Clara. I hope you're feeling okay. Drink lots of water and eat something, then text me to let me know you're okay so I don't worry all day. H.

And there went those butterflies in her belly.

This *was not* the distance she needed. Not even close.

She scrubbed her eyes, the previous night trickling back to her.

Laced brownies. Her roommate had made laced brownies. And she'd taken them to a gathering with people from the running club. People who Clara was pretty sure her roommate was investigating.

Why? To get information? Even if she was an undercover agent, that would get her fired. Even if it did get her the information she needed. The brownies had sure as hell made Clara loose-lipped last night.

She groaned as she swung her feet to the floor. She tested herself. Good. Her knees held her. She moved out of her bedroom and into the hall, stopping at the sight of folded sheets on the couch.

Had Holden stayed here for part of last night?

She was screwed. A whole Holden worth of screwed. There was no getting over the guy.

Why did he have to be so sweet and protective and cute while also being so adamant that they weren't going to be together? She was being set up to fail.

With a sigh, she moved down the hall and knocked on her roommate's door. When no noise sounded, she turned the handle and stepped inside. The room was dark, but she still spotted Scarlett hunched over her laptop at her desk, her back rising and falling in slow succession.

Jesus, that didn't look comfortable. How long had she been asleep like that?

Clara reached a hand out to wake her, then stopped. If she woke Scarlett, her roommate would probably be tired and angry. And *Clara* needed to be the angry one for this conversation. She needed answers. A whole bucket worth of them.

She was about to turn when Scarlett sighed and shifted. Only slightly, but it was enough for her to nudge the laptop and the screen to light up.

Clara frowned at the headline.

One Dead, More Sick, and Authorities Quiet: Unraveling the Mysteries of a Hospital in Crisis.

There it was—the confirmation Clara didn't really need that Scarlett was looking into the hospital staff. Still, it felt crappy knowing she'd basically been an accomplice in deceiving Malcolm, Deb, Helen, and all their colleagues. And who the heck was Scarlett's boss? Because they needed to know how she was getting her information.

This afternoon, she'd talk to Scarlett. Tell her that she was going to tell Malcolm what she was doing and ask her to move out.

It was time. *Past* time.

She headed back into her room, had a quick shower, and threw on a comfy, loose blouse and some high-waisted jeans. On her way out to the car, she saw Mildred across the road, gardening.

The older woman waved to her. "Morning."

"Good morning, Mildred. Not working today?"

"No. I have Sally on. And it's good to have a morning off to get some gardening done."

Clara chuckled. Even when the woman wasn't working in her store, she was still working with flowers. "I'm glad you have someone else in and your shop isn't closed, because I need some irises."

Mildred chuckled. "Well, I'll let you in on a little secret—if I'm ever not there and you're desperate for flowers, feel free to break in and take some using the spare key. It's in a fake rock in a hanging potted plant out front."

"You really think I'm desperate enough for fresh flowers that I'd break into a store? I am. And I'm so glad you know me well enough to realize that."

Mildred laughed. "Anytime, dear."

The drive to The Tea House was quick. Thank God, because she needed a sweet tea and she needed it now.

She'd just parked when someone by the entrance caught her attention. Malcolm. He had a phone pressed to his ear, and his hair was unkempt and disheveled.

Well, if this wasn't the universe screaming at her to tell him about Scarlett, she didn't know what was.

She climbed from her Volkswagen and reached Malcolm as he hung up. He looked angry and frustrated and a dozen other things, none of them good.

She gently touched his shoulder. "Malcolm."

He jumped and turned toward her. "Clara."

"Are you okay?"

"Uh...not really." He ran his fingers through his hair, his gaze lowering to the phone in his hand before lifting to her again.

"I need to talk to you," she said quietly. "Do you have a minute?"

"I—" His phone rang, and he cursed. "Sorry, I have to take this. Maybe later. I'll see you around."

He was across the lot before she could stop him.

Okay, maybe this wasn't the universe telling her to be honest with him. Not now, anyway.

With a sigh, she stepped into the café and spotted Jesse and Aspen in a booth. Jesse had his arm around his girlfriend, and they looked happy.

Well, at least someone did. She stopped at the counter and ordered her sweet tea before dropping into the booth opposite them.

Her brother frowned. "Hey, Clara. Are you okay?"

Did she look as exhausted as she felt? "Yeah, just tired."

Aspen reached over and squeezed her hand. "You know what you need? A big slice of Mrs. Gerald's pie. She made blueberry, and it might just be better than the rhubarb."

"You know, that actually sounds incredible." She nibbled her bottom lip before looking at her brother. "Can I ask you a sheriff question?"

"Shoot."

"Hypothetically speaking, if someone took brownies that were laced with marijuana to a social event, and everyone unknowingly consumed them, what consequences would that person face?"

Jesse frowned. "Well, marijuana's legal in Montana for medical and recreational use, but distributing or serving it to someone without their consent is not. So if it was proven to be true, they could face charges related to criminal deception and endangerment. Or worse if someone experienced a reaction to the drug."

She nodded quickly. She'd suspected that but had still wanted to ask. She really needed to talk to both Scarlett and Malcolm.

Aspen tilted her head. "Is everything okay?"

No. She was confused why her roommate would go so far for a story.

Clara opened her mouth, but before she could get another word out, Holden suddenly stopped beside the table. And he looked just as good as usual.

* * *

HOLDEN HAD BARELY SLEPT. Maybe a couple hours of broken sleep, that was it. He needed coffee and he needed it now.

He'd spent most of the night on Clara's couch and only left when the sun began to rise. He'd needed to stay and make sure she was okay. No way was he leaving her alone in a house in her state.

Her roommate had gotten home around two a.m. And that's when Holden had spoken to her. Or at least tried to. Scarlett had gone from zero to a hundred pretty damn quickly, shouting that he had no proof she'd done anything wrong before storming off to her bedroom.

It had done nothing to improve his mood. And if Clara didn't speak to Jesse today, then he would.

When he reached The Tea House, he saw Clara's Beetle in the parking lot.

Good. He'd be able to talk to Clara and see what she planned to do about her roommate. The woman was moving out of Clara's house, and if Clara didn't agree, then he'd sure as hell push the issue.

Inside, he found Jesse, Clara, and Aspen all sitting in a booth by the window. When he reached the table and Clara looked up, her eyes immediately flared.

So. Damn. Beautiful. Even when she was clearly tired.

He slipped in beside her. "Hey."

Her cheeks tinged a pretty shade of pink. "Hey."

"You feeling okay?"

She nodded quickly.

He looked up to see Jesse frowning at them.

"Why would she *not* be feeling okay?" he immediately asked.

"I've just been tired," Clara answered quickly, before Holden could.

So she hadn't told her brother about the brownies. Why the hell not? Because he was the sheriff and she was worried her roommate would get into trouble?

Screw that. Scarlett *should* get into trouble for what she'd done.

"Clara—"

"Have you ordered?"

She didn't want him to bring it up.

Mrs. Gerald stopped by their table. "Two sweet teas and two coffees."

"I didn't order," Holden said.

The lady gave a distracted smile. "I know. I saw you come in, so I made your usual. But I gave you a double shot because you look like you could use it."

He fucking loved this woman. "Thank you."

Mrs. Gerald was about to walk away when Aspen touched her arm. "Hey. Everything all right?"

The shop owner nodded. "I'm just worried about one of our new employees. She went into the hospital for a minor surgery yesterday and had a seizure while she was in recovery."

Clara visibly tensed beside him. "Do you know what caused it?"

Mrs. Gerald shook her head. "I checked on her this morning. She's never had a seizure before in her life. They're not sure what happened. I'm hoping she makes a full recovery."

"I'm so sorry," Aspen said gently. "If you need extra help, I could always jump behind the counter."

The older woman patted her arm. "That's very kind of you to offer. I'll let you know if it gets to that point."

Mrs. Gerald walked away while Clara suddenly straightened, her attention going to the counter. Holden followed her gaze— and tension swept through him.

Scarlett.

He shot to his feet and was halfway across the café when Clara grabbed his arm. "Holden! What are you doing?" Her voice was low, clearly not wanting Jesse to hear.

"I'm going to drag her to Jesse and demand she tell him what she did."

"*No.*" She stepped closer, her voice more of a shout-whisper. "*I'll* talk to her."

"I'll join you."

"Absolutely not. You look like you're about to kill someone."

Fuck yeah, he did. Clara had unknowingly consumed drugs, and the outcome could have been far worse than it was.

She squeezed his arm. "Sit back down...*please?*"

His hands fisted. That was the last thing he wanted to do.

Without a word, Scarlett finished her purchase and stepped outside. Clara hurried to follow, and Holden watched as she touched the other woman's arm outside the café. He couldn't hear what they were saying, but he saw the anger cut across Scarlett's face.

Scarlett was angry? Fuck that!

Not caring that Clara had told him to stay out of it, he stepped outside.

"I didn't do *anything* to those brownies. It sounds like you just had one too many drinks. And you shouldn't be eating my food anyway. I need to go." She started to stomp away.

"Hey!" Holden shouted when he reached Clara.

Scarlett turned. *"What?"*

"You need to explain yourself."

Scarlett's lips thinned and she stepped closer. "Actually, I don't. I didn't do anything, but even if I did, it's legal for me to have marijuana in Montana. So mind your own damn business!"

"It's *not* legal for you to serve it to other people without their consent," Clara pushed.

Scarlett cocked her head. "Has someone said that I served it to them without their consent? No. So leave me alone."

She started to turn again, but this time Clara called out, "Scarlett, I think it's time for you to move out."

Scarlett froze, the muscles in her back twitching before she turned.

"You can have a couple weeks to find somewhere else to live," Clara added, voice quieter now.

"Fine." The single word from Scarlett held barely concealed rage. Then she stormed off.

Holden turned to Clara. "Are you okay?"

"Yeah. I should have done that weeks ago."

"Why didn't you?"

She lifted a shoulder. "I don't know. I didn't want to look for someone else in case they were even worse."

He scoffed. They couldn't get much worse.

"Do you know why she did it?" he asked.

Clara swallowed. "I'm positive she's investigating the hospital. Linking that woman who died to patients who've been getting sick."

"*What?*"

They both turned to see Jesse stepping outside, Aspen close behind.

"Your roommate's looking into the hospital?" Jesse asked.

Clara wrapped her arms around her waist. "Yes. Do you already know what's going on there?"

"I know that the hospital administration has been looking into some events. But I only step in if there's suspicion of foul play, like criminal activity or someone deliberately making patients sick."

"I think that's what Scarlett thinks," Clara said quietly.

"I'll look into it." Jesse stepped closer. "But I want you to leave it alone. Okay?"

"I never wanted to be a part of it anyway," she assured him.

Good, Holden thought. Because if there was criminal activity happening at the hospital, anyone responsible would be doing everything they could to protect themselves...and no part of Holden wanted Clara near that.

CHAPTER 16

*C*lara swiped the mascara wand across her lashes as she watched her reflection in her dresser mirror.

She was tired. *Had been* tired all day. Which didn't make sense because she'd barely done anything. But if there was anything she'd learned over the years about her chronic fatigue, it was that it didn't matter if she'd seen two clients or ten, the exhaustion could sneak up on her.

Thirty. She was going to be thirty freaking years old in a week. And she'd most likely go into her thirties a virgin.

Yes, she'd told Holden that she wanted to sleep with someone before that, probably making it sound as though she'd have sex with any Tom, Dick, or Harry who came along.

But the closer she got to her birthday, the more she realized she couldn't do that.

She capped the mascara as her phone dinged with a text. Maybe it was Indie. Her cousin was five minutes late to pick her up to go to the bar.

It wasn't.

Helen: Hey. We haven't seen you at the running club lately. We miss you. Want to hang out?

Interesting. Helen didn't text her often.

She still hadn't talked to Malcolm about Scarlett. She'd tried, but the man was always either working, sleeping, or busy. And she understood. He was a doctor; he worked long hours.

Maybe she could talk to Helen about it. But would the other woman want to go to the bar after what had happened in the alley?

Clara: My cousin and I are going to CJ's tonight. You're welcome to meet us there. Completely fine if you would prefer not to though.

Helen: No, CJ's sounds good. When are you leaving?

Clara: Ten minutes.

Helen: See you soon.

There. Done. She'd tell Helen what she knew about Scarlett, and maybe even find out what had happened that night at the gathering, and then this guilt would finally lift off her shoulders. Because she *did* feel guilty that she hadn't told them what Scarlett's true profession was. She also felt guilty that she knew about the laced brownies and hadn't said anything.

Maybe Helen and the others from the hospital would then find out who Scarlett worked for and let them know her less than ethical methods of getting information. It would get her fired, but that was something Scarlett would just have to deal with.

When her makeup was finished, she stepped into the hall just as keys rattled in the door. Then it flew open and Scarlett stepped in. Except, she didn't look her usual cool, calm, and collected self. She was disheveled and her eyes were wide, almost scared.

Clara took a step toward her. "Scarlett…are you okay?"

"I'm fine." The words were mumbled as she ducked her head and moved past Clara.

She was about to follow when the soft click of heels sounded behind her. She turned to see Indie standing in the still open doorway.

Her cousin lifted her brows. "Everything okay? I watched Scarlett race in here."

"I'm not sure."

She eyed Scarlett's closed door. A part of her wanted to check on her roommate. But she was almost certain Scarlett wouldn't open up to her. In fact, she'd probably yell at Clara to leave her alone.

She shook her head. "It's not my business. Let's go." She grabbed her purse from the hall table and stepped outside.

Indie glanced back at the house. "Is Scarlett still moving out?"

"I gave her two weeks to find a place. I wouldn't know how it's going though, because she doesn't talk to me."

"I'm sorry."

Clara shook her head as she lowered into the car. "It's okay. I tried, she didn't. Her loss."

"Absolutely her loss."

As Indie started the car, Clara opened her purse. Crap. She'd left her phone on her bedroom dresser.

"Sorry." She looked up at Indie. "I need to run back inside for my phone."

"Want me to come?"

"No, I'll be quick." Clara jumped out and jogged back to the house. She quickly grabbed her phone from her bedroom and stepped back into the hall, only to stop at rustling noises from the kitchen. She frowned at the sight of Scarlett rummaging through the spice drawer.

"Is everything all right?"

Scarlett jumped and turned. "I thought you left."

"I did. I forgot my phone. Didn't you hear me open the door?" She held up her phone as if to prove her point before scanning the spices that had been taken out. "Baking?"

"Yep."

Clara nodded slowly. "You know, if you ever need someone to talk—"

"You should go, Clara."

Suddenly, anger cut through the concern. "I wish you'd given me a chance. I could have been a great friend, Scarlett."

No emotion in the other woman's eyes. None. "I don't need friends."

Argh. Why did she bother?

She turned and stormed out of the house before dropping back into the car.

Indie frowned at her. "Are you okay?"

"I shouldn't let her get to me. Tell me I shouldn't let her get to me."

"You shouldn't let her get to you."

Why didn't that help?

Indie pulled onto the road, her gaze continuing to flicker to Clara. "What happened?"

"Nothing. Just Scarlett being Scarlett. She's so unfriendly."

"You can't change a leopard's spots, Clara. She's going to be who she is."

"I know. And I thought I was okay with that because she was quiet and out a lot, but now I don't know. I just think I deserve more from her. Really, it's my fault for not asking her to leave sooner."

"Well, you've asked her to leave now."

She had. And soon, Scarlett would be out of her life.

By the time they arrived at the bar, Clara had calmed down... kind of. Until she saw Holden talking to Briar by the bar.

Great. Just what she needed.

They went to the bar, and Indie ordered a paloma while Clara got a soda water. Not exactly the life of the party, but she was here to catch up with Indie, not to drink.

She waited until they reached a standing table before asking, "So...the divorce papers. Have you opened them?"

Indie groaned. "I've tried. I really have. Every morning, I see them. Some days I even pick up the envelope. But so far, I just haven't been able to."

"That's okay. If you need more time, you need more time."

She looked down at her drink. "I saw Sylvia yesterday."

It was hard for Clara to not wrinkle her nose at Colt's mother's name. "Where?"

"The diner. I didn't know whether to smile or say hi or pretend I didn't see her. In the end, she saw me. Came over. Told me I looked tired and asked if I was okay."

"I really don't like her." Colt and Indie had been dating since high school, and at first everything had been fine. But in the last few years, Indie had received nonstop passive-aggressive comments and remarks designed to break her down.

"I don't like that I put up with her for so long. But not anymore." She took a big gulp of her drink. "I'm going to ask for more ice in my glass."

Clara watched her cousin walk to the bar, her heart aching for her. She hated that Indie was hurting. She deserved better. And one day, she'd get better.

Her phone vibrated in her pocket with a text.

Helen: Sorry, I've gotten held up. Deb asked me to stop by. Rain check?

Damn. Clara really needed to talk to her. She needed to talk to *someone* from the hospital.

Clara: Not a problem.

Then, before she could think better of it, she typed out a text to Malcolm.

Clara: Hey. Just checking if you're free? I'm at CJ's.

Malcolm: Hey, Clara. Sorry. Just got home from a twelve-hour shift. I'm wrecked. Definitely next week.

It wasn't going to happen. She just needed to accept that she was never going to speak to him. Maybe she just needed to text him the information and be done with it.

Sudden throbbing in her head made her massage her temple. Man, she was tired, and exhaustion always gave her a headache. Maybe she should have stayed home tonight.

"Are you okay?"

She jumped—and looked up to see Holden standing beside her, concern on his face.

* * *

HOLDEN STUDIED CLARA'S EYES. They weren't as bright as usual, and she had circles beneath them. "You're tired."

"I am."

She didn't even deny it like she usually did. And that made worry surge through him.

He stepped closer and touched her hip. "Let me take you home."

She shook her head and stepped away, forcing his hand to drop. "I only just got here. Plus, you're with Briar."

"I'm not *with* Briar. I came to have a drink with your brothers. They had to go, and Briar saw me before I could leave."

"You should return to her."

"She left. But even if she hadn't, I'd want to stay with *you*."

Clara swallowed and looked away. "It's okay, you know."

"What's okay?"

"Briar's pretty. And if she's what you're into—"

"I am *not* into Briar." And Clara saying she was *okay* with him choosing Briar left a sour fucking taste in his mouth. He glanced at her phone. "Who were you texting?"

"Helen. Then Malcolm. I was hoping one of them could meet me here."

That sour taste raced down to his gut and coiled. "You wanted to have a drink with Malcolm?"

She rolled her eyes. "It wasn't some prelude to sex, if that's what you're wondering. I want to tell them about Scarlett's brownies."

His muscles tightened at the mention of her roommate. "Is she still moving out?"

"As far as I know." Clara stared at her drink like it was the most fascinating thing, before looking back up at him. "Holden, I've been trying to tell you without *telling* you, but...I think we should take a break from each other."

For a second, he couldn't catch his breath. He should have been expecting it, so why did it still hurt? "A break?"

"Yes."

"No."

Her brows shot up. "You can't just say no."

"I just did."

Her mouth opened and closed. "You don't get a say."

"The hell I don't! We're friends. Family."

She shook her head. "You don't get it."

She stepped away, but he stopped her. "Clara. Don't walk away from me."

"It's too hard!"

"*What's* too hard?" But he knew. Deep down, he knew.

She opened her mouth—only to stop and suddenly sway on her feet.

He cursed and grabbed her waist, holding her close. "Clara... you're not okay."

She rubbed her forehead. "I'm tired. I probably shouldn't have come out tonight."

No, she sure as hell shouldn't have.

Indie stopped beside them, glass in hand. "Hey, is everything all right?"

"No," Holden answered for her. "I'm taking Clara home."

Indie frowned at him before looking at her cousin, concern in her eyes. "Clara?"

"I'm so sorry. I should have told you I wasn't feeling great. Is it okay if we rain check?"

"Of course. I can—"

"I've got her," Holden interrupted, already knowing she was going to offer to take Clara home.

Indie looked ready to argue, but Clara touched her arm. "It's okay. Holden can take me. Thank you though. And I'm sorry again."

The two women hugged, then he slipped his arm back around her waist to lead her outside.

The entire drive to her place, he kept one eye on the road and the other on Clara. "Have you passed out recently?"

She shook her head. "No. Apart from the last few days, I've been feeling really good. The dizzy spells can come out when I'm stressed."

His fingers tightened around the wheel. Stressed because of her damn roommate. "Has there been any more trouble with Scarlett?"

"No. She's just been her normal joyful self."

"Are you going to find a new roommate?"

"I'll need to if I don't want to increase the hours I work. But I'll give myself some time to find someone. Really vet them."

"If you need any help, I'm a great vetter."

She chuckled softly. "Thanks. I'll keep that in mind."

"You know, by not getting to know you, she's really missed out."

A small smile curved Clara's lips and she looked at him, the soft blue of her eyes boring into him. "Thanks, Holden."

When he arrived at her place, it was to see most of the lights off. Good. Maybe her roommate was asleep.

Clara reached for her seat belt. "You don't need to walk me up."

He could have laughed. "Of course I do. The gentleman in me insists." Plus, after almost passing out on him at the bar, he was making sure she got inside safely.

He climbed out and moved to her side to help her out. As they walked to her door, he kept a hand on the small of her back, letting her warmth slip into him, crawl up his arm, and heat his blood.

When the front door was open, she stepped inside and turned. "Well, thanks for walking me in."

"I don't want space." The words fell from his mouth, heavy but true.

She tilted her head, resolve in her eyes. "You don't want me in the same way that I want you. So *I* need space to move on."

More fucking kicks to his gut, these ones harder and more precise.

"I need..." She looked at the sky behind him, as if searching for the right words. "I need to breathe without you being on my mind. I need to find my person without comparing every man I meet to *you*."

"I don't want to lose you." It was unfair of him. He knew it was unfair. He was a selfish prick. She deserved to be with someone who could give themselves to her without hesitation. But the idea of her going out and finding someone who wasn't him...*fuck*, it hurt.

She dropped her head into her hands and scrubbed her face. "Let's sleep on it, okay?" She didn't give him time to respond, instead stepping back and closing the door. Cutting their connection...and making him feel fucking hollow.

CHAPTER 17

*T*he door closed, and the house was suddenly too quiet. A heavy kind of quiet that sat on her chest, making the air feel thick and her lungs tight.

She touched her temple to the wood of the door, trying to breathe even though she wanted to cry. She'd just done exactly what she knew *needed* to be done. So why had it felt so wrong? Why, when she'd asked for space, had a voice in her head begged, *screamed*, for her to give him more time? But more time for what? To love her?

She turned, hating the tears that pressed at her eyes. Hating that even though space between her and Holden would save her heartache in the long run, right now it felt wrong and hard and painful.

She stepped into her room and took off her shirt and jeans, then eyed her pajamas. She should put them on. She didn't. Instead, she rummaged through her bottom drawer before finding an old sweatshirt. Not *her* old sweatshirt—Holden's.

There was something about it that just made her feel close to him, even when she wasn't.

Man, she was a glutton for punishment.

She pulled the sweatshirt over her head, and it was so long it almost hit her knees.

In the kitchen, she was about to grab a bottle of water from the fridge when a cool breeze hit her legs. She turned to see the back door ajar.

She frowned. Was Scarlett out there?

Slowly, she crossed to the door and stuck her head outside.

Nothing. Well, nothing that she could see, anyway. It was dark though.

She quickly closed the door, but when she went to flick the lock, she couldn't. The bolt wouldn't engage. Was it broken?

All the fine hairs on her arms suddenly stood on end, and that chill on her skin intensified.

Was Scarlett home? Had she noticed something had happened to the lock on the back door?

Quickly, Clara went to Scarlett's bedroom. She knocked and waited.

Silence.

Was Scarlett even here? She knocked again, and when there was still no answer, she quietly turned the knob and stepped inside. The light was on, and just like the other night, Scarlett was hunched over her desk.

Where was her laptop? And if she wasn't working, why would she fall asleep on an empty desk?

Unease churned in her belly. She inched forward, her pulse quickening, each beat loud in her ears.

"Scarlett?"

Nothing. Not even the twitch of a finger. Then Clara noticed something else…

Scarlett's back wasn't moving.

Her heart started to beat faster, dread pooling in her gut.

"Scarlett?" Her voice was louder this time, and there was more urgency.

Still nothing.

With trembling fingers, she reached out and touched Scarlett's back. No reaction. No movement.

No. This wasn't possible. She had to be in a deep sleep or something.

Slowly, Clara reached for the pulse on Scarlett's neck.

There was none.

She shot back, her throat closing, cutting off her breath. Her knees felt so weak that she wanted to crumble.

A distant knock sounded on the front door, but Clara couldn't move. She could barely think. Black dots began to dance in her vision, bile crawling up her throat.

Dead. Scarlett was dead.

The knocking sounded again, this time louder and followed by a voice.

"Clara, it's Holden. I had to come back. We can't leave things like this."

Air. She needed air.

She stumbled to the bedroom door and grabbed the frame to keep herself upright. Her head was in a deep fog, her lungs barely allowing her to breathe. When she finally reached the front door, she yanked it open for Holden.

The second his eyes hit her, his expression shifted from concern to panic to something harder that she couldn't quite name.

"What's wrong?"

"She's dead." The words were so quiet she wasn't even sure they crossed the distance. "Scarlett's dead."

* * *

HOLDEN's entire body locked at Clara's words, years of training in the military taking over as any words he'd been about to say died on his lips. He moved quickly, stepping inside the house and locking the door before pulling his Glock from his concealed holster. He didn't always carry, but fuck, was he glad he had tonight.

He pushed Clara behind his body, shielding her. If it was up to him, Clara wouldn't be in the house at all, but there wasn't a chance in hell he was leaving her alone outside if there was a killer somewhere. It was too dark out there. Too many places for someone to hide.

He scanned her hall and living area. "Did you see or hear anyone?"

"No." Her voice was quiet, a small shake in it. "But the back door was ajar and the lock broken."

Shit. If someone had killed Scarlett, they could still be here.

He grabbed his cell.

Jesse answered on the second ring. "Hey—"

"You need to get to Clara's house *now*. Her roommate's dead."

There was a small pause. "Dead?"

"Yes. Come quickly."

Jesse cursed. "Coming."

"Where is she?" Holden asked, keeping his Glock raised.

"In her room."

"Stay close." Remaining close to the wall, he inched down the hallway, every sense heightened. If there was someone still here, they wouldn't be getting past him. Not a chance.

He scanned the hall as he moved, looking for a threat. When he reached the bedroom, he saw Scarlett hunched over her desk.

At first glance, it looked like she was sleeping. But after a few seconds, it was obvious she was too still.

He moved closer and touched the inside of her wrist.

No pulse. But there also didn't appear to be an obvious wound. Hell, there wasn't even blood. What the hell had happened?

Another scan of the room before he turned to look at Clara. "I need to check the house."

Her eyes widened and she grabbed his arm. "Wait for Jesse."

"I'm just as well trained as your brother."

"I know, but—"

"I'll be okay."

He took a step, but she stopped him again.

"I'm coming with you."

He opened his mouth to tell her that he needed to go alone, but she spoke first.

"*Please*! I don't want to be alone."

Shit. He didn't want her alone either. "Stay behind me."

She nodded.

He stepped out of the room, Glock up but close to his chest. Systematically, he went through the house, checking her bedroom, the bathrooms, then the living room. Nothing was out of place until he reached the kitchen, and just as Clara had said, the lock was broken on the back door.

That was how the asshole had gotten in.

Something sounded from the front of the house. Holden pressed Clara behind him before slowly moving toward the noise.

Someone tried the handle, then the pounding of a fist on the door. "Clara! Holden! It's Jesse."

The air rushed from Clara's chest, and she ran to the door.

Jesse immediately pulled Clara into a hug before gripping her shoulders and searching her face. "Are you okay?"

She nodded shakily, and Jesse growled and tugged her into another hug.

The next hour passed quickly, with people going in and out of Clara's house, taking prints and photos. When Scarlett's body was removed, Clara's face paled even further.

Holden never left her side.

"So there was no laptop?" Jesse asked, after Clara finished telling him everything that had happened.

"No." She ran her fingers over the edge of the couch cushion. "I think whoever…killed her, took it."

Holden tightened his arm around her, thankful as hell that she hadn't pushed him away.

"And you don't know why she was acting strange when she got home today?"

"No, but a couple nights ago..." Clara paused, glancing at Holden before looking back to her brother. "She went out with some people who work at the hospital and took some laced brownies with her."

Jesse cursed. "That's why you asked me about them at The Tea House. I'm guessing they didn't know the brownies were laced?"

"I'm not sure. I haven't had a chance to ask them. But I doubt it. She wasn't completely honest with them about her job. I'm assuming because she didn't want them finding out what she was writing. But then, I don't think she was completely honest with me about her job either, based on the ethics of how she got her information."

"We need a background check on her." Jesse shared a look with Holden. "But tonight, it seems someone might have discovered that she was a journalist who was investigating them. They said too much after being drugged—"

"And needed to silence Scarlett," Holden finished.

Clara shuddered. "You're suggesting someone from the hospital murdered her? Oh God, I'm going to be sick."

She dropped her head into her hands, and Holden barely bit back a curse as he rubbed her back. He hated that this was happening to her.

"We don't know anything for sure," Jesse said. "So nothing can leave this room. But Clara..." He waited for her to look up. "I'm going to find out what happened to her."

She nodded quickly, those tears once again shining in her eyes.

"I want you to come stay with me and Aspen," Jesse said.

Holden stiffened. No part of him wanted Clara out of his sight. Not after what had happened tonight.

She shook her head. "No. I have clients in the morning. And I don't want to be scared out of my own home."

"Cancel them," Jesse pushed.

"No. I don't want to. They need their treatment."

"*I'll* stay."

Both Clara and Jesse looked at Holden.

"No," Clara said again. "You don't need—"

"I do. I need to be wherever *you* are. And if you say no again, I'll just sit in my truck and watch from the street. I'm not going home tonight."

There was a beat of silence.

Say yes, Clara. Let me stay.

He didn't have a problem staying in his truck, but the closer he was, the faster he'd get to any danger that arose.

She swallowed, silent for a few seconds, her gaze boring into him before, finally, she nodded. "Okay. Thank you."

CHAPTER 18

*C*lara shot up, her chest heaving, sweat chilling her skin. The bedroom was dark, her loud breathing cutting through the quiet.

A dream. It was just a dream.

But it wasn't. Scarlett *was* dead. Clara *had* found her roommate's lifeless body draped over her desk, and her house *had* been crawling with deputies.

She dropped her head into her hands, trying to quiet her breathing, not wanting to wake Holden.

It didn't work. She still panted in reaction, and her skin was clammy and cold.

Quickly, she pushed the sheets off her legs and climbed out of bed. She didn't even realize she was walking in that direction until she stood in front of Scarlett's closed bedroom door. The brass was cool beneath her fingers when she wrapped her hand around the knob. Then, slowly, she turned it.

Her chest rose on a sharp inhale at the sight of Scarlett's room. All her things, sitting there, as if she was going to return. Clothes sticking out of closed dresser drawers. Reading glasses on her desk.

The memory of Scarlett lying over the desk flashed in her mind.

Her heart thumped, panic crawling up her throat.

"Clara."

She spun to see Holden. He there, shirtless, his perfectly sculpted chest on full display. But it was the concern in his eyes that held her attention. When he looked at her that way, she just wanted to fall apart in his arms. Let him hold her. Protect her.

He stepped forward. "Are you okay?"

"I was angry at her."

"What?"

"The last thing I said to Scarlett was that I could have been a great friend. Then I stormed off."

"You couldn't have known what was about to happen."

She swallowed hard as she turned back to the bedroom. "I need to know who killed her. I need to know if it was anyone from the hospital. I need—"

"Hey." With gentle but firm fingers on her waist, he turned her back to him. "We *will* get answers. Jesse will make sure of it."

She nodded, even though she wasn't as confident as Holden. But maybe that was because she wasn't used to this kind of stuff, while he'd spent years in special operations.

He tilted his head toward the hall. "Come on."

"I can't sleep. Every time I close my eyes, I see her." She fisted her hands to stop the trembling.

He saw. Of course he did. He saw everything.

Gently, he took her hand, uncurled it, and slipped his fingers through hers. "Not sleep. We're going to heat up some croissants."

She frowned. "What?"

"I saw them in your freezer. Come on. We'll add some Nutella."

"It's the middle of the night."

"You're right…we need hot cocoa too."

He led her toward the kitchen. Then, without a word, he lifted her to sit on the island.

She gasped. "What are you doing?"

"I'm making you Nutella croissants and hot cocoa. And you're going to sit right there so you don't feel the urge to help. In fact…" He opened her pantry door and searched for a moment before finding her jar of Nutella, uncapping it, and shoving a spoon inside. He handed her the jar. "You can eat this to keep you busy."

Despite the night they'd had, a small hint of a smile stretched her lips.

She watched as Holden moved around the kitchen like he'd lived there for months.

"Distract me," she said quietly, as she swirled the Nutella with the spoon. "Tell me if you're happy you moved to Amber Ridge."

"Very happy. There wasn't much left for me in Minnesota. My best friend and his family were here."

"*Your* family too."

He gave her a gentle smile before taking the croissants out of the freezer and turning on the toaster oven. "My family too."

She lifted the spoon to her mouth, and the sugary Nutella hit her tongue. "I'm sorry you lost your mother."

He paused for a moment, every part of him going still. Then he looked back at her. "Thank you. It was just the two of us for a long time. My father left before I was born."

"Losing her must have hurt."

"She was my whole family."

"Did you have much of a chance to say goodbye?"

"I had a million chances." Pain wove through his words. "She was diagnosed with breast cancer when I was eleven. I didn't understand it then, and she always told me she'd be fine. But as I got older, I watched her deteriorate, and I started to realize that the cancer could, and probably would, kill her. I also realized that I couldn't protect her. I spent years looking after her. Hoping and praying that she'd pull through. But there was nothing I could actually do. I couldn't take away her pain. I couldn't fight her cancer. I just had to watch her die."

Her fingers tightened around the jar as little pieces of this man started to slot together. "I'm sorry."

Something clicked in his jaw. "The day she died, I realized how it felt to be so utterly alone in the world. It was a darkness I didn't know existed until then."

His words cut into her, hurting. "I can see how that would make you scared to need someone."

"Terrified. I'm terrified to experience that darkness again." His quiet words were so much more than he'd ever shared with her before.

She swallowed hard and looked down at the Nutella, swirling the spread with the spoon once again. "One time when I was in the hospital and feeling sorry for myself, a nurse said to me that God always tests his strongest soldiers. I remember thinking that I didn't want to be strong. I didn't *ask* to be. And if that were true, if I was so strong, why was I being punished for my strength? Everything felt so inherently unfair."

"I know that feeling." He shot her a look. "What got you through it?"

She lifted a shoulder. "I had to choose between letting a sense of inequity take over my life...or accepting that this *was* part of the life I'd been dealt and fight the cancer."

"Your strength still amazes me, Clara."

She tilted her head. "You're strong too."

"I wouldn't say that."

"I would. You just can't always see it."

His gaze held hers for a moment, the hazel so intense...but also wounded.

He went to move past her, but instinctively, she reached out and touched his cheek. "Hey. You *are* strong. You were in the special forces. You had to be."

That took a mental strength that very few in the world possessed.

His eyes shifted between hers, and he stepped closer, standing between her thighs. "I would argue that's a different kind."

"Strength is strength." She touched his chest, feeling the strong beats of his heart beneath her palm. "I'm sorry you couldn't save your mom. I wish we could save everyone, but that's not how this world works."

"I hated this world for a long time because of that."

"I've felt that anger, Holden. I've held it in the palm of my hand. And I've felt the loss of a parent. Granted, I was young, and I had my mom and brothers to support me, but I know it hurts."

"I wish I could let it go. I wish I could think about a future with someone I love and not feel this unbearable weight on my shoulders, pressing me to the ground."

"Maybe that's the problem. You're thinking too far into the future. Maybe you just need to think about here and now."

His eyes flared, and his fingers pulsed against her waist. "That could be dangerous."

Her next words were barely a whisper. "Live dangerously with me."

His eyes darkened, and long seconds of silence passed.

Then he growled, dropped his head, and kissed her.

And she fell. She fell fast and hard into everything that was Holden. She swam in him. Suffocated in him. Took everything he offered while begging for more.

His tongue slipped between her lips, and it was an explosion of sensations. He tasted good, a heady combination of mint and whiskey.

His hands went to her hips, shifting her to the edge of the island. She wrapped her legs around his waist, needing to eliminate any remaining space between them. She only wore a shirt, and God, there was so little between them in the way of barrier, yet still, it was too much.

When his mouth slid down her neck, she wasn't sure whether to focus on that or the way his hands slid up her waist, beneath her shirt, touching bare skin.

"Tell me we shouldn't do this, Clara," he whispered, his warm breath grazing her skin. "Tell me to step back and let you go."

"I can't do that, Holden. I want this. I want you. *You* need to decide if you want me too." And God, she prayed he did.

For a second he was still, then an almost strangled sound slipped from his throat as he lowered his mouth. He found her nipple and took the pebbled bud between his lips, sucking. Even through the material of her shirt, his lips felt like electricity. Like energy and life surging into her.

With desperate fingers, she yanked her shirt off. Then his lips were around her naked nipple. She cried out, her fingers latching onto the locks of his hair, her head tipping back while that dull throbbing built in her lower belly.

This man, who had consumed her for so long, now blocked out the world around her.

He switched to her other breast, his tongue circling her nipple before flicking it back and forth.

She hummed and moaned, her nails digging into his shoulders.

"You're like a drug," he whispered, his words weaving into her. "I'm addicted to you."

"I was an addict long ago."

Those hands on her waist tightened and he lifted her, his mouth returning to hers, his bare chest hot against her breasts as he walked through the house, only stopping when he reached her bedroom.

Gently, he lay her on the bed, his weight pressing her into the mattress. Then he looked at her—*really* looked at her. "Are you sure? Maybe now, after what happened today, isn't the best time…especially considering it's your first."

Her blood pumped faster, the beats of her heart stumbling

over one another. "I want it to be you. I've wanted it to be you since the day we met."

His eyes darkened, and he dropped his head once again, but this time his mouth moved down her body, kissing over her chest, her belly, until he reached the waistband of her panties. Gently, he pushed them down her thighs.

Her breathing grew faster, her heart racing as he paused over the V between her legs. Then he lowered his head and his tongue swiped her clit.

She cried out, her back arching, her lower belly pulsing.

He swiped her again, this time wrapping his arms around her thighs, keeping them separated.

The blood in her veins heated to lava, his every touch a lick of fire on her skin. She squirmed and moaned under his onslaught, the pressure of his tongue on her clit sending her wild.

But she wanted more of him. Desperately, she grasped at his arms.

He ran kisses up her body before finding her lips again, this kiss slow. Like a gentle exploration of her mouth.

She pushed at his chest until he was on his back. Then she was on top of him, tasting him...nipping his bottom lip as she reached between them. When she slipped her hand inside his briefs, wrapped her fingers around him, the muscles in his chest grew harder beneath her.

She slid her hand over his length, exploring. Touching him base to tip. Every time the air hissed from his teeth, she grew more confident. Learning what he liked.

"Clara..." One growl of her name and suddenly he was spinning them and she was beneath him again. Then a pained expression crossed his face. "I don't have anything."

It took her a second to realize what he meant.

She swallowed. "It's not the right time for me. You're safe."

An emotion she couldn't place crossed his features. "Are you sure?"

"Yes." No pause. No hesitation.

He lowered his mouth and kissed her again, his tongue diving straight in. And she felt him right there between her thighs, at her entrance.

Her heart drummed in her ears, a symphony of chaos and longing...but not nerves. Not with Holden.

He lifted his head, his gaze boring into hers. "You are the most perfect soul I have ever met, Clara."

"And I'm yours."

Another darkening of his eyes. "Mine."

Slowly, he inched inside her, stretching her walls. Filling her. There was a flicker of pain that made her gasp.

He stopped. "Are you okay?"

Her chest rose and fell before she gasped out two words. "Kiss me."

He studied her eyes, her face, like he saw all of her. Then he lowered his head and caressed her lips with his own. She wrapped a leg around him and encouraged him deeper.

A low rumble sounded from his chest. She wiggled her hips and moaned, needing more of him. Needing everything this man had to give.

* * *

HIS. Clara was his. The words kept rolling through his mind, making every territorial part of him want her more. *Crave* her.

Her walls hugged his cock like a glove, so damn tight it scared him to move or even breathe. Scared to do anything but remain exactly as he was.

He watched the thousands of expressions play over her face. "Clara...are you sure you're okay?"

She reached for his head, tangling her fingers through his hair, then drew him down. But before her lips touched his, she whispered, "Take me."

It was like gas on the fire of his need.

He lifted his hips and gently thrust back in.

She moaned, a deep, throaty sound that drove him to thrust again. He moved in and out of her body slowly, his lips returning to hers over and over so he could drown in the taste of her.

How had he denied himself this woman for so long? Clara was made for him—everything she was belonged to him.

He cupped her breast and ran his thumb back and forth over her nipple, absorbing every sound she made, like music written just for him. He circled the tight bud, and she cried out.

She was so damn responsive.

He lifted her thigh higher, thrusting at a new angle, his breathing now coming out in short puffs, his heart crashing against his ribs.

"Holden..."

The way she sighed his name...it fucking tormented him. Phantom fingers wrapped around his heart, squeezing.

He reached between them and circled her clit with his thumb. Immediately, her body jolted. He did it again, this time running his thumb up and down.

Her chest heaved beneath him, her moans growing louder.

One more swipe and her back arched and she broke.

He dropped his head and swallowed her cries with his kiss, moaning with her, continuing to thrust, feeling the throbbing of her walls against his cock.

He moved faster, every thrust pushing him closer to the cliff's edge.

When her nails bit into his shoulders and her body continued to clench his cock, he lost himself. He fell and broke—and the very foundation of his world shifted.

His growl was loud, punching through the silence of the room. Two more brutal thrusts, until finally he had nothing left. Until there was no sound in the room except their heavy breathing. No movement, bar their chests.

He just lay there, holding his weight on his elbows, his head tucked into her neck.

When he finally lifted and looked down, it was to see Clara's eyes half hooded, her cheeks a pretty pink and her chest finally slowing.

"Are you okay?" he whispered, concern now mounting. Concern that he hadn't been gentle or slow enough for her first time.

The smile that spread across her lips was fucking gorgeous, like when the stars wake up in the dark of the night.

"No," she whispered.

His heart stopped.

Until she added, "I'm so much better than okay."

She tugged his head down and planted another kiss on his lips.

Even *that* made blood rush between his ears.

He dropped beside her and gathered her into him, wanting her as close as possible.

What they'd shared wasn't just sex. It was more. And it made him feel things, *want* things, that he'd never allowed himself to feel or want...

And no matter how much he told himself not to be scared, that fucking terrified him.

CHAPTER 19

$\mathcal{A}$ ray of sun danced over Clara's eyelids, making her scrunch them and groan as she rolled to her side.

She frowned at the dull ache between her thighs. At the hard, warm body beneath her chest.

Then she remembered.

A breath slipped from her lips as everything from the previous night came back to her. Finding Scarlett. Waking in the middle of the night. Holden.

The arm around her suddenly felt hot and heavy, the heart beating beneath her cheek loud.

Her heart started to thump. Nervous thumps that made her rib cage rattle.

He was awake. Did he know *she* was awake?

"Morning, honey."

She wrinkled her nose. Yep. He knew.

Slowly, she forced her head up to see Holden's intense hazel gaze on her, his day-old stubble looking ridiculously sexy. "Morning. Have you been awake for long?"

"Long enough to watch the sun rise through the curtains."

A small weight lifted from her chest. Because a part of

her had wondered if he'd leave before morning came around. If he'd feel the magnitude of what they'd done and run from it.

But he was here.

He slid a lock of hair from her face. "How are you feeling?"

Her skin tingled where his finger grazed. "Good. Last night was nice."

"Nice?"

Whoops. "Better than nice. Definitely better."

"You mean I made your first time un-fucking-believable?"

He was joking, but she didn't even crack a grin. "Yeah. You did."

His hand slid up and down her side. "I could touch your curves all day and never tire of them."

A rush of warmth spread over her skin. "You know, I went through a period where I hated my body."

"How could that possibly be true?"

"I felt like my body betrayed me by getting sick."

There was a small tightening of his eyes. "What changed?"

"I realized it wanted to heal as much as I did. That we were on the same side, fighting the same disease."

"Your body fought with you." He set a soft kiss on her forehead.

She smiled, but the smile slipped when some of that old fear slipped back in. "Holden...I need to know what last night was for you. Did you sleep with me just because what happened with Scarlett scared you? Or did it mean more to you? Because it meant more to me."

Something flickered in his eyes, a hesitation...a fear. Then he blinked and it was gone. "It meant something to me too."

"You're not going to pull away from me, are you?" A million fears came alive in her belly at the possibility. Because the longer she was with him, the deeper she'd fall, and the more it would hurt if he ran.

For a second, he didn't say anything, and his face was so unreadable that the fear simmered and rippled inside her.

Maybe now wasn't the best time for this conversation. Her heart was too vulnerable after last night.

She started to get up, but he snagged an arm around her waist and tugged her back down before rolling them. "I'm not going anywhere, Clara."

He was everywhere. Over her. Around her. He was all she could see or feel.

"Promise me," she whispered.

"I promise."

His words were whispers, but he looked so deeply into her eyes that she believed him.

Relief had air rushing out of her lungs.

Then he kissed her. A slow, gentle kiss that made the last wisps of fear slip away. His tongue tangled with hers, his hand slipping down her body, heating her skin.

She was just wrapping a leg around his waist when an alarm went off.

Her eyes flashed open. "What's the time?"

"Hm...not sure." His mouth moved down her neck.

"I set it for seven thirty. I have a client at eight."

"I agree with Jess. You should cancel."

She wanted to. But she couldn't do that to her client. They booked because they needed her. Whether it was for their mental health or physical, every appointment was important.

She pushed at his chest. "I need to get up."

He nipped her neck. "Reschedule."

"No." She pushed again. "You need to go."

He laughed as he lifted his head, but not his body. "If you think I'm leaving you alone in this house, you're out of your mind."

"Holden...I don't need you babysitting me all day, and I'm sure you have things you planned to do today."

"I'll cancel."

"No, you will not. I'll lock the doors and only let my clients in. I'm not in any danger. *I* wasn't writing an article on the hospital. I don't know anything about what's going on there."

Her heart gave a sad kick at the memory. At the possibility that someone she knew had hurt Scarlett.

She shook her head. She couldn't think about that right now.

"Clara—"

"I'm seeing my client, and you're doing whatever you planned to do today. Okay?"

His jaw clicked. "If I leave, I expect hourly updates from you. And I'm returning this afternoon."

"Are you coming to watch out for me or to be with me?"

He lowered his mouth, hovering it over hers. "I'm coming because I care about you."

Then he kissed her again, and the alarm was suddenly the last thing she could think about.

* * *

COOL MORNING AIR sliced over Holden's skin as he ran, the rhythmic pounding of his shoes against the earth competing with the sounds of the mountain around him. His breathing came out in sharp bursts, his chest tight. But that tightness wasn't from exhaustion.

It was Clara.

Memories of the previous night played over in his head. The feel of her skin beneath his fingers. The sounds she'd made when he touched her.

He tightened his fists and forced himself to move faster.

One night with her and he was already craving another. *Needing* her with this new intensity...new desperation. And he didn't want to be afraid of it. He wanted to love her without letting the fear of losing her rule him.

In every other aspect of his life, he could be fearless...so why not this one?

Branches snapped beneath his stride, the chill of the morning biting the back of his throat.

Waking up this morning with her in his arms had felt right. He needed to be strong enough to keep her.

He reached his house and the second he stepped inside, he texted her.

Holden: Hey. Are you still okay?

When she didn't reply immediately, he had to physically stop himself from calling. She was probably with a client. If he needed to wait, he needed to wait.

But fuck, he was worried. Her roommate was dead. The back door lock had been broken and someone had murdered her.

Yeah, he'd replaced the lock last night, but that didn't make him feel any better.

He took a quick shower, then called Jesse.

He picked up after a couple of rings. "Holden."

"Do you know anything about Scarlett's cause of death yet?"

"No. And we won't for a couple weeks. There were no signs of physical trauma, so we need to wait for the toxicology report."

Holden's back teeth ground together as he headed to the kitchen for a bottle of water.

"But I did get that background check on Scarlett."

Holden paused. "And?"

"Her real name was Rosie Thorpe. She used to be an investigative journalist and did a lot of undercover work, but she crossed the line of ethics too many times and burned all her bridges, so according to her old bosses, no one would hire her."

"If she couldn't publish any of her findings at any legitimate newspaper or magazine, then what was she doing investigating the hospital?"

"My IT person linked her to articles that she blasted on conspiracy and exploitative sites on the internet. She also had her own site under a pseudonym with some serious firewalls. She got good exposure."

"Shit. It explains the less than ethical methods of getting information from people."

"Exactly."

The question still stood…who'd killed her? "I don't like Clara still being in that house."

"If you hadn't offered to stay last night, she wouldn't have been there. Was she okay?"

Guilt cut through Holden's chest that Jesse was in the dark about everything that had happened recently between him and Clara. He just needed to tell his best friend. But not over the phone. And he needed to talk to Clara first. "Yeah, she was okay."

"Good."

"You're looking into the hospital staff, aren't you?"

"We've been interviewing the staff this morning, starting with the running club. Briar Winslow was at the bar, then went to Helen Monroe's house. Malcolm Trundle was at home, but no one can verify that. We're just heading to Deborah Fuller's house now."

Holden straightened. "I want to be there."

"No. This is a sheriff matter—"

"I don't fucking care. It involves Clara."

Jesse growled. "Holden—"

"I'm leaving now." He hung up, grabbed his shit, and ran to his truck. He wanted to be in on at least one of these interviews. He wanted to hear what Deb had to say, not only about last night but also about the night Scarlett laced the brownies.

When he reached Deb's house, Jesse pulled up behind him almost at the same time, his deputy, Luke, in the passenger seat.

Jesse climbed out of his car, his jaw set. "You can come in if Deb say it's okay. If she says no—"

"I'll go." But Deb liked him, so that wasn't happening.

He said a quick hello to Luke before moving to the front door, not missing Jesse's exaggerated huff.

When Deb opened the door, she gasped. "Oh my...am I in trouble?"

Jesse shook his head. "No, ma'am, but we were hoping we could ask you some questions."

"Oh, yes, sure."

Jesse shot him a glare. "Holden Forbes is invested in this case and would like to listen to your interview. But say the word, and we'll send him away."

Holden gave the older woman a kind smile. "Hi, Deb. I hope that's okay."

She returned his smile. "Of course. I don't have anything to hide."

Jesse sighed before stepping inside, Holden and Luke following.

"Have a seat," Deb said, gesturing toward the round dining table. "Can I get coffee for anyone?"

"No, thank you." Jesse sat and waited for everyone else to take a seat before asking his first question. "Deb, I need to know where you were last night between the hours of eight and midnight."

"Last night?" An orange cat jumped onto her lap. "I was here."

"Can anyone corroborate that?"

"Well, Biscuit can, but unless someone speaks cat..." She laughed, but when no one joined her, the laugh died off. "Do I need a lawyer?"

"Not at this stage," Luke said.

Jesse leaned forward. "A few nights ago, did you have drinks with Scarlett Calloway?"

"Yes. She came here, and so did Malcolm, Briar, and Helen."

"Do you remember much about that night, Deb?" Holden asked, receiving a warning look from Jesse for the question.

"Oh, yes, it was a great evening." She blushed. "I'm afraid we all drank far too much."

"Did you eat some of Scarlett's brownies?" Jesse asked.

"I did! They were divine. I actually need to get the recipe from her."

Jesse's brows rose. "Are you aware that she laced them with marijuana?"

Deb gasped and pressed a hand to her chest. "Oh, no. She wouldn't do that."

"She would, and she did," Holden pushed.

"Oh my." She started petting her cat, her hand shaking.

"Do you remember much of what was said that evening?" Jesse asked. "Any conversations that might have upset anyone? Many conversations about the hospital?"

"The hospital? No. We try not to talk about work when we're away from it. We talked about the weather and the brownies. Helen made these meatballs that we all obsessed over. Briar spoke a bit about work, but she tends to do that. She complains a lot."

"It's the same as the others said," Jesse told him quietly.

"Will Scarlett be in trouble?" Deb asked.

There was a small pause before Jesse answered. "Scarlett is dead, ma'am."

She paled, and it was a moment before she spoke again. "Dead? What do you mean? What happened?"

"We're not sure yet," he answered. "We're just gathering information at this stage. Can you tell me how things have been at the hospital?"

"The hospital?"

"There've been patients getting sick, haven't there?" Jesse asked.

"You know about that?" When Jesse nodded, she continued, "Well...yes, but the hospital administration said we're not allowed to talk about it while they're investigating things."

"Now *I'm* investigating things," Jesse said. "And I'd like you to tell me what's been happening."

She took a deep breath. "Well...Lauren Tabs died of heart failure after rotator cuff surgery. It shook everyone, because no one knew what happened. Since then, perfectly healthy patients have been randomly getting sick, everything from respiratory depression to seizures, but no one knows why."

"Is there anything connecting the patients?" Holden asked. "Rooms? Medications? Procedures?"

"There's only one thing connecting them," Deb said quietly. "Malcolm's their doctor."

CHAPTER 20

*H*olden's eyes shot open, and he went from dead asleep to wide awake in under a second.

What had woken him?

He looked down to see Clara's body half on top of his and her back rising and falling in steady succession.

The last few days, they'd fallen into this easy rhythm of living together. Cooking in her kitchen. Sleeping in her bed.

But it wasn't Clara who'd woken him just now.

He scanned the bedroom, only the dim glow of the moon poking through the curtains giving him a bit of light.

Nothing was out of place in the bedroom. He checked the closed door, the eerie quiet loud in his ears.

Then a sound cut through the silence—the click of the front door closing.

Someone was in the house.

Gently, he shook Clara's shoulder.

She moaned and scrunched her eyes.

He set his lips close to her ear, his voice barely a whisper. "Clara, I need you to wake up."

She opened her eyes with a frown. "Holden?"

"There's someone in the house."

Her eyes popped open wide and she tried to sit up, but he gripped her shoulder, keeping her in place. "We need to be quiet. Go to the bathroom and lock yourself in."

"What about you?" she asked.

Without making a sound, he reached into the side drawer where he'd stashed his gun, before looking back to Clara. "I'm armed."

Her eyes flared with fear, but she pushed the blankets back and climbed out of bed.

He moved with Clara across the room, waiting for the soft click of the bathroom lock before crossing to the door.

Another noise sounded from the hall, this time the light shuffle of movement.

He slipped back into the man he'd been in the military, calling on his training and maintaining his calm.

Silently, he turned the knob and opened the bedroom door, his Glock immediately pointing around the hall and living area. Even in the darkness, he saw everything. The hall table. The couch. The mugs they'd left on the coffee table.

But no intruder.

He slipped out of the bedroom and closed the door behind him, his movement slow and deliberate. His bare feet didn't make a sound against the wooden floorboards.

He was about to check Scarlett's old room when he heard another shuffle, this time from the kitchen. Then the crackle of what sounded like plastic.

Quickly, he shifted to the opposite wall and stepped into the living room. When he reached the kitchen, he aimed his Glock. At first, it appeared empty. Then a figure stepped out of the pantry. A familiar figure.

"*Indie?*"

The woman screamed, a bag of balloons flying into the air as she grabbed her chest. "Oh my God, Holden! What the hell are you doing?"

"What am *I* doing?"

"Yes! You scared the life out of me! I think I'm dead. Am I dead?"

He lowered the pistol. "What are you doing here?"

"It's Clara's thirtieth birthday." She frowned like *she* was the one confused. "I texted you last night."

He hadn't checked his phone since dinner. He and Clara had gotten...distracted. "You texted to tell me you were breaking into the house?"

"It's not breaking in if I have a key."

He disagreed. And he had a mind to remind Indie that they were already on high alert since Scarlett's death, but he gritted his teeth. "Why are you here so early?"

"So I can blow up thirty balloons, set her favorite flowers in the middle of the table, and serve her almond croissants. That takes time."

He scrubbed a hand over his face, setting his gun on the island. It was too damn early for this.

Footsteps sounded behind him. "Indie?"

He cursed. "Clara, I told you to stay locked in the bathroom."

"It's just Indie."

"You didn't know that!"

Indie suddenly screeched, "Happy thirtieth!" She ran around the island and flung her arms around Clara.

Clara chuckled. "Thank you."

When they separated, Indie grinned. "Now you need to march your butt back into the bedroom so I can set this room up, then pretend you didn't see me and come out in thirty to sixty minutes and act surprised. Okay?"

"Okay." Clara squeezed his arm before leaving the room.

Indie turned back to him. "And *you* should not pull a gun on me ever again. Colt taught me self-defense, and I *will* use it on you."

He bit back the laugh. The woman was five foot nothing. "Have you spoken to him lately?"

There was a small tensing of Indie's muscles. "No. Not for a while."

Holden nodded. Colt was a Marine, and they hadn't been in Amber Ridge at the same time a lot, so Holden didn't know him well. But he'd seemed like a good guy.

He stepped forward. "Need help?"

"Nope. I'd like you to go and give Clara a big happy birthday kiss and keep her occupied for as long as this takes me. Oh—and take that gun with you. I don't need to look at it. It's killing the party vibe."

"Shout if you need anything."

He grabbed his Glock and returned to the bedroom, but it was empty and the bathroom door was closed. Once the weapon was secured in the bedside table again, he went to the bathroom to find Clara in front of the mirror while the shower ran.

He stepped inside and wrapped his arms around her waist, his lips going to her ear as he whispered, "Happy thirtieth birthday, Clara."

A little shudder coursed down her spine. She leaned back into him and placed her hands over his. "I made it."

He froze. Had she not expected to?

"When you've been diagnosed with stage four cancer, every year feels like a gift," she clarified.

He pressed a light kiss to her neck. "You've got a hell of a lot more birthdays in your future."

She turned in his arms, her gaze shifting between his eyes, the small smile slipping from her lips. "Will you be there to celebrate with me?"

She still doubted him. He shouldn't be surprised. That fear

still snuck up on him, usually when he least expected it. "I'll be wherever you want me."

"Here," she whispered. "Right here by my side."

He lowered his head and kissed her. "Wait here. I have something for you."

In the bedroom, he pulled a small box from his suitcase.

When he returned to her, Clara frowned. "What is it?"

"Your present."

She grinned. "You got me something?"

"It's your *birthday*, Clara."

"It is, isn't it?" She looked down at the box and opened it. Then she gasped. "An amethyst gem…"

The gem sat on a gold chain and was identical to the one she'd lost.

Tears shone in her eyes when she looked up. "You remembered."

"You never replaced it."

"I'm not sure why. I guess it just never felt like the right time to replace it."

It was a gift she'd bought herself after chemo because it signified growth and transformation. "It was important to you."

She smiled as a tear ran down her cheek. "It was. Thank you."

He took the necklace out of the box and slipped it around her neck.

She touched it before giving him a teary smile. "I think you're the most thoughtful man I've ever met, Holden Forbes."

"And the best-looking?"

She laughed as she leaned into him. "Definitely the best-looking." Then she lifted to her toes and kissed him.

* * *

CLARA WALKED beside Indie as they strode down the street, Holden and her mother trailing a bit behind. It was almost evening, and she'd spent her day eating croissants, laughing with her favorite people, and being a couch potato.

Last year, she'd gone bungee jumping, and the year before, she'd flown to Australia to see Uluru. But this year, with everything going on, a quiet birthday was exactly what she needed.

She had no idea where they were headed, just that Holden, Indie, and her mom had organized a dinner somewhere. All she knew was that it wasn't a fancy restaurant, because that was something she'd firmly vetoed.

Today, she just wanted to spend relaxing time with the people she loved most.

"So…" Indie started slowly. "I've been holding this question in all day, but now that we're finally semi-alone, I need an answer."

Oh God, why did Clara's belly flutter at that? "Okay."

"I know that Holden's been sleeping over to watch out for you. I also know from my early visit this morning that he's sharing your bedroom. I know you've kissed, but—"

"Holden and I had sex."

Indie's eyes widened, and Clara squeezed her arm before she could scream.

"Shh! Mom and Holden are behind us."

"You tell me that you finally lost your V-card, then ask me not to scream?" Indie shout-whispered. "Are you crazy? When?"

"The night Scarlett died…and every night since."

That was like five nights ago!

"Shh!" Jesus Christ, did the woman want to alert the entire street?

"Why did you not immediately call me over and tell me over champagne and croissants?"

"You *know* why. Scarlett had just died, and celebrating *anything* didn't feel right. Plus, you and I haven't had a lot of alone time."

Indie cringed. "I'm sorry. I haven't checked in enough these last few days."

"Don't apologize. I know you're going through your own stuff."

"Still…I should have been there more." Indie glanced over her shoulder, then back at Clara. "So…how was it?"

"It was amazing. Soft and slow and…it was Holden, you know? So it felt right."

Indie's arm tightened around hers. "Does this mean you're together?"

"Yeah."

A glimmer of tears shone in Indie's eyes. "Oh, Clara. I'm so happy for you. You've loved him for so long, and you deserve to be happy. So that stuff about being scared—he's over that?"

"He says he is."

"But you don't believe him?"

"Maybe I'm just projecting my fears. I don't know. But time will tell."

Indie frowned, silent for the next few steps.

Clara bumped her cousin's hip. "Say it."

"I don't want to project what happened to me onto you, but… be careful. I know how much you love him. And losing someone you love that much hurts." Real pain wound through Indie's words.

Clara wanted to tell her friend that she wasn't scared. But that wasn't true. Something had changed in her after sleeping with Holden. Her love for him had deepened, something she hadn't thought was possible.

She opened her mouth to respond but realized they were at The Tea House. And through the glass, she saw a dozen people. Her family. Clients who'd become friends. Even Mildred.

The Tea House wasn't even supposed to be open. But there were balloons and streamers and…was that a wall of printed photos?

She stopped and turned to Indie. "You did this?"

"*We* did this. Because you love this place and their almond croissants and sweet teas, and we love you."

Holden slipped an arm around her waist and kissed her head while her mother gave her a soft smile. "Happy birthday, darling."

She hugged all three of them, tears in her eyes.

When she finally stepped inside, the entire crowd shouted, "Happy Birthday!"

She laughed and, yeah, she was almost crying. Happy tears, that was.

She went around the room and hugged everyone one by one. When she got to Mrs. Gerald, she grinned. "Thank you for allowing us to do this."

"Thank *you* for always getting your sweet teas from me. You keep me in business."

"Not true. *You* keep you in business by being amazing. And even if someone else in town started selling sweet tea, I'd still go to you."

"You're too kind, dear."

Mrs. Gerald got called back to the counter just as Clara's phone vibrated with a text. She frowned when she saw who it was from.

Malcolm: Hey, Clara. Is it okay if we chat?

She bit her lip. Holden and Jesse had told her about the interview with Deb. They'd asked her not to speak to Malcolm or anyone else from the running group until they got to the bottom of this.

Clara: I'm sorry, I can't see anyone from the running club while my brother's actively investigating the hospital. I hope you understand.

She hit send and winced. She hated writing that.

Nothing about Malcolm being a suspect felt right. She didn't believe he'd intentionally make his patients sick. Heck, she didn't believe he could murder Scarlett. Sure, they weren't super close, but her gut told her she was right on this one.

"Hey."

Her eyes flashed open to see Jesse in front of her. "Hey, big brother."

He studied her face. Something he did often. "Everything okay?"

"Of course. But I'll be better when you tell me what Scarlett's cause of death was." Holden had already told her what Jesse had found out about Scarlett's job. It had just been one shock after the next lately.

"Respiratory depression."

Clara gasped. Like others at the hospital. "What triggered it?"

"We're still waiting on the tox report to find out."

"What are you thinking?"

"I'm thinking...that your broken back door in combination with her investigating an open case is suspicious. And people from the hospital have better access to drugs than the general public."

A knot formed in her belly.

"You're staying away from them, right?" Jesse stepped closer. "You're not in contact with anyone from the hospital?"

She glanced at her phone, then back up. "I—"

"Darling, it's time for gifts."

Clara gave her mother a look. "Gifts? I said I didn't need anything."

Her mother rolled her eyes. "It's your thirtieth birthday."

The next hour and a half was a blur of people and presents and cake. The cake was in the form of a big acupuncture needle and was the best she'd ever tasted.

She was just taking her empty plate to the trash can when a car passed The Tea House. She frowned at the sight of Malcolm behind the wheel and he frowned back. Suddenly, he was pulling over and climbing out.

Crap. If he came in here, her brothers and Holden would lose their minds in front of everyone.

Before she could think better of it, she rushed outside. "What are you doing here?"

Malcolm stopped in front of her. "I need to talk to you." He shot a glance at The Tea House, then back to her. "It's your birthday?"

"Yeah. Thirty."

"Happy birthday."

"Thank you. But you need to go."

Frustration flickered in his eyes. "I need to know if your brother's said anything about Scarlett's death."

He was trying to get information from her? "Why?"

"Because…" His chest rose and fell. "I'm pretty sure he thinks I did it."

"Did he say that?"

"No. But he was asking me what I was doing the night she died. I was home alone, and I know he didn't believe me. I could see it in his eyes. And if Scarlett's cause of death is linked to Lauren's and the others who've gotten sick…this won't look good for me."

No…not if they were his patients as Holden had told her they were.

"What was that?"

She frowned. "What was what?"

"That expression. You know something."

"Malcolm—"

He grabbed her arms. "Clara, you need to tell me what he's said."

"Malcolm, stop it. If you didn't do anything wrong, then you have nothing to worry about."

"At the beginning, I thought that too. But it just keeps happening."

The door opened behind her.

"*Hey!*"

She turned to see Holden stepping outside, hands fisted, jaw set.

"Get your hands off her," he growled, stepping toward them.

Malcolm's hands dropped. "I'm sorry! I just needed to talk to her."

"No, you don't."

Anger flashed over Malcolm's face. "Well, considering her roommate was investigating my workplace and her brother thinks I'm a murderer, yeah, I kind of do!"

Holden stepped forward, towering over Malcolm. "She has nothing to do with *any* of that."

Clara grabbed his arm. "Holden. We were just talking."

The door opened again, and this time Jesse and Becket stepped out.

Oh, Jesus.

"What's going on?" Jesse asked.

Malcolm cursed. "Nothing. I was just trying to talk to Clara."

"Why?" Becket asked.

Clara turned to her brothers and put her hands on their chests. "Stop. *I'm* fine. I voluntarily came out here to talk to him, but he's leaving now." She threw him a pointed look over her shoulder.

Malcolm's jaw visibly clenched, but he turned and hurried toward his car. The three men around her didn't move or take their eyes off him, each of them looking ready to attack if needed.

When Malcolm drove away, Becket turned to Clara. "What were you thinking?"

"He saw me in there. I came out here to avoid a scene." Ha. That hadn't worked.

Holden crossed his arms.

Jesse stepped forward. "You should have gotten me. You need to stay away from him until the investigation's over."

She rubbed her temple, the beginnings of a headache coming on. "I know. I'm sorry."

Becket scrubbed a hand over his face. "She made a mistake. Come on, Jesse, let's go back inside."

"Promise me, Clara," Jesse warned.

She sighed. "I promise."

Jesse's face gentled, and he leaned down and kissed her cheek while Becket squeezed her arm, then they both returned to the café.

Holden stepped closer. "Why did he come here, Clara?"

"He texted and asked to talk. I told him no, and it was just dumb luck that he was driving past."

His eyes narrowed. "What did he want to talk about?"

"He wanted to know if Jesse had spoken to me about him. He's worried Scarlett's death is being pinned on him."

"Did you tell him anything?"

"No. I don't know anything except that she died from respiratory depression. And he didn't tell me anything."

He gently folded her into his arms. "I'm sorry you're dealing with this."

"It's not your fault. I just want to know what happened to Scarlett."

"We'll find out. I promise."

She nodded, but one question burned in her mind...when?

She rubbed her temple a second time.

"Are you okay?" Holden asked, concern in his eyes.

"Yeah, just a headache. I think I need to drink more water."

He studied her for a moment before he nodded. "Let's get you some water then."

Then he slipped an arm around her waist and led her inside. She shot one more glance behind her to the road, but Malcolm was long gone. And she couldn't help but wonder...if she didn't think he was the murder, why was all the evidence pointing to him?

CHAPTER 21

*T*he smell of ground coffee beans filled the kitchen as Clara poured hot water into the French press.

For some reason, the exhaustion was hanging around. It was a strange exhaustion. One she'd felt for days. The type that dragged at her limbs and made her feel heavy and her head foggy. And she still had that headache from her birthday even though it had been almost a week. She hadn't felt like this since—

She shook her head.

No. She wasn't going to go there. She was fine, just stressed. Jesse still didn't have Scarlett's toxicology report back, and that had been playing on her mind.

Once her mug was filled with coffee, she took a sip. She didn't usually drink coffee, but this morning she needed it.

She took a few deep breaths…only to press a hand to her chest.

It wasn't just the fatigue these last few days. She'd also been short of breath.

Acupuncture. That's what she needed. Calming music, a dark room, and some of her fix-everything needles.

Her phone vibrated, and she lifted it to see a text from her cousin.

Indie: I have an idea and I need you to tell me it's as crazy as I think it is.

Clara: I'll call you now.

Indie: No. This is definitely an in-person conversation. Are you free later today?

Clara: Absolutely. Lunch? And remember, crazy ideas aren't always bad ones.

Indie: You haven't heard this one yet. See you soon.

Clara set her phone back down on the counter. Did this crazy idea involve Colt? Maybe she was finally thinking about flying out to California and really talking to him. God, she hoped so.

Indie had shared a little bit about the night they'd broken up. Well, the night Indie had broken up with Colt. Emotions had been high with her getting the news that her tenth and final embryo hadn't taken and she wasn't pregnant. And to make things worse, Colt was supposed to be with her to receive the call, only he hadn't been. Of course, the reason for that had involved his mother.

Clara didn't know exactly what Indie had said to Colt when he'd finally gotten home, but whatever it was, Clara was certain it had been a buildup of years of frustration.

Clara could still remember the moment Indie had told her they were done. She'd assumed it was just a fight, and Indie was making it sound worse than it was. But almost a year later, Indie was filing for divorce.

Her heart gave a sad twist as she sipped her coffee again, only to immediately scrunch her nose.

Argh.

How did people enjoy the taste of this stuff? Sure, she'd drunk it a lot when she'd lived in New York, but that was because she'd been chronically sleep-deprived and had relied on the caffeine to keep her awake and functioning.

The front door opened and Holden stepped in. His gaze immediately went to her, scanning her body as if needing the reassurance that she was okay.

"Hey."

She smiled at his deep, raspy voice, but her eyes remained fixed on the width of his chest. The light sheen on his skin. He'd gone for a run, and man, did he look good. It chased a bit of her exhaustion away.

"Hi."

He took slow, almost predatory steps toward her. "Did you do okay without me?"

"I survived, but it was tough. I might need a reward for my bravery."

A slow grin curved his lips. "What did you have in mind?"

"I'm partial to kisses. And cuddles. And touching in any form." She set her mug on the counter.

"Is that right?" When he reached her, he slipped an arm around her, hauling her against him.

"Yeah."

He lowered his head and kissed her neck. "That sounds a bit like a reward for me too."

"Mm, win-win."

He kissed her shoulder, and she sighed.

Suddenly, a wave of dizziness washed over her. She swayed and grabbed his shoulders.

His hands tightened around her waist. "Hey. Are you okay?"

"Yeah. I'm just really tired today."

"You've been tired for the last week. Are you sick?" He touched her head and frowned. "Shit, Clara, you're hot."

She was? Maybe she *was* sick. "I might go take a shower and rest."

"I'll come with you."

She shook her head. "No. I'm okay."

"Clara, you just almost passed out. I'm not letting you stand in a hot shower by yourself."

His phone rang.

"Answer it," Clara said softly. "Then join me." She lifted to her toes and kissed his cheek before heading out of the room.

When she reached the bathroom, she touched her forehead. He was right—she *was* hot. Was it a virus?

Once the shower was on, she stripped and stepped under the stream. The hot water beat down on her shoulders, and for the first couple minutes, the warmth made her feel better. Then that light-headed feeling returned, this time hitting her with force, making her sway again.

She tried to grab the wall to catch herself but missed and hit the floor of the shower.

"It was just a client about a cabinet I'm—" The bathroom door opened, and Holden cursed before sprinting to her, turning off the water, and dropping to her side. "Clara, are you okay?"

"Yeah, I think the heat made the dizziness worse."

"We're going to the hospital." He grabbed a towel from behind him, wrapped her in it, and lifted her. She barely had to do anything as he dried her and helped her pull on leggings and a shirt. Then they were in his truck and he was speeding to the hospital.

* * *

HOLDEN FELT SICK, and if a fucking doctor didn't come and check on Clara in the next five minutes, he was going out there and finding one himself.

He shot a glance at Clara on the bed. They'd been shuffled into this small room where a nurse had asked a few questions, but so far, no one else had come to see her.

The rhythmic beeping from other rooms drummed in his

ears. The smell of antiseptic and something metallic made that nausea in his gut ripple.

Fuck, he hated hospitals. His skin crawled just standing in this room, but he couldn't let Clara see that. This wasn't about him— it was about her.

He shifted his gaze back to her on the bed, but the memory of her on the shower floor replayed in his head, and he could almost feel that fear again like he was right there.

He'd found his mother like that a few times. As young as fourteen years old, he'd had to call an ambulance for her. One second she'd be fine, the next she'd be on the floor.

"Where's the damn doctor?" Holden growled. "We've been here an hour."

He went to step away, but Clara grabbed his arm. "Holden, they're busy. They'll come when they can. And I'm actually feeling a bit better with the rest and water."

How was she so calm?

When her thumb stroked his elbow, the edge of his anger smoothed. Not all of it, but a bit.

He sat on the bed beside her. "I hate that you're not feeling well."

"Me too. But it's probably just a virus."

There was something in her voice, a hint of uncertainty, that made a knot form in his gut. Did she *not* think it was a virus? What was she not saying?

The door opened, and Clara looked up first. Her fingers immediately tightened on his arm. He followed her gaze to see an older man with white hair and a mustache. In his hands was a folder.

"Dr. Bennett," Clara said. "I didn't know you were in today."

To anyone else, her voice would sound normal. But he heard the ring of nerves that shadowed each word.

"Hi, Clara. Fortunately, I was here seeing patients when the nurses told me you were in."

She nodded, but the move was jerky. She turned to Holden. "Holden, this is Dr. Bennett. He was...*is* my oncologist."

Oncologist—the word hit him at full impact in the midsection, knocking the breath from his body. Why would her oncologist be needed?

"He works between here and Bozeman, so he isn't always in Amber Ridge," Clara finished.

The doctor moved to Clara's bedside. "You passed out in the shower, is that correct?"

"Yes. I was already feeling light-headed earlier. I've also had a headache."

"And you told the nurse you've been having some shortness of breath?"

"Yes. For a couple of days."

Holden flinched. She'd had shortness of breath for *days* and hadn't told him? And how had he missed her telling that to the nurse?

Dr. Bennett placed the diaphragm of his stethoscope on Clara's chest and listened. "Any other symptoms?"

"Tired...really tired. And a bit of a fever."

The oncologist nodded, shifting the diaphragm to another part of her chest. "Well, Clara, I'm sure it's nothing. But I'd like to do a physical examination and take some x-rays just to be sure. You were due for your annual checkup in a month anyway, so this can just replace that."

The tightness in Holden's muscles grew stronger, and it was suddenly accompanied by a sharp pain in his chest. How many oncologist appointments had he sat in on with his mother? And the constant helplessness he'd felt then matched the concern crawling through his body right now.

Clara turned to him. "You should go."

"No. I'm staying."

"Holden, I know you hate hospitals, and this may take some time. Get a coffee, go outside, and get some air. I'm okay."

He gritted his back teeth together, another "no" on the tip of his tongue. But then Clara squeezed his hand.

"Please," she said softly, a note of desperation in her tone.

He didn't want to leave her side. But maybe him leaving was more for her than him. He forced himself to rise and press a kiss to her temple. "Call me when you're done."

She nodded, worry in her eyes as he turned. Worry about what her oncologist was going to say?

Almost on autopilot, he walked into the hall. He'd only taken a few steps when Deb turned a corner and bumped into him.

"Oh. I'm sorry." She looked up. "Holden?" She wore her nurse's uniform and her hair was pulled up into a slick bun.

He tried for a small smile but was almost certain he didn't pull it off. "Hi, Deb."

"Is everything okay?"

"Clara isn't feeling well." A fucking understatement.

Her eyes widened. "Oh, that's not good. Do you need anything?"

"No. I'm just going to grab a coffee. But thanks."

She nodded quickly. "Okay. Text if you need me."

He continued down the hall. But he didn't step outside or get a coffee. He didn't want to leave the hospital, and he couldn't stomach anything right now.

Instead, he went to the waiting area and paced. Then paced some more.

Back when his mother had been sick, he'd sit and wait for hours. Sometimes by her side in her room. Sometimes in the waiting area. And it had always felt like he was waiting for the worst news. Like every day was both a gift and a ticking time bomb.

What if Clara's oncologist told her the cancer was back?

His skin turned to ice, and a fist wrapped around his heart, squeezing and twisting...yanking him back into the past. Into a time when the world had been dark and lonely.

His phone rang, and he looked down to see Jesse's name on the screen. "Hey."

"Hey, you got a sec?"

He had a million seconds, because he didn't want to spend a single one of them just waiting and thinking about worst-case scenarios. "Yep."

"I've got Scarlett's cause of death."

Holden straightened. "Tell me."

"A mix of fentanyl and morphine was injected into her neck. She then went into respiratory depression and the lack of oxygen killed her. This possibly happened while she was sleeping over her desk."

So she was murdered...probably by the medical staff member she was investigating. He glanced around. Fuck, was Clara even safe in this hospital?

He started moving down the hall.

"Where are you?" Jesse asked.

"At the hospital. Clara passed out."

"*What?*"

"She's with her oncologist now—"

"Her oncologist?"

"He was already here, so he's running some tests."

Jesse cursed. "I need to call Mom. But Holden, I need you to do something for me."

"Anything."

"Don't let them give her anything unless absolutely necessary, especially fluids."

"Why?"

"It's looking like that's how some of those patients got sick. We think something was added to the bags of fluids."

Holden cursed and ran down the corridor, not stopping until he reached her side.

CHAPTER 22

"*I*t's a combination of a virus and the chronic fatigue, which was probably induced by stress."

"So the cancer isn't back?" Clara asked her doctor, almost breathless.

"No, the cancer isn't back, Clara."

Air rushed from her chest while tears pressed at her eyes.

The cancer wasn't back. It was just a virus.

Holden's fingers tightened on her thigh. Since returning to her room, he hadn't left her side. But he'd been quiet. Almost silent. Offering her support with gentle touches here and there. Little squeezes of her leg or hand.

Dr. Bennett kept talking, but Clara just nodded. A mixture of relief for herself and concern for Holden swirled inside her. He didn't like hospitals. And he was already scared at the prospect of losing her to illness. This was the last thing he needed.

"Now, I need you to get plenty of rest and fluids at home."

Clara nodded. "I will."

"Great. Well, you're cleared to go, and I'll see you again for our next annual checkup. But if you have any concerns in the meantime..."

"I'll call you."

"Good."

When the doctor left, Clara grabbed her things and let Holden escort her out. They were halfway down the hall when she heard a familiar voice.

"You *know* that this is bullshit. Someone's setting me up."

Then she spotted him. Malcolm stood in a small office off the hall. He wore jeans and a sweater and was arguing with an older man in a white lab coat.

"Malcolm, you're the only common denominator."

"I know I am, but it's not me!"

Holden's arm tightened around her waist and he urged her forward. "Come on."

Was Malcolm losing his job?

She looked at Holden, about to ask what he thought, but that deep frown was set into his brows, the same one that had been there since she'd passed out.

Suddenly, she didn't want to talk about Malcolm. She wanted to know what was going on in his head.

She waited until they were in the car and driving to break the silence. "Thank you for staying with me."

"I didn't want you to be alone."

She studied his body. The way the muscles in his arms seemed thicker and tenser than usual. The whites of his knuckles as he held the wheel. "Are you okay?"

"I'm fine."

She didn't believe him. The words came too quickly, like they were rehearsed.

"Are *you*?" he asked softly.

No. But that had nothing to do with their hospital trip. "I'm glad Dr. Bennett confirmed I'm okay."

He nodded, and she wanted to ask him a hundred more questions. About what he was thinking. About the fear in his eyes. But she forced herself to wait, because something in her gut told her that this wasn't a car conversation.

When they got home, she kicked off her shoes and headed toward the kitchen for water. "I think it's a takeout and early-to-bed kind of evening," she said over her shoulder.

"I might take the couch tonight."

She stopped, her chest rising on a deep inhale before she slowly turned, a flicker of panic kicking at her ribs. "The couch?"

He scrubbed a hand over his face. "Yeah, so you can have the space to rest."

That was bullshit. She rested best when he was holding her, and there was no doubt in her mind that he knew that.

"You're pulling away from me." Her words were barely a whisper, but they sounded loud. They cut through the air, sharp like a knife, slicing through the silence.

He looked up at her, and a million emotions passed over his face. Fear. Sadness. Even regret. "I'm not—"

"Don't lie to me." She stepped forward. "Be honest, Holden. You owe me that. I can take it."

At least, she *should* be able to take it. She'd survived cancer—she should be able to survive anything he threw at her.

One deep sigh before he spoke. "I was scared today. And that fear reminded me of every reason I ran from this for so long."

"This… You mean *us*."

He didn't respond, but the confirmation was in his pained expression.

Suddenly, it was hard to breathe. To maintain the flow of air in her lungs, when that air felt thick and stuck in place. "It's okay to be scared. I was scared too. It's what we do with the fear that matters."

He ran his fingers through his hair and looked down. And without words, she knew what was about to happen. The floor was crumbling beneath her feet.

Finally, he looked at her again. "I think maybe we should take a pause on us."

If a heart could break from simple words, then hers shattered into a million pieces.

"After everything it took for us to get here," she whispered, "you're ending things because of a small health scare today?"

"Small? Clara, you were having symptoms that could have led to a cancer diagnosis."

"But it wasn't cancer. And the cancer didn't kill me five years ago." She stepped closer. "We can't live in a state of fear."

"I just...I don't know if I can do it."

"Not *it*—*us*. You're talking about you and me."

His silence was so loud it rang in her ears, and God, it hurt. An all-over, every-limb kind of hurt.

"I *love* you." His eyes flared at her words. "I've loved you for so long, Holden. And you promised me you weren't going anywhere."

"I'm not. I'll still be in your life."

It wasn't the same, and they both knew it. He was running, and she'd been a fool to think this was going to end any other way.

"You're right," she whispered. "You *are* scared. We both are. You're scared to live and to love...and I'm scared not to."

He swallowed.

"I was told I had cancer." She stepped forward, needing him to hear everything. "Stage *four*. And when I heard those words, I felt like all these moments were ripped away from me. Smiles and laughs and loves and experiences. They just disappeared." She tilted her head, more tears falling. "Then I did the work and the day came where they told me there was no more cancer in my body, and I got all those moments back. So I can't wait for life to happen, because I'm so viscerally aware of how any second, every future plan can be ripped away."

Pain...it was all over Holden's face. "I've felt loss too, Clara.

But the difference is, I didn't get those moments back with my mom."

"No, but you got the ones before she passed. Now you have the memories of her." Her chest started to heave, the heartache making each breath a battle. "I just...I wish you could see how much more you're going to miss."

"What would you have me do? What's the alternative here?"

She closed the distance between them and set a hand on his chest. "The alternative is to feel the fear and love me anyway."

"I don't know if I can do that."

"You can. But you don't know if you're willing to take the risk." She didn't want to lose that small contact, but she forced her hand to drop. Her feet to step back. "I'd like you to leave."

A muscle clicked in his jaw. "I don't want to leave you alone."

Didn't he get it? By deciding not to love her, even if he physically stayed in the house, she *would* still be alone.

She was on the verge of breaking, but she forced her legs to move. Forced her hand to reach for the door and open it. "I'll call my mom to come over. I need you to go."

Still, in that moment, when she thought she'd lost all hope, there remained a part of her that wanted him to stay. To tell her she was worth fighting for. That she was worth the risk.

Three seconds passed of him remaining exactly where he was...then he finally moved. He walked straight past her, and had just stepped outside when he stopped and turned. "I'm sorry."

"Me too."

She closed the door. And that's when she fell apart. When she allowed the heartache to squeeze her entire body and the pain to swallow her whole.

* * *

THE CLICK of Clara's front door closing was loud and hit Holden like a gut punch.

He stormed down the walk and into his car, where he slammed the door.

What was wrong with him? What *the fuck* was wrong with him?

He punched his fist into the wheel, then did it again. It did nothing. The pain and fury shooting through his limbs were still there, festering and rolling inside him, poisoning.

Feel the fear and love me anyway.

He closed his eyes and hit his head back against the headrest. Why couldn't he be what she needed? Why couldn't the love be stronger than the fear?

He shot a glance toward her door. He wanted to go back. Tell her he'd messed up, that he was there to stay, but that thing inside him that had urged him to run was still there, dictating everything.

He cursed and started the engine.

He wasn't even sure how he made it home, his head was such a mess. One second he was outside Clara's house, the next he was parking in front of his own place. He frowned when he saw Jesse sitting on the steps of his porch, two beers beside him.

What the hell?

Holden climbed out of the truck. "What are you doing here?"

"Clara had a cancer scare."

He said it like that was it. That was the entire answer to Holden's question.

"Don't worry, my mom's with her," he added.

Holden lowered beside Jesse and dropped his head into his hands. "I'm a fucking mess. And worse than that, I'm an asshole. Clara has a cancer scare and I tell her I'm not sure if *I'm* strong enough to date her. I broke up with her because I'm pathetic."

"Well…at least you've finally admitted you were dating."

Shit. "I'm—"

"Don't say you're sorry. You're the best man I know, Holden, and I trust you to love and protect my sister."

"You shouldn't. Not the love part, anyway." He shook his head. "I don't know what's wrong with me."

"You're scared. You're scared to watch the person you love most get sick and die, again. You're scared of having to sit on the sidelines, unable to protect her from something you can't fight." Jesse handed Holden a beer. "We're cut from the same cloth. We're both protectors. It's why we joined the military. To then not be able to protect the most important person in our lives feeds into our worst fears."

He was right. "You know, I always thought that I joined the military to find family because after my mom died, I had no one."

"But now?"

"Now I think I spent so long unable to fight my mother's cancer, I needed to face enemies I *could* fight to gain back some of that control."

Jesse laughed, but there was no humor in the sound. "You certainly did that. We all did."

"I don't know if I can do it again, Jess."

"You're already doing it."

Holden looked at his best friend. "What are you talking about?"

"You love her. I can see it when you look at her. When you talk about her. You're in love with Clara."

He swallowed hard, his throat so dry it felt like sandpaper. "I am." Two words, and they both hit so hard they almost knocked the breath right out of him.

"So it's too late to turn back. You're already in too deep. If you break up with her, you lose her anyway."

Holden's fingers tightened around his beer, that familiar panic gnawing at his skin. "I shouldn't be this scared."

"I'll tell you something very few people will admit. Loving someone—*really* loving them—is scary as hell. You become vulnerable. And you have to be okay with that person having a level of control over you. But you gain so fucking much."

"How do I get past this?"

"You show up. Even if you're scared. You show up and you stop running."

He *had* been running. He'd been running from this thing between him and Clara for so damn long that he was exhausted. Could he ever stop?

He lifted his gaze to the forest around him. "After today, she might not take me back."

And he wouldn't blame her. She'd had a cancer scare and he'd made it about himself. Right now, he should be looking after her.

Jesse laughed, and this time there was some real humor behind it. "We *are* talking about the same person, right? Because my sister loves you. And yeah, depending on what you said to her before you left, you might need to put in some work to earn her trust back. But she *loves* you."

"And love conquers all? Is that what you're saying?"

"Hell no. I'm saying Clara always gets what she wants, and she wants you." Jesse rose and took the keys from Holden's fingers. "I'm going inside. I'm going to make sure you eat before I leave."

Holden watched his best friend go into his house. He rose slowly, but the weight of the day still felt heavy.

Jesse was right. It was too late to run. He *did* love her. And he needed to man the hell up and love her the way she deserved to be loved.

CHAPTER 23

"*H*ow are you doing?" Indie asked as they walked down the street. "And don't tell me fine if you're not."

Oh, Clara definitely wasn't fine. A week had passed since she and Holden had separated. Every day she woke up, expecting the pain to ease and things to feel easier—they didn't.

"Not too good." She frowned down at her sweet tea. They'd grabbed drinks from The Tea House, but Deb had been there and the woman talked a lot, and Clara hadn't really felt like talking so they'd gone for a walk. She needed to get out and move anyway. "He's been calling and texting every day to check in, asking if we can talk, but after the way he left, I just need some space."

Her mother and Indie had been amazing over the last week. Making her meals. Staying over. If it wasn't for them, she'd probably have drowned in self-pity by now.

"What if he wants to tell you that he made a mistake and wants you back?"

Yearning and fear competed inside her. "What about the next time I have a health scare? Will he just desert me again when I need him most? He already promised me once that he wouldn't leave, and he did it at the first opportunity. I need a partner who's going to stick around during the hard times, not just the good."

Indie reached out and squeezed her arm. "I'm sorry. Do you want me to drive over to his place tomorrow and kick him where the sun don't shine as penance for being an idiot? Because I will."

Clara chuckled, and it felt good to laugh. "I don't know if that's a good idea."

"Why? Because he's former special forces? You forget, I was married to a Marine. I have skills."

As if mention of her husband had conjured the woman, Sylvia Reed, Colt's mother, walked around the corner.

Indie stopped in her tracks. "Sylvia."

"Indie, what a surprise." She glanced at Clara. "Hi, Clara."

She gave the older woman a tight smile. "Hi."

"How are you?" Indie asked politely.

Sylvia was a short, thin lady. She came from old money and looked the part. Her hair was always perfect, clothes expensive, and there was always jewelry—today a pearl necklace and beautiful pearl earrings.

"I'm good. You still look tired, dear." Sylvia scanned Indie's body in an almost intrusive way. "Not sleeping well since the split from Colt?"

Clara almost gasped, and she was a second away from telling the woman that her cousin looked great, but Indie spoke first.

"I'm sleeping fine, Sylvia."

"It's nothing to be ashamed of. I spoke to Colt last night. He's not sleeping well either. Such a tough thing you're putting him through."

Her cousin straightened. "I'm not putting him through anything. Couples separate."

"You know, after all that stress from the procedures and disappointments, I don't blame you for needing a break from each other."

Clara's jaw dropped. She was actually bringing up Indie's struggle with IVF?

"IVF wasn't why we separated," Indie said firmly.

"It couldn't have helped." Sylvia perked up. "Speaking of which, did you hear that Julia Stratton just had twins? Natural conception after they stopped trying. Just shows, God has a plan, and we just need to surrender to it instead of forcing things."

That was it! Clara was going to kick this woman in the shin.

She stepped forward, but Indie grabbed her arm. "We should go."

"I'll pass on to Colt that I saw you."

Indie tensed before walking around the woman.

Clara waited until they were at least ten steps down the road before letting it out. "That woman is—"

"The Devil," Indie cut in. "She's the Devil."

"Why did Colt not put an end to it?"

"She usually didn't do any of that in front of him. And when she did, she was a lot more subtle with her passive-aggressive digs. Do you know she once told me that some women just aren't meant to be mothers?"

"You should have let me kick her."

"I should have." Indie shook her head. "I also should've been more honest with Colt about how his mother treated me. But it only started in the last few years, when I moved back here, and by then our relationship was already under stress with the IVF and him being away so much. Plus, he worked such a dangerous job. It didn't feel right to add to all of that."

"He would have lost his mind," Clara said quietly, as they made it back to The Tea House.

"It would have killed him. He loves his mother. She's his entire family. She's always relied on him so much. And maybe that's another reason I didn't say anything."

"Have you opened the divorce papers?" Clara asked gently.

"No. But I will. I don't know when. But...I will."

Clara wasn't sure if Indie would ever feel ready. Those two had been so in love with each other.

A bit like how she felt about Holden. The way she'd *thought* he felt about her. But he couldn't have. Because if he loved her the way she loved him, he would have fought for them.

Her phone vibrated with a text from her back pocket, and she pulled it out, only for her heart to give a sharp thud. "It's Holden."

"Another text asking to talk?"

She opened the text. "No, this time it's just to say that he misses me."

"Maybe..." Indie started slowly, "he realizes he made a mistake and he'll do better next time."

"Maybe."

Sympathy darkened Indie's eyes. "I'm sorry this sucks so much."

"It does suck." Ugly-crying, don't-want-to-get-out-of-bed kind of suck.

They stopped at her Volkswagen Beetle in The Tea House parking lot.

"Any news on Scarlett or the hospital?" Indie asked.

A car pulled in beside Clara's, but she ignored it. "Not since we found out it was fentanyl and morphine that killed her."

She hadn't seen Malcolm since she'd walked past that office and heard him arguing. But that was mostly because Jesse had basically prohibited her.

"I can't believe patients were probably being drugged by someone who worked there," Indie said quietly.

"I know. I still don't think Malcolm is responsible. Scarlett must have figured out who was behind it, and it got her killed. But her laptop was taken, so unless there's another way to figure out what she—" She stopped, a memory crashing back to her.

Indie stepped closer. "What?"

"That night she died, Scarlett was acting really strange."

"Strange how?"

"Remember how I ran back into the house?"

"Yeah, you forgot your phone."

"She was rummaging through the spice drawer. But there were no other ingredients on the counter. There was no cake or cookies in the fridge when I got home. No dirty bowls. I can't believe I'm only realizing it now!"

"I don't—"

"What if she wasn't baking anything—what if she was hiding something? Maybe she knew someone was onto her and she needed a safe place to put something?"

"Put what?"

"I don't know. But I'm going to find out." She turned and opened her car door, but Indie grabbed her arm.

"Clara, maybe you should call Jesse."

"I will. I'll call him as soon as I've checked the spice drawer. This might be nothing, and I don't want to waste his time." She gave Indie a quick hug. "I'll let you know what I find."

This was good. Something to focus on other than the heaviness of the last week that tried to swamp her. And maybe she'd also learn something about Scarlett's death.

When she pulled into her driveway, her pulse sped up in anticipation of what she might find. She sprinted to the kitchen and opened the spice drawer. Then, one by one, she took everything out, tipping the spices onto the counter, not caring that she was going to have to replace everything or that she was making a mess.

She was halfway through when doubt started to flicker in her mind. Was she being ridiculous? Maybe Scarlett *had* baked something. Maybe she'd eaten it or given it away and cleaned up after herself?

She was on the verge of giving up when she lifted a jar of peppercorns. Quickly, she opened the lid and poured them out... and that's when she saw it.

A USB.

Her breath caught. She lifted it from the kitchen counter, her pulse picking up speed.

"Scarlett…what did you find?"

She was about to call Jesse when a rustling noise sounded. From the hallway?

She turned to see her front door ajar.

The back of her neck prickled. Had she left it like that? She couldn't remember. She'd been in a rush to search the jars, so it was possible.

She took out her phone, and with her cell in one hand and the USB in the other, she walked toward the door, pressing Jesse's number on the way.

"Clara, hey. Is everything okay?"

"I'm not sure."

"What do you mean, you're not sure? Where are you?"

"I'm at home. I found something but I think someone's here."

"There's someone in your *house*?" Jesse's voice was harder and louder now, and movement sounded over the line.

She stepped into the hall. "I'm—"

An arm suddenly wrapped around her neck from behind and pushed her into her bedroom doorframe.

She gasped, both the USB and phone dropping from her hands. She took three quick steps back, turning with each step and hitting the person behind her against the wall. The attacker grunted, and she quickly threw an elbow to their gut, nailing them in the midsection.

When their grip on her loosened, she tried to run but a body hit her full force from behind, sending them both to the floor. Her head hit the floorboard, her gaze going blurry.

An arm wrapped around her neck once again, this time pulling so tight that the air cut off in her throat.

For a second, panic rendered her completely useless. Then her fight instinct kicked in, and she turned her head toward the person's elbow to try to create space to breathe before grabbing at the arm around her throat. When that wasn't enough, she bucked her hips up and rolled so that she was on top, her back pressed to their front. She lifted her leg and brought her foot down hard on their shin.

They cried out, and she pushed up and ran. She wanted to run outside, but her keys were in the kitchen and the attacker might force her into their car. So instead, she ran into her bedroom, then the bathroom, and locked the door.

* * *

HOLDEN GUIDED the smooth edge of the cabinet door through the table saw, the blade whirling as it sliced through the wood.

Cool air blew in from the open workshop doors, and sawdust and fresh-cut pine scented the air. He'd been working out here for hours. Doors lay on the workbench, their edges rough because he'd yet to sand them.

He'd barely slept over the last week. Clara was all he could think about. The tears in her eyes when she'd told him to leave. The pain in her voice.

He'd messed up. Fuck, he'd messed up so badly that he didn't know how to fix it. She wasn't answering his calls or responding to his texts. Was what he'd done completely unfixable?

His lungs tightened at the idea that it was. That he might never get Clara back.

He paused and checked his phone. He'd texted her not long ago, but still no response.

Being apart from her was killing him, and not just because he needed to fix things. She'd been sick. He needed to make sure she was okay, and right now the only information he was getting was secondhand through Jesse, Becket, and Pam.

Fuck it. He was going to go see her.

He turned everything off, took a quick shower, and climbed into his truck.

On the way, he went over so many scenarios in his head. Things he wanted to say. Apologies he needed to make. None of it felt like enough.

Maybe he should have stopped for flowers or an almond croissant or one of those sweet teas she liked.

He pulled over in front of her house.

Too late now.

This was it. This was when he *begged* her to forgive him.

He was just taking off his seat belt when his gaze caught on the front door.

It was ajar.

The *fuck?* She wouldn't have done that, not after Scarlett's murder.

A pulse picked up speed in his temple. Quickly, he reached for his pistol in the glove box and slipped out of the car. He scanned her yard, then street as he jogged up her front steps.

Nothing looked out of place outside.

Quietly, he gave the door a little shove, aiming the Glock in front of him.

Nothing.

He lowered his gaze to the floor—and saw blood on the floorboards.

His muscles locked, his gaze immediately lifting again. "Clara?"

Silence. And it was so fucking loud.

He moved into the living room, then the kitchen, always keeping his back firmly against the wall and his weapon raised. Empty spice jars lay scattered on the counter, their contents spread everywhere.

What the hell happened here?

A siren wailed in the distance.

He turned and made his way into the bedroom. "Clara? Are you here?"

He stepped toward the bed, about to look beneath it, when he heard her.

"Holden?"

He swung toward the bathroom and took three quick steps forward. "Yeah, honey, it's me. Can you open the door?" A few seconds of silence passed. When nothing happened, he took another step forward and gentled his voice. "Clara...you're safe."

One more beat, then the click of the bathroom lock sounded. The door opened, and Clara stood there, blood on the side of her head, her neck a deep red.

"Clara—"

He didn't have a chance to finish his sentence before she fell into him, her body shaking.

He wrapped one arm around her tightly and holstered his pistol as the air whooshed from his chest. For a moment there, when he'd seen the blood and the empty house, he'd wondered if he'd been too late.

He closed his eyes, thanking every fucking god out there.

"What happened?" he finally asked.

"I—"

"*Clara?*"

They both looked up at the sound of Jesse's voice.

Jesse found them in the bedroom. "Holden?" He looked from Holden to Clara to the cut on her temple and cursed. "What happened?"

She swallowed. "It's a long story."

"We've got time."

Holden curved an arm around Clara's waist and led her out to the couch. He studied the wound on her temple. "Maybe we should go to the hospital to have that looked at."

She frowned and touched the wound, as if she was surprised

it was there, before shaking her head. "No. I'm okay. I just need a bandage."

"Clara—"

"I'll get one of my guys to look at it," Jesse said, still far too calm. He glanced at Holden. "Did Clara text you?"

"No, I came to talk to her. The door was ajar, so I assumed something was wrong."

"They must have left," Clara said softly, almost to herself.

"Who?" Jesse asked.

"I don't know." Clara swallowed, then winced. "Whoever wanted the USB."

Holden sat beside her on the couch, his hand going to the small of her back, the need to touch her consuming him. "USB?"

"I was with Indie in the parking lot of The Tea House when I suddenly remembered that on the night Scarlett died, she was rummaging through the spice drawer. So I ran home and found a USB that she'd hidden in the peppercorn jar."

"What was on it?" Jesse asked.

She dropped her head into her hands. "I don't know. Just as I found it, I heard someone else in the house. That's when I called you. They attacked me and I dropped it. If it's not on the floor in the hall, I'm guessing they took it."

Holden frowned at Jesse. "Pretty big coincidence that they came in at exactly the right time."

"I don't believe in coincidences." Jesse looked back at Clara. "Was anyone around to overhear your conversation with Indie?"

"I don't—" She stopped, her brows dipping. "A car pulled in beside mine, but I didn't look over, I only heard it. I guess they could have rolled down their window and listened."

"And then followed you home," Jesse finished.

Holden cursed. This was getting too fucking dangerous, and he didn't like Clara being in the middle of it.

"Did you see who it was?" Jesse asked. "Did you recognize them, or could you give us a description?"

She shook her head, her brows tugging together again. "I didn't see them. They were always behind me. I don't even know the color of their car. I'm sorry. But there *is* something I'm certain about."

Holden leaned closer. "What?"

"It was a woman."

CHAPTER 24

Clara's fingers wrapped tightly around the mug of hot cocoa. She hadn't taken a single sip since Holden had placed it in her hand. People moved around her, deputies leaving her house while her brother and Holden spoke in the hall.

It was nearing evening, but she'd barely absorbed anything anyone had said after talking to Jesse.

She touched her neck. She could still feel that arm wrapped around her. And her throat still felt light, like the air wasn't getting through.

It was hard to breathe suddenly, and she couldn't look away from the spot in the hall where the person had grabbed her.

"Clara."

Jesse crouched in front of her.

"Are you okay?"

"I don't know."

Rage flickered over his features, but it came and went so quickly she almost missed it. He was trying to shield her from his anger. But he couldn't. Not completely. "What do you want to do? I've still got a few hours left of my shift, but you can stay with Becket until I finish."

"Or you can come with me," Holden added quietly.

God, nothing seemed like the right choice. She didn't want to intrude on her brothers. Things weren't good with her and Holden. And she no longer felt safe in her own home.

"Sheriff."

Jesse turned as one of the deputies tilted his head toward the door. He looked back at her and squeezed her thigh. "I'll be right back."

The second he left, it was just her and Holden. There were so many emotions she probably should have felt at being alone with Holden, but after the day she'd had, all she could feel was safe.

He sat beside her on the couch, his gaze boring into her, his muscles looking big and tense. "I'd like to stay with you."

She swallowed, wanting to say yes. Wanting this man to remain by her side and keep her safe.

But then what? He would leave in a week when Jesse solved the case? Where would that leave her and her heart?

"I don't think that's a good idea." She rose and took her hot cocoa to the kitchen, where she set it in the sink. She didn't hear Holden behind her, but she was aware of him. His heat. His strength.

A lot of people would argue that they couldn't feel strength, but with Holden, it was everywhere he went.

"Clara—"

She turned. "You broke up with me."

Pain cut across his face. "I know. It was a mistake."

"No. A mistake is forgetting to turn on the dishwasher after you fill it. It's leaving the house without your phone or forgetting to set an alarm for the morning. Breaking up with me because I had a *virus* was you running scared, after you promised you wouldn't. It was intentional."

His eyes were so dark, they almost looked black. He stepped forward, and she moved back, needing the distance between them.

This time, it was hurt that flashed through his eyes. "I'm sorry."

His words were quiet. And God, they sounded genuine.

"I'm sorry I hurt you," he continued. "I'm sorry that I couldn't be the person you needed me to be."

She swallowed and looked down, her fingers tightening on the counter behind her to stop from touching him. Drawing him toward her.

"Let me be better," he whispered, taking another step closer. "Let me prove to you that I *can* be better."

A mixture of hope and need snuck into her chest, teasing her with the idea that she could trust him. "What happens if I say yes, and I have another health scare? Or I get hurt or something really bad happens?"

"I'll be with you the entire time, by your side."

She wanted to believe him. She really did.

He lowered his mouth to her neck, but before his lips could touch her skin, she whispered, "Don't."

He paused, his head lifting just enough for her to see his eyes. She could still feel his breath on her skin.

"Why not?" he whispered.

"Not here. Not now."

His gaze flickered between her eyes. "Okay. Not now. But I *will* earn back your trust. For now, let me stay. Let me be close so I know you're safe."

She closed her eyes, the feel of him, the smell, making her body sway toward him.

"Okay." The single word came out as barely a whisper. "But on the couch."

"Thank God." He touched his forehead to hers.

She closed her eyes, letting his heat seep into her. They remained exactly as they were until Jesse stepped back into the house.

"Did you decide—" Her brother stopped.

Holden took a slow step back. And damn her, but she wanted to pull him back again.

"I'm staying," Holden said, no hesitation in his words.

Jesse looked at Holden before studying Clara's face. Even though Holden was his best friend, Clara knew he'd only leave her with him if he knew she was okay.

She gave a small nod before moving around the island and lifting to her toes to kiss her brother. "I'll call if I need anything."

"Good." He wrapped his arms around her in a tight hug.

When they finally separated, he shook Holden's hand, and the two men shared a look she couldn't decipher before her brother left.

Then it was just her and Holden...and suddenly she was nervous. Scared that she'd wrap her arms around him and not let him go.

She took a few big steps back. "I might, um, take a bath."

He nodded, watching her so closely that she wanted to squirm. "Call me if you need anything."

Nope. She wouldn't be needing a thing.

She turned and walked quickly, almost *ran* out. The second she reached her bedroom, she closed the door and let her breath rush out.

Time. She needed some time to trust Holden again. She *could not* just fold because he was here, and he was beautiful and strong and he smelled really good.

In the bathroom, she turned on the tap and undressed. Once a candle was lit and the lights were off, she sank into the tub.

Usually, a warm bath relaxed her. But tonight? Tonight her body was tight and stressed and she couldn't sit still.

She leaned back and closed her eyes, trying to allow the tension to ease from her body.

It did nothing. Diddly-squat. Absolutely no relaxing happening here.

Maybe some magnesium flakes would help.

She reached for the jar on the counter but accidentally knocked it off. The glass hit the floor and shattered.

She gasped—and that gasp turned into a cry when the door flew open and Holden charged in, fury on his face.

* * *

HOLDEN PLACED the almond croissant on a plate with some cucumber sticks, hummus, and olives. Aspen had dropped off the croissants and he'd found the rest in Clara's fridge.

Thank fuck she'd let him stay. If she hadn't, he wouldn't have slept. Not one damn minute. Someone had broken into her house. *Attacked* her.

His feet itched to go out and find the person. Show them exactly what happened when they lay their hands on his woman.

Was Clara right? Was this person a woman? Who? Someone from the hospital? Briar? Helen? Deb? Hell, there were dozens of women who worked there, it could be anyone. Was it someone who was working with Malcolm, or trying to protect him?

They needed answers and they needed them now.

Jesse had told him that Malcolm was temporarily suspended from practicing until everything was sorted out. All the sick patients were his. Not only that, but he didn't have an alibi for the night Scarlett was murdered.

Holden was about to head to the bedroom when his phone rang, Briar's name on the screen.

He tensed, considered not answering, but…fuck. He was still in the middle of her kitchen renovation.

"Hey, Briar."

"Hi! I just wanted to call to let you know I paid the final installment for the kitchen."

"Great. I'll start installation next week."

"Perfect, well—"

"Did you have a good afternoon?"

There was a small pause. "Uh, yeah, I guess. I was at work. A twelve-hour shift. Although, as usual, we were understaffed. And who do they expect to pick up the extra patients? Me."

Holden's fingers tightened around the phone. If Briar was working, then it couldn't have been her. "Can I ask you about Malcolm?"

"Malcolm Trundle? Sure. I heard about his suspension. I should probably be more surprised about what he did than I am."

"You're not surprised that he made his patients sick?"

"He was a man whore. Slept around like he was Casanova."

Holden frowned. "How does that—"

"He's not a good person. And people who aren't inherently good obviously do bad things. Plus, all that sepsis treatment fame probably went to his head and he started getting a God complex." Briar huffed. "Anyway, I need to go. See you next week for the kitchen install."

She hung up, and Holden lifted the plate and headed toward the bedroom. If Malcolm slept around, could he have pissed off the wrong person and someone was framing him? Or had he pulled a woman in to help him, and that woman had attacked Clara tonight to protect him?

There were too many possibilities.

He stepped into Clara's room and had just set the food on her dresser when glass shattered in the bathroom.

He cursed and ran, crashing through the bathroom door to find Clara, naked in the tub, broken glass on the tiles.

Clara cried out and pulled her knees up. "Holden! What the hell?"

"What happened?"

"I broke a jar of magnesium."

He scanned her, needing the confirmation that she was okay.

When his heart rate started to return to normal, he finally focused on other things. The drops of water trickling down her arms. The smooth thighs tucked against her body.

Shit. He scrubbed a hand over his face. "I'll clean it up."

"*After* my bath, you mean."

"Now, Clara. I don't want you to cut your feet. I'll be quick. I've also brought you food."

Her brows lifted. "Food?"

He smiled as he left the room to grab the plate of food and the dustpan and broom.

There was a small gasp when Clara saw the croissant. "I didn't have that in my house."

"Aspen brought it over."

"Remind me to kiss her feet when I see her next."

He handed her the plate before squatting to clean up the glass and magnesium. "You don't get sick of croissants?"

"Do you get sick of breathing?"

He laughed. "Guess not."

She picked at the flaky dough. "I've loved croissants since I had my first, and when I tried my first almond croissant, I thought I'd died and gone to heaven. Although, I didn't eat them a lot while I lived in New York."

"Why not?"

Her knees remained pulled up, covering her body. "Often, I was so busy that I just forgot to eat, period. And when I *did* eat, it was usually a can of tuna and some microwavable rice that I kept in a work drawer." She shook her head. "I really did lead a different life."

"Do you miss it?"

She scoffed. "Never. It was one of those situations where you think you want something, but then you get it, and you're like...is this it? And it just kind of feels hollow."

"So what does living in Amber Ridge and working as an acupuncturist feel like?"

"The fresh air I didn't know I was being starved of." She frowned, popping a little bit of croissant into her mouth. "Or at least, it did until everything started happening with Scarlett."

He scooped up the last bit of glass before looking at her. "It'll be over soon."

Yeah, that wasn't something he could promise. But fuck, he'd do anything to give the woman some peace.

She swallowed. "I'm sorry I lost the USB."

"You have *nothing* to be sorry for. You protected yourself, which is what you needed to do." He rose. "I'll get rid of this and set up the couch."

He turned and started toward the door.

"Holden…"

He turned.

"Why did you come here today?"

"To tell you that I'm the biggest idiot on the planet and beg for your forgiveness."

Her brows dipped. "What changed between last week and today?"

"I realized it was too late to run."

That frown deepened.

"Let me know when you're going to bed so I know you're okay." He closed the door quietly and stepped into the living area.

He'd just finished setting up the couch when his phone rang. "Jesse, you found something?"

"I've got a list of the hospital staff who weren't on today. I'll interview them tomorrow."

"I spoke to Briar. She told me she had a twelve-hour shift."

"She did. Deborah Fuller wasn't on."

Could she be involved? She was fit for a woman in her sixties, but in a fight, he'd put his money on Clara winning. But he didn't know her well enough to say it couldn't be her. "What about Helen?"

"She also worked a twelve-hour shift."

He nodded absently. "Keep me updated when you have more information."

"Will do. And you look after my sister for me."

"I'll protect her with my life."

"I know you will."

Holden hung up. After eating something, he had a quick shower in the hall bathroom before checking all the locks in the house. He was just sitting down on the couch when Clara poked her head out of the bedroom. She wore an oversized T-shirt, and fuck, she looked cute. But then his gaze caught on the cut on her head. The bruising on her neck. And that familiar anger slipped through the shield.

"I'm going to sleep now," she said quietly.

"Call out if you need anything, honey."

Her chest rose. "I will."

The door closed with a soft thud, and he had to fist his hands to stop from pushing up from the couch and going to her. He just wanted eyes on her. To hold her. Tell her he'd messed up and beg for her forgiveness.

He turned off the lights and climbed beneath the blankets on the couch. But he didn't sleep. He lay there, memories of that afternoon playing over in his mind. The open front door. The blood on the floor. The fear when he couldn't find her.

He squeezed his eyes shut, trying to force the memory away.

He wasn't sure how much time passed, maybe an hour, maybe three. But at some point, a soft shuffle sounded from the bedroom, followed by her door opening.

It was dark, but he could still see the shine of her eyes as they met his. The length of her legs left uncovered by the shirt.

Without a word, she made her way over to him, pulled back the blanket, and slipped in beside him. When she looked up, her eyes were wide and vulnerable. "Is this okay? I can't sleep. If it's not—"

"Yes." He wrapped an arm around her and tugged her closer. "Sleep. You're safe with me."

She sighed before laying her head on his chest. Slowly, her breathing evened out. And finally, he could sleep too.

CHAPTER 25

The hum of Clara's breathing whispered across Holden's arm. Damn, she was soft. Her back was pressed to his front while one of his arms lay over her waist and the other under her cheek.

Perfect. She was perfect. And last night, he could have lost her. Hell, even before that, he'd lost her by being an idiot. What would happen when she woke up? Would she put that distance between them again? Distance that was his own doing?

He tightened his arm around her as if that could somehow keep her in his life.

When her breathing shifted from long, slow breaths to shorter ones, his muscles tensed.

What's the plan, Clara?

Long seconds passed where she was completely still.

Instinctively, he stroked his thumb against her stomach.

She sighed. "You're awake."

Gently, so gently it was barely a graze, he lowered his head and kissed her neck. "I am."

Her breathing shifted, moving faster now. "What are you doing?"

"I've been wanting to kiss you there for hours."

"You've been awake for hours?"

"Yeah. I couldn't get back to sleep, but I didn't want to leave you."

She rolled onto her back. The pink of her cheeks, the red of her lips—all of her was damn breathtaking.

"Holden...we can't."

"Can't what?"

"Kiss...say things like that."

"Why not?"

"Because it makes the distance between us even harder."

"I don't want distance." He lowered his head again, but she touched her fingers to his lips.

"You *did*."

"I messed up." So fucking badly.

"I don't know how to trust that you won't run again."

He gently took her wrist and kissed the inside of it. She gasped softly, and when she didn't pull away, he kissed her jaw, then her cheek, before whispering, "You're the one who told me to take a chance. Now it's your turn—take a chance on me."

A shudder rippled through her body. "I spent so many years waiting for you."

"I'm here." He lifted his head to see heat in her eyes...and need.

She watched his expression carefully. Slowly, so slowly it felt like time had stopped, she slipped her hands up his chest, then curled them around his neck. They slid into his hair, and he lowered his head. And when he finally found her lips, she hummed, and he ate that sound up.

Her lips separated, and he slipped inside, tasting her.

And fuck, she tasted familiar and good and like every damn craving he'd had for the last week.

He moved on top of her, holding his weight on his elbows.

Her leg curved around his waist, and he felt all of her. Her heat. Her softness. The desperate tugs of his hair that matched the fire in his chest.

A week ago, he'd been scared to fall deeper. Now? Now he was scared to lose everything. And Clara *was* everything. He just hadn't realized it until he'd lost it.

His hand was caressing her body, about to cup her breast, when she stiffened. "Holden, what's the time?"

He didn't know and he didn't care. "Why?"

"I'm meeting someone at eight."

She pushed again, but he kept her caged to the couch. "Who?"

An uncomfortable expression crossed her face. "Holden—"

"*Who*, Clara?"

Her chest rose and fell. "Malcolm."

Every muscle in his body tightened. "No."

"Yes."

She shoved him again, but he didn't move an inch. "Clara… don't be stupid."

"I need to talk to him. My attacker was a woman. It wasn't him. And he might know something. I need to know what he knows in case it can lead me to Scarlett's killer."

"That's Jesse's job."

"I'm going to talk to him."

His back teeth ground together. He didn't want to move a muscle. But he did. And he watched Clara rise, grab her phone, and jog to her bedroom.

As she did, he pulled on his shoes.

She stepped out of her bedroom and stopped. "What are you doing?"

"I'm coming with you."

"No. He won't talk to me if you're there."

"Too damn bad."

She moved to the door, only to stop and turn when he tried to follow her. "Holden—"

"There is no scenario, none, where you go to Malcolm's house alone. Do you understand? It's me, or nothing."

Her jaw visibly clenched. "Fine. But you're waiting outside."

He could have laughed. He was going wherever Clara was going, whether she liked it or not.

* * *

CLARA'S HEART beat hard in her chest as Holden drove them to Malcolm's house, doubt flickering in her mind.

Maybe she shouldn't be doing this. But it wasn't him who'd attacked her last night. It was a woman. And there were things Malcolm hadn't told her. Things that might help her figure out who it was. And yes, it wasn't her job, but for some reason, even though she and Scarlett weren't friends, she felt like she owed it to the other woman.

She shot a glance at Holden. He was mad. His fingers were so tight around the wheel that his knuckles were white.

"You're not going to wait outside, are you?" she asked quietly.

"Not a chance in hell."

She sighed as they pulled up in front of a ranch-style home.

Those nerves hit her again, but she tried to hide them as she climbed out. Holden scanned up and down the street, his hand going to the small of her back as he led her toward the door.

She knocked.

She wasn't nervous that Malcolm would hurt her—she was almost certain he wasn't involved. Maybe she was nervous about the information he might have.

When no one answered, she knocked again. "Malcolm?"

Another minute passed. Still nothing. She pulled out his phone and tried calling, and even though he didn't answer, she heard the ringing inside the house.

She frowned as she looked up at Holden before trying the door.

Unlocked.

"Clara..." There was warning in Holden's voice.

"He's expecting me. If he's not answering the door, something must be wrong." She stepped inside. "Malcolm? Are you here? It's me, Clara."

Nothing.

Had he left? She *was* ten minutes later than she'd said she'd be. But his phone had rung from inside the house. No one left their phone at home when they went out.

She tried to take a step, only for Holden to grab her arm. "We're leaving."

"Holden—" She stopped when she saw him looking at something. She followed his gaze to the couch. "Malcolm?"

He sat there, his back toward them.

Clara took a step toward the couch, but Holden tugged her back, stopping her.

"He's so still," she whispered.

Holden stepped forward, and Clara followed to see Malcolm's head tilted to the side at an odd angle, his eyes closed.

Her heart crashed against her ribs.

Holden lowered beside him and touched his pulse before cursing and pulling out his phone. "This is Holden Forbes. I need an ambulance to two forty-eight Turner Court. I've got a man in his thirties who's barely breathing."

Oh God...had he been drugged too? Who did this?

The door behind them swung open and Jesse entered.

Her brother frowned at her. "Clara?" Then he looked from Holden to Malcolm before cursing.

"Did you call him?" Clara asked Holden.

He shook his head as he rose.

Things moved quickly after that. Jesse and his deputies worked to try to help Malcolm until the paramedics arrived. Then they checked the house.

Clara just stood there, Holden by her side, feeling cold and useless, her gaze never moving from the place they'd found Malcolm.

Why him too? And how many more victims would there be?

"What are you doing here?" Jesse asked when he finally returned.

"I wanted to talk to him. I was attacked in my home last night, and I thought he could help me figure out who it was."

"That's *my* job." Jesse rarely let his anger get the better of him, but right now, he looked right on the edge.

He was right. Of course he was. She was just so desperate for everything to end and Scarlett's killer to be brought to justice.

"How did you know to come?"

"We came to take Malcolm in for questioning. That woman who died, Lauren? Malcolm was her masseuse client, and he was sleeping with her. A witness says she tried to break it off the day before she died, and he didn't take it well. He's also been the primary caregiver for every patient who's gotten sick. And he didn't have an alibi for Scarlett's attack."

She swallowed. Okay, all of that made him look bad. Really bad.

A hand suddenly touched her back. A warm, calming hand. "Jesse...it's done. Why don't we focus on how to move forward?"

She swallowed, so incredibly glad Holden had come with her, even if she'd pushed to do this alone.

"We found a syringe beside his body," Jesse said. "We'll get it fingerprinted, and if the prints are his, it's possible he realized he was going to be arrested and panicked."

Clara frowned. "You think he did this to himself?"

"It's a possibility. We'll wait and see if he pulls through. If he does, we'll question him."

"Why would he agree to talk to me if he was going to do that?" she asked, genuinely confused.

"I'm not sure," Jesse said, voice gentling now. "What time were you supposed to meet?"

"Eight. But I was ten minutes late."

When Jesse was called over by his deputy, Holden's warm hands slipped to her waist and turned her. "Hey. Are you okay?"

"I should have listened to you. I'm sorry."

"It doesn't matter now."

But it could have mattered if she'd come alone and gotten here a couple minutes earlier. Because either Malcolm was the bad guy or the bad guy would've been there. Either way, she would have been in danger.

Her focus once again returned to the empty couch where they'd found Malcolm's body. "I don't want to be here."

"Let's get out of here."

"Are we allowed to leave?"

"I don't care. You don't want to be here, and I don't want you here."

She let him lead her toward his truck, her gaze sweeping the room one last time before stepping out as she wondered yet again what the hell was going on.

CHAPTER 26

*H*olden pulled up in front of Briar Winslow's house. He didn't want to be here finishing the kitchen installation. He wanted to be with Clara, making sure she was okay. Convincing her she could trust him.

Three nights had passed since they'd found Malcolm's body. He was in a coma. A high dose of fentanyl had been found in his blood and his prints were on the syringe, so the signs pointed toward him injecting himself. But Clara was adamant her attacker had been female, so there were still unanswered questions.

He'd remained on Clara's couch for the first two nights, but last night she'd stayed at her mother's house. He'd barely slept.

Before getting out of his truck, he sent another text to Clara.

Holden: Hey. Sleep okay?

Clara: Kind of. You?

Holden: Barely an hour.

The three dots popped up, then disappeared. When she didn't immediately respond, he shoved his phone into his pocket and climbed out. At Briar's front door, he knocked and waited, frowning when no one answered. He tried again...and again, nothing.

Was she not home? She knew he was coming.

He pulled out his cell, about to call her, when a car pulled into the drive and Briar rushed out. "Holden, I'm so sorry. I got caught up at the hospital."

He shoved his hands into his pocket and stepped back while she opened the door. "Is everything okay?"

"Not really. We're all a bit shaken by what happened to Malcolm." She sniffed, a hint of tears glittering in her eyes. "I just hope he wakes up and can tell us why he did it. Has Jesse said anything?"

"No."

Her face dropped.

"But if there's anyone I trust to find answers, it's him."

"I hope you're right." She shook her head. "Anyway, sorry I'm late. Come in."

"I'll just get the cabinet doors from my truck."

He went back to his truck and grabbed some of the doors. They were the last items the kitchen needed, then he'd be done.

When he returned to the house, he didn't see Briar. But then, she might have gone into the bedroom or study.

As he worked, he continued to check his phone, wanting to be ready if Clara needed him. How long was he supposed to give her space when she was in danger?

An hour later his phone rang, Jesse's name on the screen.

He answered on the second ring. "Hey."

"Hey. Just thought I'd give you an update. Our two most likely suspects are currently Helen and Deb. Both their shifts give them the opportunity to be at Malcolm's house at the right time, although Helen was working at the time Clara was attacked."

Which meant Deb was the prime suspect. "Have you interviewed them?"

"No. That's the plan today."

Holden nodded, even though his friend couldn't see him. "Keep me updated."

"Will do. You still staying with Clara?"

"She stayed with your mom last night. Any news on when Malcolm might wake up?"

"Not yet."

"Do *you* think he did it to himself?"

There was a small pause. "I think he's involved in whatever's going on...but I think someone else is too. The woman who attacked Clara."

Holden's fingers tightened around the phone.

He hung up and turned to see Briar standing in the doorway, arms wrapped around her waist. "Was that Jesse Hayes?"

"Yeah."

"Did he...I mean, is there an update on what will happen to Malcolm when he wakes up? Will he be arrested for murder?"

So everyone at the hospital just assumed it was Malcolm. "He didn't say."

Holden wouldn't be sharing about the woman who'd attacked Clara, not when Briar worked with the two main suspects.

She nodded. "Everyone's so upset by what happened."

"I assume people have been talking about it at the hospital."

"It's all *anyone's* talking about."

He nodded slowly. "Helen and Deb weren't close to Malcolm, were they?"

"They were friends. We're all friends."

Didn't really tell him much. "I'll probably be another hour here."

"Not a problem. It looks great."

"It does."

She left the room and he got back to work. He was just heading back out to his truck to get the last few cabinet doors when her phone on the hall table lit up with a text. But it wasn't the text that caught his attention—it was the background photo.

It was a group of people from the hospital, but what *really* caught his attention was the way she and Malcolm stood so close. His arm was around her waist, and everyone was looking at the camera except Briar...

She was looking straight at Malcolm.

* * *

A COMA. Malcolm was in a coma.

Clara sucked in a sharp breath. It didn't feel real. None of it did. It was like she was in a movie, but not a happy one.

The back door opened and her mother walked out onto the deck, two cups of chamomile tea in hand. "Here you go, honey."

"Thank you, Mom. And thank you for letting me stay last night. I just needed to get out of the house."

Her mother shook her head. "Don't ever apologize for coming over, Clara. This is your home too."

Warmth filtered through her chest. This was exactly why she'd moved back to Amber Ridge when she'd gotten her diagnosis. Because this was home.

"How are you feeling?" her mother asked gently.

"Confused. I just want to know what's going on. Who killed Scarlett? Did Malcolm hurt himself or did someone else do it? And mix that into my mess of a personal life."

"Why's your personal life a mess?"

She swallowed hard. "Because I love Holden, and I don't know what to do about it." She'd never admitted that to her mother. But by the look in Pam Hayes's eyes, she knew.

"He's been really good at running from you."

"You saw that?"

"Clara, I saw *everything*. And I can tell you that whenever that boy's in your vicinity, you are all he sees."

"I thought he loved me too, but then I had that scare at the hospital and he was so quick to end things."

"I'm not surprised."

She frowned. "You're not?"

"He knows what it feels like to be alone in this world and to have no one. And he blames that on cancer. Then you—this beautiful, kind woman who he loves—has her oncologist walk into the room, and it suddenly hits him that he could go through that pain all over again. He panics. He does the only thing he knows how to do to protect himself and pushes you away."

She made it all sound so obvious. "So *many* things could happen to me. Health isn't guaranteed. I want someone who'll stand by me during my hardest times."

Her mother nodded slowly. "Letting him back in would be a risk. But loving someone is always a risk."

She swallowed hard. Since going into remission, she'd prided herself on taking risks. "Do you regret loving Dad, because you lost him?"

"Not for a single second. That man was the love of my life. He gave me you kids and you're my world. He also gave me some of my best memories. They're gifts. And they're still alive inside me. No one can ever take them away."

Her heart did one of those massive thumps. Because she *wanted* that. She wanted those memories and that love and everything that came with it. And yeah...she wanted to take that risk.

She stayed outside with her mother for another hour, talking about everything and nothing. Just something else she loved about her mother—they never ran out of stuff to talk about.

When the doorbell rang, her mother stood and squeezed her shoulder. "I'll get that."

She was looking out over the yard, a million thoughts running through her head, when the door opened. But it wasn't her mother who walked through.

Holden stood there, looking big and powerful and protective.

His eyes were intense, emotions flickering in the hazel depths. When he started moving toward her with slow, intentional steps, her heart began to beat faster. Hard thuds against her rib cage that made her breaths shorten and her skin tingle.

He crouched in front of her, so close that she could see the laugh lines beside his eyes. The dark specks in his hazel eyes. "Hey."

His deep, rumbly voice ran over her skin. "Hey."

"I've missed you."

"It's only been a day."

"Too long." He reached out and slipped a lock of hair behind her ear, and God, her entire body wanted to lean into that touch. The need was so great that it hurt not to. "How are you doing?"

"My mom is filling me with tea and croissants and some pretty great advice."

He didn't smile, just kept his intense gaze on her. "Doesn't really answer my question, Clara."

"Not too good."

Concern...maybe a bit of anger...flickered over his expression. "Let me take you home. Let me look after you."

Her fingers tightened around her mug.

He lowered his hands to her thighs, just above her knees. "Please. It's killing me to be away from you."

It was killing her too. "Okay." The single word slipped into the air, quiet but powerful.

"Okay?"

"Yeah. I want you to take me home."

Relief washed over his face, then he whispered, "Thank God."

CHAPTER 27

"So he's staying with you tonight?"

Clara tugged at a thread on her bedsheet as she pressed the phone to her ear, Indie on the other end. "Yeah, he's staying with me tonight. He made me dinner, refused to let me help him clean up after, and now he's doing a perimeter check."

"Will he stay tomorrow night as well?"

"I don't know. He'll probably want to stay until we figure out all this hospital stuff." Not probably—definitely.

"Clara…can I give you some advice?"

"Always." Even when she didn't like her cousin's advice, she usually needed it.

"You love him. So love him."

She hung her head. Her mother had said something similar.

"I know he hurt you when he ended things after the hospital trip," Indie continued. "But I think he wants to be better. And maybe this little break with you has scared him enough that he'll do better next time."

"I *do* love him," she whispered.

"I know. And take it from someone who never felt like she got enough time with the man she loved—if he's there and he loves you, don't waste another second."

She frowned. "Indie, maybe you should just call Colt and talk to him. You had that fight a year ago and have barely spoken since."

There was a small pause. "Because it hurts to talk to him."

"Sometimes you have to hurt before you can feel better again."

"I think there's just too much that's happened." She sighed. "I *do* need to speak to him though. He didn't sign the papers."

Clara straightened. "What?"

"He sent them back blank. Actually, not blank. He wrote a note in black pen saying, 'You're dreaming if you think I'll ever sign this, Cricket.'"

Cricket…it was the nickname Colt used for Indie. "What are you going to do?"

"He doesn't have to sign them for me to get a divorce. I can let the courts handle it if I have to."

There was something in Indie's voice…some regret, but also uncertainty. Was she having second thoughts about the divorce? "If you need anything from me, you know I'm here."

"I *do* know. Thanks, Clara."

The click of the front door opening sounded from the hall, and Clara sighed. "I've got to go. Holden's back."

"Remember what I said."

Clara smiled as she said goodbye and hung up. She needed a shower, then maybe if she felt brave, she'd go out and see Holden in the living room.

She stepped into the bathroom and her gaze went straight to her neck. The bruising from the break-in was just about gone, but sometimes she swore she could feel that arm around her neck.

Gently, she touched the skin, her chest rising on a deep inhale.

When a figure appeared behind her, she gasped, only for the air to rush out of her when she recognized Holden. "I didn't hear you come in."

"Sorry. Your door was ajar and I wanted to check on you." He stood behind her, dwarfing her as he looked at her neck. Fury flashed over his face before he lightly grazed her skin right where her fingers had just been. His touch was gentle and warm. "I hate that you got hurt."

"I got off fairly lightly compared to Malcolm and Scarlett."

Holden growled. "You shouldn't have been in danger at all." He lowered his head and kissed her shoulder. "The thought of someone hurting you kills me."

A shiver ran down her spine.

He kissed her neck this time. It was so light that it felt like a whisper over her skin. "I need you safe."

"Safety's never guaranteed."

He paused, maybe because he knew she wasn't just talking about the kind of safety that came from external factors.

Then he kissed her again. "I will do everything in my power to protect you. But if I can't, if the enemy is some kind of sickness, then I'll look after you in every other way. I'm not going anywhere." He said the last four words slowly, like he knew she needed them said emphatically.

"You won't run?"

He gripped her hips and looked up at her in the mirror, fire in his eyes. "Never again."

She believed him.

He kissed her again. Her eyes shuttered and all she could do was feel him. The strength of his body against her back. The power in his hands as he held her. And the softness of his kisses up her neck.

She tilted her head, giving him more access. Her fingers threaded through his hair, and when she turned to look at him, their gazes held for a split second before his mouth claimed hers.

She groaned, leaning into him as he slipped his tongue between her lips. Humming at the feel of his hands trailing over her body. She closed a hand over his and guided it toward her breast. When he cupped her, he growled, a low, deep sound that shot straight between her legs.

He found her nipple and grazed it back and forth, making her insides turn molten.

When he released her breast, she wanted to protest. But then his hands went to the hem of her shirt and she lifted her arms to help him. Once the shirt was off, he immediately unclasped the button of her jeans. Every time his fingers grazed her belly, her skin burned.

When she only wore a bra and panties, he lifted her and set her on the counter before stepping between her thighs. She removed his shirt and jeans just as quickly as he'd dealt with hers.

As she pushed his pants down, his mouth returned to her neck. He stepped out of his jeans, but his entire focus remained on Clara as he flipped down the cup of her bra and took one nipple between his lips.

She gasped, her head flying back, and pulled at his hair...as her fingers played over the strength in his shoulders.

He was everything. And he made her burn for him.

As he sucked her nipple, she writhed against him. Needing more, she reached down and slipped her hand inside his briefs.

His muscles tensed, and she wrapped her fingers around his length, not missing the sharp, masculine gasp that cut through the air.

She moved her hand up and down, exploring and feeling and loving him.

"What do you do to me?" he growled.

She reached up with her other hand and cupped his nape, bringing his mouth back to her. As she did, she guided his cock toward her entrance before sliding her panties to the side.

"Clara—"

"I'm ready for you, Holden. I've been ready for you for so long."

His eyes were all fire. Slowly, he slipped inside her. Filling her. Loving her. Giving her everything.

* * *

BLOOD ROARED between Holden's ears, a flame burning inside him. He could drown in Clara, and he'd die a happy fucking man.

He found her lips again, kissing her. Tasting her. Taking everything that she had to give him and giving it all back.

She wrapped her legs around his waist and drew him closer. He growled at the feel of her walls hugging his cock.

"I love you, Clara." The words fell from his lips, so damn overdue. "I've loved you for so long."

Tear gathered in her eyes. "I feel like I've waited a lifetime to hear you say that."

"I'll say it every day."

"I love you too, Holden. You own my love."

His world narrowed to just her. To the indigo of her eyes. The wisps of hair, and all the lines and shadows that made up Clara.

He would spend the rest of his life loving this woman.

He slid out of her before plunging back in.

The air that escaped her lips was somewhere between a gasp and a sigh. And he felt it too. All of it.

He started moving in slow, deep, rhythmic thrusts as he once again found her neck with his lips…kissing and sucking.

It never felt like enough.

He reached for her nipple and ran his thumb over the hard peak, grazing it back and forth.

Every sound she made was fucking music to his ears.

He lifted her and turned, pressing her to the cool tiled wall, never separating them.

His thrusts became deeper…faster. He slid his hand down her

UNTOUCHED

side, and when he ran his thumb over her clit, her entire body shuddered and arched. Her head tipped back, and her eyes closed as a moan cut from her throat.

There was no hesitation or inhibition...this was all Clara, and she was fucking gorgeous.

Her fingers dug into his skin, her head dropping forward and burrowing into his chest. She was close. And he wanted to see her fall. To feel her walls pulse around his cock.

He pressed his mouth to her ear and nipped her lobe. "Let go, honey."

One more roll of her clit with his thumb, and suddenly her entire body tensed. Her fingers curled around his shoulders and she cried out, her scream bouncing off the walls, her body wrapped so tightly around him, he could barely move.

And he couldn't take his damn eyes off her. For a moment, he forgot time and place. He forgot everything but her.

He kept thrusting, but too soon the sheer fucking sight of her losing control tipped him over the edge. He growled as he shattered, his head dropping into the crook of her neck, sucking her skin as he continued to move until he had nothing left.

Then, finally, there was stillness. He leaned into Clara, breathing her in as both their chests moved quickly.

When he finally had the strength to move again, he stepped away from the wall and carried her into the shower. He took his time washing her. Exploring every inch of her body as he pressed light kisses to her skin, loving her.

And it was there, under the stream of water while Clara was still in his arms, that she cupped his cheeks. "We're done running, right? This is it?"

"It's you and me, Clara. We're in this forever."

She studied his eyes. "You're not scared?"

"I'm terrified. But someone told me to feel the fear and love you anyway. So that's what I'm doing."

Her eyes softened and she kissed him again, but this kiss was

243

softer. Slower. A gentle admission of love and a promise of forever.

CHAPTER 28

*T*he ringing of a phone cut through the room, jolting Holden from dead asleep to wide awake.

His eyes shot open. Clara was the first thing he saw. Her hair was splayed over his chest, her cheek lying right over his heart.

Then he looked at the sun piercing through the curtains. He'd slept in. He never slept in.

Gently, he slid out from under her. When a soft hum slipped from her chest, he almost ignored the call and lay back down.

But the call could be important. It *better* be.

He stood and lifted his phone to see Deb's name on the screen.

So probably not that important.

With a sigh, he stepped out of the bedroom and closed the door with a soft click before answering the call.

"Deb, is everything okay?"

"Hi, Holden. Sorry to call so early, but I went to leave today and the lock you installed won't engage properly. It's happened a couple of times, but I've always managed to get it. Today, I just can't seem to make it lock at all, and I'm late for work."

Holden ran his fingers through his hair. "It could be that the strike plate isn't aligned properly, but that's something I would have picked up on at installation."

"Is there any chance you're free now to come by? I really need to get going."

Footsteps sounded behind him. Then warm arms curled around his waist and a cheek pressed to his back.

Fuck, he loved it when Clara was close.

He set a hand over her smaller one. "I can be there in ten."

A relieved sigh sounded over the line. "Thank you. I'll let work know I'll be late."

Holden hung up and turned, his arms going around Clara's waist.

She looked up at him. "Is everything okay?"

"Something's wrong with Deb's door. I need to run over and fix it so she can get to work." He hated the idea of leaving her alone though. "Maybe you should come?"

"Holden, I need to get ready. It's the Amber Ridge street party today."

"We're not due to get there until ten."

"Exactly. And before then I need to shower and wash my hair and dry it. I have to choose something to wear. Do my makeup…"

He frowned. "We're just going for a couple of hours."

"Don't you want me to look pretty?"

He could have laughed. "You are always the most beautiful woman in every room."

"Pfft. You have to say that."

"I don't. And I don't like leaving you alone."

"I'll lock the door. I'll be fine."

He still didn't like it. "On one condition. You call me at the first sign of trouble."

"Does that include croissant withdrawals?"

"Clara—"

"*Yes*. I'll call you at the first sign of trouble." She lifted to her toes. "I love you."

"You have no idea." He kissed her, slipping his tongue inside her mouth and holding her body tighter against his. He growled. "Deb can wait."

She playfully whacked his chest. "She cannot wait. She'll be late for work."

"I don't care." He began lowering his head again, but Clara put a finger against his lips.

"I do. And so will Amber Ridge Hospital."

She was right. Dammit. "Fine."

Quickly, he threw on some clothes. When he reached his truck, he sent a quick text to Jesse.

Holden: Is Malcolm awake yet?

When Jesse didn't respond, he headed toward Deb's house. She lived about ten minutes away, a bit farther out than most of his clients. But it should take him *less* than ten minutes to fix her door.

When he reached Deb's house, he grabbed his tools from the back and crossed to the door. Thank God he kept his tools in his truck and didn't need to make a stop at his place first.

He knocked. When a few seconds passed and she didn't answer, he tried again. Same thing.

Frowning, he tried her door. It wasn't locked, but then, of course it wasn't. That was the entire reason he was here.

He stepped into her hall. "Deb?"

Silence.

What the hell was going on?

He moved into her living area. "Deb? It's Holden. Are you here?"

He turned toward her kitchen—only to stop at the sight of blood on the kitchen floor.

The fuck?

He sprinted into the kitchen and found Deb on the floor behind the island, a bullet wound in her chest.

Fuck.

247

He dropped beside her and touched her pulse. Faint but there. Quickly, he reached for the towel that hung from the oven and pressed it to the wound with one hand before pulling his cell from his pocket.

First, he called for an ambulance. Once they were on their way, he called Jesse, who picked up after a few rings.

"Holden—"

"Deborah Fuller's been shot."

"What?"

"She asked me to come fix the lock on her door, and I found her on the floor in the kitchen."

"Shit. I'm on my way." There was a small pause. "I was just going to call you...Malcolm had a setback last night."

"What kind of setback?"

"Not the natural kind. It looks like someone drugged him and he almost died."

Holden's heart beat faster. Was Clara in danger? Shit! He shouldn't have left her alone. "Jesse...Clara's alone."

* * *

CLARA STEPPED out of the shower, steam thick in the air.

She couldn't wipe the smile off her face. Hadn't been able to wipe it off her face since she'd woken.

Holden loved her. He loved her, and he wanted to be with her. Not for a night. Or a month. Forever.

Her heart sang at that thought.

For so long, this was what she'd wanted, but after she'd told him how she felt three years ago, she'd thought it wasn't going to happen.

She pulled on jeans and a cropped tee and was about to make the bed when a knock sounded at the door. Not the front door, but the acupuncture studio door.

She frowned. She didn't have any appointments. Everything

was closed the day of the street party because that's where everyone went.

Moving into her studio, she looked through the peephole to see Briar.

Her brows flickered. She shouldn't open the door. But what was she going to do? Yell through the thing?

With a deep breath, she cracked the door open. "Briar. What are you doing here?"

The other woman frowned and looked at her watch. "Eight thirty? Sorry, I'm fifteen minutes early."

Clara shook head. "*I'm* sorry, I think you must have your days mixed up. We're closed today."

"No. I booked for Saturday at eight thirty."

That wasn't possible. "Do you have a confirmation email?"

The other woman pulled out her phone and started scrolling. "I do. I only booked it last night. It says…" She stopped. "Crap. It's the thirteenth of *next* month, not this one." She looked up, rubbing her brow. "Look, is there any chance you could fit me in? Normally I wouldn't care, but with everything that's going on at the hospital and Malcolm…I really need something for the stress."

Clara opened her mouth to say no—of course, in the nicest way possible—when tears gathered in Briar's eyes.

"Please," she said softly. "I kind of feel like my head's under-water right now."

Guilt pricked at her chest. "It'll have to be a short appointment, though."

Relief filled the other woman's face. "Thank you!" Briar stepped inside.

"To make it quick, we don't need to do the usual sit-down-and-chat first," Clara said. "I know what points to do to help you relax and de-stress. Why don't you lie on the table, and I'll check your pulse."

"Sure." Briar slipped off her shoes and climbed onto the bed, and Clara lifted her wrist. "Why do you check the pulse?"

"To assess the flow of energy and balance in your body. It helps me understand your overall health and identify any areas that may need attention so I can create the most effective treatment plan."

Briar scoffed. "Bet my energy and balance aren't feeling too good."

"It's a bit irregular. It could be from stress or something else."

"Bucket loads of stress."

Clara turned and prepared her needles before facing Briar again. Minutes later, once they were all in, she turned the soft music on, dimmed the lights, and set the buzzer by Briar's hand. "Press that if you need me."

"I will. Thank you."

"You're welcome."

Clara grabbed her laptop and stepped out of the room, closing the door quietly behind her. She waited until she reached her room before sitting on her bed to log onto her booking system.

Yep. Briar had booked the wrong month. She canceled that appointment and went to stand, only to knock her phone to the floor. It slid under the bed a bit, so Clara dropped to her knees to grab it.

That's when she saw something poking out from behind one of the frame legs.

Wait…was that the USB?

No. It couldn't be. But her bedroom was right off the hall where she'd been attacked.

There was no way her attacker would have left without it though. Unless they saw on her phone that she'd called for help and run?

Quickly, she crawled under the bed. Her heart started to beat faster as she reached for it. When it was in her hand, she rose to her bed and slipped it into her laptop.

There was one file on the USB, labeled *A Prescription for Revenge*.

She frowned. Revenge? Revenge for what?

Her fingers trembled as she clicked into it.

It started off as an affair. It ended in murder and sabotage.

Briar Winslow, a nurse at Amber Ridge Hospital, has been targeting a well-respected doctor, Malcolm Trundle, after a brief romantic encounter gone wrong. According to insiders, Winslow was hurt and angry after Dr. Trundle, who had reportedly engaged in several affairs, ended his relationship with Winslow without warning or explanation.

His affair with local massage therapist Lauren Tabs then spurred Winslow to take matters into her own hands, manipulating the care of Dr. Trundle's patients.

Clara's pulse pounded in her temples as she skimmed the rest of the report in disbelief.

It was Briar? Briar who was, right now, in her treatment room?

Oh God.

She was just reaching for her phone when a noise sounded from somewhere in her house. The soft click of a door opening. Her treatment room door?

Her heart lurched, panic seizing her body.

Quickly, she dragged the file over to save it on her desktop before yanking the USB from the laptop. Then she turned and slipped it inside a pillowcase. She'd just risen when the bedroom door opened, and Briar appeared.

"Briar." Clara worked hard to keep the panic from her voice. "Is everything okay? Where are the needles?"

"I pulled them out because I was feeling a bit dizzy. Any chance I could get some water?"

"Oh, of course." She swallowed, grabbing her phone from the mattress and passing Briar to move into the kitchen.

She grabbed a bottle from the fridge, but when she turned, Briar wasn't behind her.

Where—

Briar stepped into the kitchen, laptop in one hand, gun in the other.

Clara gasped. "What are you doing?"

"I see the article your roommate wrote is right here on your laptop screen. You must have found the USB."

The report...she'd forgotten to click out of it. Shit. "I didn't read it."

"I'm not stupid, Clara, so don't treat me like I am. Give me the USB."

Her heart pounded. "You killed that patient. Then Scarlett. You've made people sick. If I give you that USB, you'll kill me too."

Briar lifted a brow as she shortened the distance between them. "I'll kill you if you *don't* give it to me."

"No, you won't." Her phone started to ring, and her gaze flashed down.

"Answer it and I shoot your shoulder. Throw the phone over here."

Dammit.

She slid her phone across the floor and watched as Briar stomped on it.

"Now," Briar said slowly. "I just forced Deb to call Holden to get him out of the house, all so I could get into this house to search for that USB again. Of course, Deb started asking too many questions, so I killed her. I'll kill you, too, without so much as blinking."

Clara's breath stalled. "You killed Deb?"

"Last chance, Clara."

"You won't kill me, because I'm the only one who knows where the USB is," she said firmly, refusing to let her voice shake. "And I've already told Jesse I found it. He's on his way right now."

"You're lying."

Of course she was lying. Her life *depended* on not just lying, but lying well. "I'm not. He's coming right now. You won't have time to find it before he gets here, and if I'm dead, he'll scour this house for the USB. He won't stop until he finds it."

Anger distorted her features, and she lunged.

Clara moved instinctively, grabbing the fruit bowl and smashing it over Briar's head.

She cried out and fell, the gun discharging with a deafening crack, causing a wall tile to shatter.

Clara took advantage of the distraction and ran, sprinting around the island and toward the front door.

A growl followed by footsteps sounded behind her.

She grabbed keys from her hallway table, flung the door open, and sprinted outside.

Her hands shook as she opened her car door and slid behind the wheel. The engine was loud as it roared to life.

Briar appeared at the front door, pure rage in her eyes. But she didn't shoot.

As Clara backed out of the drive, she watched in the rearview mirror as Briar sprinted toward her own car.

Clara's tires squealed as she swerved onto the street, pressing her foot to the floor, praying she made it away in time.

CHAPTER 29

With one hand on Deb's wound and the other gripping his phone, Holden tried Clara's number. His heart beat so fucking fast it felt like it was going to punch out of his chest.

It was the fourth ring when he knew she wasn't going to answer.

Fuck.

He tried again. Same thing.

He needed to go to her, but he couldn't take his hand off Deb's chest. Jesse might take too long, but maybe Becket was closer.

He tried her brother's number.

"Holden, hey."

"I need you to go to Clara's house and check on her right now."

"What's wrong?" Becket's voice was harder now, with a dangerous edge.

"I'm with one of the hospital staff. She's been shot, and Clara's not answering her phone. Jesse's on his way but—"

"I'll be at her place in less than five."

A siren sounded. The ambulance. Thank God.

He hung up and when the paramedics finally ran in, Holden lifted his hand and let them take over. Then he was running. Sprinting out of the house, toward his truck.

He sped out of the drive, a bad feeling in his gut that was just getting worse by the second.

If Clara was okay, she would have answered her phone.

He tried her again, already knowing what was going to happen.

She didn't answer.

He pressed his foot to the floor, forcing his truck to move faster.

Who had shot Deb? The same person responsible for the other deaths and sick patients? She and Malcolm had been the top suspects. If it wasn't them, then who?

When he reached Clara's house, her car was gone and only Becket's was in the drive.

Both he and Jesse climbed out of their vehicles at the same time while Becket came out the front door, Glock in hand.

"She's not here," he growled. "But there are signs of a struggle. Bullet hole in the kitchen wall tile, a broken bowl on the floor, and someone smashed her phone."

Anger pulsed through Holden's veins.

Needing to see for himself, he ran inside the house.

And he saw it. The broken tile. The smashed bowl. The phone.

It was true. But it felt like a fucking nightmare.

Jesse and Becket stepped inside, Jesse's gaze sweeping the area before he pulled out his radio and put out an APB on Clara's car.

"The dimmed lights and music are on in the studio," Becket said. "Looks like she had a client."

Holden shook his head. "No. Today's the street party. She was closed to appointments."

"Someone was definitely in there," Becket pushed.

"All the evidence pointed to Malcolm or Deb," Jesse said as he scanned the room. "But it wasn't Deb in this house, and if this person tried to frame Malcolm before killing him, then it's someone who *really* wanted to hurt him."

"Someone who works in the same hospital," Holden said. "Who knows all his shifts and patients. Someone with opportunity and motive."

"What motive?" Becket asked.

Holden frowned. "Deb said he was a womanizer. Slept around. What if he did that to someone at the hospital? They wanted a relationship, he didn't, and it pissed them off. They still worked with him though, so they had to watch him date everyone else. Maybe it tipped them over the edge."

"But no one else's shifts match all the events," Jesse argued.

Footsteps sounded near the door, and all three of them turned and aimed their guns.

Mildred stepped in, only to stop and gasp. "Oh my!"

Holden lowered his Glock. "Mildred, what are you doing here?"

"I-I saw Clara drive out of here really fast...and I saw a woman go after her."

Holden stepped closer. "Who?"

"I don't know. But she was blonde. She had really tight curls that were pulled up into a ponytail. She was tall and she drove a blue Ford."

Air seized in Holden's lungs. "That's Briar Winslow. She drives a Ford Escape and fits the description." Something flickered back in his mind. "And at her house, there was a photo where she was looking at Malcolm like she cared about him. Maybe even loved him."

"But Briar was working the day Clara was attacked," Jesse said.

"A twelve-hour shift," Holden said quickly, his mind working fast. "She could have left for her lunch break. Gone to The Tea

House but before getting out of the car, she overheard Clara and Indie's conversation about Scarlett."

Jesse cursed and pulled his radio from his belt. "I need an APB on Briar Winslow's blue Ford Escape."

* * *

CLARA'S CAR engine roared as she sped toward the sheriff's station. No matter how fast she drove though, Briar's Ford remained in her rearview mirror. It was faster than Clara's Volkswagen.

Dammit.

If it wasn't the day of the street party, she would have driven straight through town, but Main Street would be blocked off and people would be everywhere. She couldn't risk any pedestrians getting hurt. *Kids* getting hurt. She had to go around.

She took a sharp right, her tires squealing, heart pounding hard in her chest.

Her eyes swung to the rearview mirror. Briar took the same right turn.

She took another right, then a left. When she looked in her rearview mirror again, her chest tightened.

Briar was gone. Had she given up? Was Clara getting too close to potential witnesses?

Relief was just starting to slow her heart when a car flew out of a side street to her right.

Clara screamed as Briar's Ford slammed into the side of her Volkswagen. Metal scraping metal screeched through the air, and the force snapped her head to the side, into the window. Pain ricocheted through her skull. She tried to regain control, but the car swung, hitting a tree.

Then there was stillness.

A deep fog clouded her head, and a loud buzzing filled her

ears. She felt tired and heavy, every inch of her hurting. All she wanted to do was keep her eyes closed and wait for help.

But there was no help. Businesses on this street were closed for the street party. There was no one around to call police or an ambulance. She had to run, and she had to run now.

With trembling fingers, she forced the seat belt off and shoved her door open. The second her feet touched the ground, her knees buckled and she fell.

The world swayed around her and nausea crawled up her throat.

Run, Clara! You have to run!

The voice in her head, the need to survive, was louder than the exhaustion. She stumbled to her feet, glancing over her car toward the Ford.

Briar was hunched over her wheel.

Thank God.

Clara started moving. Running up the road as fast as her legs would take her, the party a few streets over getting louder.

She was about to turn when glass shattered in the shop beside her.

Clara screamed before looking behind her to see Briar out of her car, blood running from both her nose and a wound on her temple. She looked unsteady.

Her gun was pointed toward Clara—and she looked ready to kill.

Air caught in Clara's lungs, so thick she could barely breathe. She turned and ran, not thinking about the gun or how much her body hurt. All she could focus on was getting away.

More bullets were fired around her. But she couldn't let that slow her down.

She quickly ducked into a short side street before turning right at the end.

Two shops down she saw the florist.

The key…Mildred had told her about a hidden key. She could

call for help.

She reached inside the hanging potted plant and wrapped her fingers around the rock. Beneath it, she found the key.

The first time she tried to get it into the lock, she missed, the trembling in her fingers too violent. She tried again, and the key slid in and the door opened. She dove into the shop before slamming the door and clicking the lock. Quickly, she raced to the counter and dropped behind it.

Then there was silence, just the sound of her heavy breaths soaring through the room. She dropped her head into her hands and felt the world sway around her.

Phone. She needed a phone to call for help. But the possibility of coming out from behind the counter and Briar seeing her through the glass made panic burn through her limbs.

A few more minutes, then she'd search.

She was just closing her eyes and focusing on her breaths again when the rattle of someone trying the doorknob sounded.

Her heart stopped.

No. It was fine. She'd locked the door. She was safe.

Suddenly, the shattering of glass filled her ears, almost making Clara scream. Then the click of the door opening and closing.

Her heart stopped, an icy dread filling her belly.

Briar was here.

"When I saw you run onto this street, then lost you, I knew you'd be here." Footsteps sounded. "You think I don't know Mildred lives across the street from you? It's a small town, Clara. Everyone knows everything. Did she give you a key? Come out before I start shooting. If you're behind the counter, these bullets will go straight through the wood."

Clara winced, then rose to her feet. Her body swayed, but she grabbed onto the counter to stay upright.

Briar stood a few steps inside the shop, gun raised. "Good choice."

"I'm not telling you where the USB is."

"Of course you are. Because if you don't, I'll go back to your house and shoot your brother in the head."

She could have laughed. "You and I both know you don't have the skill or training to get the jump on him."

Her eyes narrowed.

Shit. She shouldn't be making Briar angry. She needed her to talk. To waste time and pray that someone saw either the crashed cars or broken shop glass and alerted the sheriff's station.

"So, you've been behind everything?" Clara asked, trying to keep the fear from her voice. "Lauren and Scarlett's deaths...the sick patients."

"Lauren was a *whore*. I left my husband for Malcolm, and what does he do? Sleeps with his massage therapist! She deserved to die. And Malcolm deserved to be blamed for it, and for every other patient who got sick. He needed to learn that actions have consequences."

"So you poisoned his patients?"

"Kind of brilliant, huh? All I had to do was steal drugs from patients' medication carts and replace them with saline. Some I managed to inject into IV bags. Others, I just snuck into patient rooms and injected."

God. This woman was a monster. Some patients didn't even get their medication because of her. "You took drugs that patients needed and allowed other patients to get sick and almost die because you were *angry* at Malcolm?"

"Blame *him*. If he hadn't cheated on me after I left my husband for him, I wouldn't have needed to do any of it!"

She didn't blame him. The blame was solely Briar's to bear. "And you killed Scarlett."

"She drugged us! I'd already heard around town that she was a reporter, and the day I killed her, Malcolm confessed to me that he told her about our affair. About how angry I was about Lauren. I approached her, tried to figure out what she knew, and it was clear she knew everything. I saw the hate in her eyes. The disgust. I lost my temper. Might have even threatened her."

"That's why she was scared when she got home."

"I *had* to kill her."

"No. You *chose* to kill her. To save yourself."

"You would have done the same thing. I took her laptop, but then I heard you talking in the parking lot of The Tea House that day. Thank God I followed you back to your place. But after you ran into the bathroom, I saw you'd called Jesse, and I had to leave without the damn USB." She shook her head. "I can't have Jesse or any of the deputies finding out. I've hurt too many people. Lauren. Scarlett. Deb."

"Did you really kill Deb?"

She rolled her eyes. "I went over there this morning and asked her to call Holden over so he'd leave you unprotected. She wouldn't do it. Demanded to know why. So I had to hold a gun to her fucking head while she called. The bitch was so dumb! What did she think, I was going to just let her go after she got off the phone?"

Jesus. "What about Malcolm? Did you drug him too?"

She frowned. "No. He OD'd because he couldn't take the thought of going to prison."

Was that true? Had Malcolm really done it to himself?

Briar stepped forward. "So…now that we have all that stuff out in the open, you have exactly five seconds to tell me where that USB is before I cut my losses and shoot you in the head."

Shit. She opened her mouth, not sure what words were about to come out, when a figure suddenly appeared on the other side of the glass…

Helen.

Clara's heart beat faster.

No. Run, Helen!

But it was too late. Helen was looking at them through the glass, eyes wide—and Briar had already seen her.

CHAPTER 30

olden wanted to punch something. To ram his fist so far into a fucking wall that the pain drowned out the other stuff. The anger that rushed through his veins. The dread that sat in his gut at the possibility that he wouldn't find Clara in time.

"What if we're too late?" he asked, his fear spilling out into the air.

"We're not going to be too late." Jesse took his eyes off the road to glance over at him. "You know that as well as I do."

"I can't lose her."

"You won't. *We* won't."

Holden scanned the streets. Nothing. And the half dozen deputies in addition to Becket who were also looking for her hadn't found Clara yet either.

Dammit.

"Maybe she drove to the street fair," Jesse said, almost to himself. "She could have wanted to blend into the crowd. Hide where there were lots of people."

Holden shook his head. "No. There are families and kids there. She wouldn't have put anyone else in danger. She didn't have a phone, and she needed to get to safety. The only place I can think that she would go is—"

"The sheriff's station." Jesse sped up.

"I still can't believe it's been Briar this entire time," Holden said quietly, so fucking mad at himself. "She was right there. I've been to her house a dozen times. I built her a damn kitchen."

"It doesn't make sense to me either. She was working the morning Malcolm was drugged. She only would have been one hour into her shift when his attack happened. There's no way she would have had the opportunity to drug him."

"Maybe Malcolm *did* do it to himself."

"Maybe." Jesse's radio suddenly crackled, and he lifted the mic. "You got something?"

"A civilian just called in a car crash involving a red Volkswagen Beetle and a Ford Escape."

"Clara and Briar." Holden cursed.

"Where?" Jesse asked.

"At the end of Fifth Avenue and Oak Street right in front of the hardware store."

Jesse sped up. "We're only a street away. Clara and Briar weren't spotted?"

"No."

Holden lifted his Glock, pulse speeding up and muscles tensing, ready to move.

Jesse turned onto the street, and Holden saw it. The Ford had hit the side of Clara's Beetle, and shit, it looked bad. The side of the Volkswagen had a huge dent, and the Ford's airbags had deployed. Neither of them would have come out unscathed.

The second Jesse stopped, Holden was out of the car and running. He checked her Volkswagen while Jesse checked the Ford.

"Empty," Jesse said.

"They're gone." Holden scanned the street.

"We need to search the streets. I'll go this way, you go that way."

Holden nodded and went to step away, when Jesse called out to him again.

"And Holden, if Briar wasn't the one to drug Malcolm, and Malcolm didn't do it to himself, then—"

"There are two of them."

* * *

Clara tried to tell Helen with her eyes to keep going. To not step foot inside the florist.

But the other woman didn't walk away. She gripped the handle of the door and stepped inside the shop.

Clara frowned, confusion swirling in her belly. Why would she step in instead of running for help? And why was she wearing gloves?

"Is everything okay?" Helen asked.

Briar kept the gun trained at Clara's head. "You showed up right on time."

Clara's heart stopped. They were in on this together?

"This bitch won't tell me where the USB is," Briar continued. "But I don't care anymore. She needs to die, and she needs to die fast."

Helen nodded, like this was a perfectly sane conversation.

Briar shot a look at Helen. "I got Lauren and Deb. You only took out Malcolm. You owe me."

Clara's jaw dropped when Briar handed the gun to Helen. Helen looked at the pistol. Then, she reached out and wrapped her fingers around the grip.

Clara's heart beat so hard that she could hear it. Feel it through her limbs.

This was it. Helen was going to shoot her.

Briar was just turning back to face Clara when Helen lifted the gun, pressed the muzzle to Briar's temple, and fired.

Clara screamed and stumbled back, hitting the wall behind her. *Jesus Christ.*

"Wh-what did you do?" she gasped. She was going to be sick. Bile crawled up her throat, threatening to break free.

"Murder-suicide," Helen said calmly, as if it made perfect sense. "Things need to be wrapped up, and I can't risk Briar sharing my involvement with anyone."

"I don't understand."

Helen removed the magazine and checked the bullets in the gun. "Well, Clara, seeing as you've got about a minute left to live, there's no harm in sharing that Malcolm *really* pissed me off."

"You had an affair with him, too?"

She scoffed. "Fuck no. You know that revolutionary sepsis protocol everyone keeps congratulating him on?"

Clara frowned. "Yeah."

"*I* developed it." Helen finally looked at her, fire in her eyes. "I spent *years* refining the approach through direct patient work. There's documentation, emails, meeting minutes—all proving it was *my* original idea. Malcolm made a couple of minor contributions and received not only all the credit but consulting opportunities, speaking fees, and *all* the recognition."

"Why didn't you tell anyone?" she whispered.

"I *did*. But he was louder, and then it was too late because of the press, and hospital politics prevented any correction."

Clara shot a look at Briar and immediately regretted it. Blood...there was so much blood. "How does Briar fit into this?"

"I knew what happened between them. I knew how angry she was that she'd divorced her husband for Malcolm, only for him to leave her for that massage therapist. She's always been stupid, so I floated the idea of making his patients sick to discredit him and get her payback. At first, she didn't go for it. Then she learned that Lauren was due to come in for surgery. Suddenly, she was all in."

Jesus, they were sick. Both of them.

"I made it sound like we were a *team*," Helen continued. "And I guess we kind of were. We covered for each other. Took turns stealing patient drugs so no one knew who was responsible."

"But *you* tried to kill Malcolm," she whispered.

"Because even after *everything*, he was still getting congratulated for my fucking protocol! Do you know how many times I tried to talk to him about it? Reason with him? He wouldn't bend. I knew it wouldn't end until *he* did. And yeah, he's not dead...*yet*." Helen aimed her gun. "I'm sorry about this, but I can't afford to keep you alive."

Clara dropped behind the counter a second before a bullet exploded into the wall behind her. She grabbed a pair of scissors off a shelf, opened them, and held one side like a knife.

"Clara...you're just making this harder than it has to be."

Blood roared between her ears as she heard Helen's footsteps grow closer.

Calm, Clara. You can do this.

The quiet words in her head made the shaking in her fingers lessen.

The second Helen's leg appeared, Clara kicked.

Helen cried out and dropped, and the moment she was on the floor, Clara lifted the scissors high and plunged them into her shin.

As Helen screamed, Clara pushed to her feet and lunged toward the gun. She'd just grabbed it when Helen snatched her ankle and yanked her down. Her cheek hit the floor hard, the pistol falling from her hand and sliding across the shop as pain radiated through her skull.

Immediately, she rolled to her side and kicked Helen, getting the other woman in the shoulder, then the nose.

A loud crunch sounded, and Helen dropped, suddenly unmoving.

Was she unconscious?

Clara didn't wait to find out. She pushed to her feet and scanned the floor, quickly searching for the gun, but when she couldn't see it, she ran, sprinting toward the door.

When she reached Briar's body, her foot slipped on blood and she hit the floor again. Blood coated her front, the wet, sticky liquid slipping between her fingers as the metallic smell hit her nose.

Bile filled her throat but she ignored it, forcing herself up.

She opened the door and ran out, only to scream when she hit a large chest.

CHAPTER 31

*H*olden jogged down the side street, his gaze continuing to scan his surroundings. Searching.

His time as a Ghost Ops soldier was the only thing keeping him calm. But fear and dread still clawed at his insides.

Where was she? Had she gotten away from Briar? And if there was a second person, then who the fuck was it and were they also a threat to Clara right now?

He turned right onto the next street.

That's when he saw it—shattered glass on the sidewalk.

He sped up and had just reached the front of the florist when the door flew open and a woman ran straight into him.

Air cut off in his throat. "Clara!"

Her gaze shot up, fear and relief swirling together. "Holden!" She dropped against his chest and he tightened his arm around her.

"Shit, Clara, you're covered in blood." Panic soared through his lungs. Had she been shot? Stabbed? Where was the wound?

"No. It's not mine. It's Briar's."

"Briar's?"

"Yes! Helen killed her and is still in there. So is a gun, but I think she's unconscious."

"Helen?" *She* was the second person?

"They were working together."

Fuck. He stepped in front of Clara. "Stay behind me."

He didn't want to take Clara back inside the florist, but there was no way he was leaving her on the sidewalk by herself when they didn't know *how* many threats there were.

He grabbed his phone and sent a pin of his location to Jesse with two words: "She's here."

Then he stepped inside.

Briar lay on the floor, a bullet wound in her temple and a pool of blood around her head.

Jesus. He hated that Clara had witnessed the woman being killed.

He inched farther inside, scanning the shop as he went. He couldn't see Helen. Had she slipped behind the counter? When he reached the counter, he swung his weapon around, only to stop. She wasn't there either.

Clara's breathing grew louder. "She's gone…"

Holden looked into the room behind the counter. He saw the muzzle of the pistol a second before it fired. He lunged on top of Clara, sending them both to the floor and covering her body with his own before crawling them to the other side of the counter.

He pulled his second gun from the holster on his ankle and handed it to Clara, whispering, "If she gets past me, shoot."

Clara's eyes widened, but she nodded.

There was no way in hell Helen would get past him. But having Clara armed gave him peace of mind.

He lifted a fallen vase. "When I get to the other end of the counter, I need you to throw it in the opposite direction. Can you do that?"

She nodded again, a bit of color returning to her face.

He pressed a firm kiss to her temple before moving to the other end of the counter.

The vase shattered, and Helen popped out from behind a doorway, taking aim near the broken porcelain.

Holden fired, hitting her gloved hand.

The woman screamed and dropped the gun.

Holden ran forward but just as he reached her, Helen grabbed the nearest pot with her uninjured hand and swung. He dodged the makeshift weapon and grabbed her wrist, twisting it behind her back and forcing her to the floor.

Helen bucked her hips, trying to dislodge him. "Get off me! I don't deserve this! All I wanted was some fucking recognition."

He had no idea what she was talking about, but whatever it was, it didn't justify having a hand in everything that had happened. "Any second now, this room will be swarming with the sheriff's department. You're not going anywhere."

Right on cue, the door to the florist opened and Jesse burst in, closely followed by three of his deputies. He ran straight to Clara and wrapped her in his arms while the deputies took Helen.

The second Jesse released Clara, Holden pulled her against his chest. "Are you okay?"

"I'm not hurt."

Didn't answer his question. He inched back and studied her eyes, but her stare returned to Briar's body on the floor.

He had a million questions. He wanted to know everything that had taken place after he'd left this morning. But now wasn't the time. Right now, he needed to get Clara the hell out of this shop.

He slipped an arm around her waist. "Let's go."

She leaned into him and let him guide her out, and after almost losing her, the feel of her against him was everything.

* * *

CLARA'S THROAT tightened as she watched Helen get wheeled out of the shop on a stretcher. Jesse walked beside her. The wrist of her uninjured hand was cuffed to the gurney.

This entire time, she was involved. Not just involved—the instigator.

Clara barely felt the paramedic cleaning the wound on her head. She sat in the back of the ambulance after telling Jesse everything. And each word had felt more surreal than the last. Like she was talking about some movie she'd watched, not her life.

"I can't believe it was her," Clara whispered, still shocked. "She shot Briar. She tried to kill Malcolm…and she put all those ideas in Briar's head."

A deep shudder coursed down her spine.

Holden inched closer, curling an arm around her waist. "She hid her involvement well."

"They both did," she whispered. "And they both had such different motives. I never would have thought either of them could be involved. Well, Briar maybe. She always seemed to have a chip on her shoulder."

"She was angry, and she let that anger dictate her actions."

Clara shook her head. "So many people have been hurt or killed."

"I know."

"I never liked Scarlett, but she died trying to discover the truth to let people know. Even if her methods were a bit unethical. And how could they have hurt someone like Deb? *Everyone* likes Deb."

"People like them will do anything to protect themselves. They don't care who gets hurt."

She nodded absently, hating that it was true. That some people—the awful kind—had such a low moral compass that they didn't care what happened to anyone else.

The paramedic stepped back. "Okay. All done. Try not to get

it wet for twenty-four hours, and go into the hospital if you feel dizzy or if the wound looks like it's getting infected. And get some rest."

"She will," Holden answered for her.

She leaned into his side. God, she was grateful to have him. And her family. Becket had come and gone, and she'd also received a call from her mother and a text from Indie.

She'd taken one step away from the ambulance when two men stepped out of the florist holding a gurney, but this time there was a sheet covering the body.

Briar.

She tried to swallow, but it felt like there was a lump in her throat.

"Are you okay?" Holden asked softly.

"I watched her die."

"I'm sorry."

She sucked in a sharp breath before turning to face him. "Thank you."

"For what?"

"Being my knight in shining armor today. You saved me."

He shook his head. "*You* saved you. You got out of there, and I have no doubt that you would have outrun her."

"But then she might have gone free, and we'd all be looking over our shoulders until we found her. You took her down."

"If I hadn't, someone else would have."

She stepped closer and laid her temple against his chest, closing her eyes when he pressed a kiss to the top of her head.

This was safety. And right now, it was the only place she wanted to be.

A hand touched her back, and she turned to see Jesse.

"Hey." He studied her face like he was trying to assess if she'd break.

"I'm okay, Jess." She was sounding like a broken record. "I'm glad it's over."

He nodded. "Me too. Mom wanted to come, but I told her to hold off."

"Thank you."

"You're going to let Holden stay with you tonight, aren't you?"

She looked up at Holden. "I'm not letting him leave my side."

"Thank God," Holden said, before pressing another kiss to her head.

She sank further into him. Today hadn't been a good day. The people who loved her made it easier.

CHAPTER 32

*H*olden scanned the street outside The Tea House window, his untouched coffee held tightly between his fingers.

Where was she?

It had been a month since everything had happened with Briar and Helen. Briar was dead and Helen was locked up, but that day hadn't left him. It probably never would.

Deb was alive, thank God, and even Malcolm had pulled through. But Holden had almost lost Clara. If she wasn't as strong and smart as she was, he *would* have lost her.

"Where's Clara?" Becket asked, as he and Sky took seats across the table.

"She wanted to go for a walk with Indie to buy some flowers from Mildred." She'd been going to the florist daily since the place had reopened. His house was starting to look like a competing florist.

"And you weren't invited?" Jesse asked, as he and Aspen took their seats at the table.

"No. Apparently, I've been *hovering*." What the fuck even *was* hovering? He'd been staying close to her because she'd just experienced something really damn traumatic. And yeah, maybe he was a bit traumatized too, and the staying-close part was as much for him as it was for her.

Aspen looked up at Jesse, eyes sparkling with humor. "We've been there."

"Absolutely," Sky agreed, bumping Becket's shoulder. "But we know you guys mean well."

"Hell yes, we do." Becket nodded.

Jesse chuckled before turning back to Holden. "How's it going with Clara moving into your place?"

"Good. Her client room at the front of the house is almost done. I'm hoping it's starting to feel like home for her."

"And you're still on track to sell Clara's place by the end of the month?" Aspen asked.

"We've already had a couple of offers." When they'd been deciding whose house to live in, Clara said she wanted it to be his. She'd decided that she needed a fresh start somewhere new.

He didn't care where the hell they lived as long as it was together.

The group around him started to talk about what they were ordering, but his gaze went back to the window.

What was taking her so long?

He'd told himself he wasn't going to message her, but right now, he didn't care. He wanted to hear from her, even if it was just through a text.

He lifted his cell.

Holden: Are you close?

The three dots immediately appeared.

Clara: Just leaving the florist now, lilies in hand.

Holden: I bought you lilies yesterday.

Clara: I know, but you bought me red lilies. These are pink.

Holden: Pink and red are basically the same color.

Clara: They absolutely are not. I'll see you in ten.

Holden: Straight here.

Clara: Yes, Mr. Protective.

He was, and he wasn't even sorry about it.

"Is she on her way?" Jesse asked, as Holden set his phone down.

"Ten minutes."

"Good." A crease formed between Jesse's eyes. "How are *you* doing?"

"Probably as well as you. What happened to her was hard on all of us."

"Yeah, I'm not good either." Jesse scrubbed a hand over his face. "This better be the last damn thing like this in our town for a while. When I took this job, I was told my days would be filled with traffic violations and domestic disputes."

Holden's lips twitched. "You'd get bored if that was the case."

"Maybe. But my life would be a lot less stressful."

Jesse's phone vibrated from the table, and his frown deepened.

"What is it?" Holden asked.

"My cousin Noah."

"Indie's brother?" He was a Marine who didn't tend to make it back to Amber Ridge very often.

"Yeah."

"Everything okay?"

"He's coming home."

Holden straightened. "He's leaving the Marines?"

"His contract's up and he's done. Says he'll be here in a month."

"Wow."

"My thought too." Jesse looked up. "I wonder if Indie knows."

* * *

"I'm STARTING to think I should have gone with lilies."

Clara looked at Indie's bouquet as they walked down the street. "What are you talking about? Your roses are beautiful."

"Yeah, but they're starting to remind me of the flowers Colt gave me at prom."

Well, that was an easy fix. She took the roses from her cousin and traded her the lilies.

Indie shook her head. "No, you wanted the lilies. You spotted the pink the second we stepped in the door."

"No, I wanted flowers that both smelled and looked nice, and I also wanted to support Mildred. It's the least I can do after I broke in and caused her to have a broken window and the huge mess I left in my wake."

Indie cocked her head. "*You* didn't leave a mess."

"A person died in her shop because of me."

"*Not* because of you."

"If I hadn't run in there—"

"You were running for your life, and Mildred understands that. If we're going to blame anyone, it's Briar and Helen."

"Yeah, well, Briar's paid for her crime, and Helen will spend the rest of her life paying for hers." She ran her finger over a petal, hating even thinking about everything that took place last month.

Indie bumped her hip. "Hey. Are you still doing okay with it all?"

"Better than I should be. I've been resting. Eating lots of almond croissants and drinking all the sweet teas. Holden's been amazing and I'm acupuncturing the crap out of myself."

Indie laughed. "Well, you're the one who says acupuncture heals all."

"It's definitely helping."

"And you feel okay about your house being up for sale?"

"I feel fine about it. It's a new start with Holden, and his place is great. Plus, no one's been attacked there."

Indie's features softened. "And how's Holden been?"

"He's been…a lot. But in a good way. I prefer the Holden who doesn't want to leave my side over the one who runs in the other direction."

"I knew you two would find a way to make it work."

"You did not."

"I did. Even after everything happened with Colt and my view on love became a lot more pessimistic, I still thought you two would come together."

Clara swallowed at the mention of Colt. She'd been meaning to ask her cousin about him for a couple of weeks now. "Have you called or texted Colt about the divorce papers?"

"I did. He didn't answer, and then a day later he called me back, but that time *I* didn't answer." She wrinkled her nose. "I should have. I watched the phone ring. I just couldn't bring myself to pick it up. Even listening to him on voice mail hit me so hard I couldn't breathe."

"I'm sorry." If she could take this pain away for her cousin, she would.

Indie picked at the lilies. "I've actually been thinking about doing something."

"Oh my gosh…is this the crazy thing you were texting about over a month ago? With everything going on, I completely forgot to ask about it."

"I didn't want to bring it up while you had so much to deal with."

"Well, I've got nothing going on now. Tell me."

Indie peeked at her. "Well, I'm getting old."

Clara scoffed. "You're thirty-four."

"Exactly. One more year and a pregnancy would be considered geriatric. My biological clock is ticking. Colt and I tried for so many years but nothing worked, not natural conception or the rounds of IVF. But I want to be a mother. I crave it *every day*. When I see a baby, my heart physically hurts."

"Oh, Indie…" She knew her cousin wanted to be a mom, but the pain in her voice had never been this bad.

"So…" Indie continued. "I think I'm going to give IVF just one more go."

"But you and Colt aren't together anymore."

"With a sperm donor."

Clara stopped. "You're going to have a baby with a sperm donor?"

"I've made an initial appointment just to get information about the process."

She wanted to be happy for her friend. Indie would make an amazing mother, and she'd wanted this for so long. But the idea of her doing it without Colt just felt wrong.

"You think it's crazy," Indie said.

"No. Absolutely not. I just…I always thought you and Colt would enter the parenting world together."

Grief cut through Indie's eyes.

Crap. Wrong thing to say.

"But," she rushed to add, "you'll be an amazing mother, and I'll support you on any path you take. You want me to help pick a baby daddy from a printed bio? I'm there. You want help with IVF injections? I'm great with needles."

Tears shone in Indie's eyes, but she blinked them back. "Thank you. You're the first person I've told."

"I'm on your side, always, crazy ideas and all."

"Thank you." Indie wiped her eyes and started walking again.

"Maybe you can choose a guy with super-sperm."

"Super-sperm?"

"Yeah. Fast swimmers. Aggressive little guys who really attack the egg."

Indie laughed. "I'm not sure that will be in the bios."

"It should be."

When they reached The Tea House, they were just stepping

inside when Indie's phone rang. She looked down at the screen. "It's Noah."

"Talk to him. I'll order you a chai spiced latte."

"Thanks."

Indie walked over to a quiet corner while Clara found Holden at a table with her brothers and their partners.

The second her gaze met Holden's, she was hit by the same things she was always hit with. Love. Protection. And a bit of disbelief that they'd actually made it.

God, she was grateful to have him.

He rose from his seat and she stepped into his arms. "Hey, you."

He watched her expression. "Hey. You took too long."

"Miss me?"

"Always." He frowned at the flowers in her hand. "I thought you got lilies?"

"I swapped with Indie. Do you like the roses?"

"I do. But I like you more."

She grinned. "You sweet talker."

"For you, I'll be any kind of talker you like." He lowered his head and kissed her. "You know I love you, right?"

"I know. But you can say it again."

"I love you."

Her smile softened. "I love you too, Holden Forbes." She lifted to her toes. "So...damn...much."

Then she kissed him again, letting his lips soften hers, loving the way his body warmed every inch of her.

"Hey. I'm trying to enjoy my coffee. I don't need to watch my sister get pawed over by a guy I consider a brother."

Clara laughed as she dropped her heels and looked at Becket. "You can still enjoy your coffee while I kiss Holden."

"I absolutely cannot."

Jesse sighed. "He's right, Clara. To us, you'll always be our ten-year-old little sister."

She rolled her eyes and lowered to a seat, and Holden sat beside her, but his hand immediately went to her knee beneath the table.

A second later, Indie returned, her face paler than it had been seconds earlier.

Clara stood. "Indie, what is it?"

"It was Noah. He, uh, he's coming home."

"Oh my gosh, that's great. So why don't you look happy?"

Indie liked her brother. They had a good relationship, even though he was away ninety percent of the time. It was her sister she didn't get along with.

"Colt's coming home too," Indie said quietly.

Clara frowned. They were both Marines but assigned to different units. Maybe their discharge dates had lined up.

"And Noah asked me how I'd feel about them reopening the old Wilderness Adventure Park together."

"You're joking." She hadn't even known the two men had remained in contact.

Indie shook her head. "I am not. He said he'd kill the idea if I don't like it."

"What did you say?"

"Nothing for the first ten seconds...then I said it was fine."

"But it's *not* fine." In what universe would her brother and her ex starting a business together be fine?

"I was in shock. But even if I wasn't, I shouldn't be the one to stop them. If they both want to do it, then they want to do it. It has nothing to do with me."

That wasn't true, and they all knew it.

"It'll be fine," Indie repeated, as if trying to convince herself. Then she breathed out three words, the disbelief ringing through her voice. "Colt's coming home."

CHAPTER 33

$\mathcal{C}$olt Reed watched the familiar streets pass outside the window.

Home. Finally. And not just for a short stay between missions. He was home for good.

He hadn't told many people he was coming back. His mom, Noah...that was it. He'd tried to call Indie, but she hadn't answered, just like she hadn't answered any of his other calls over the last year.

But he was back now. And he was going to make things right with his wife.

His phone rang, and he didn't need to look at the screen to know it was his mother. She'd known what time his flight got in, and even though he'd told her he was making a stop first, she'd probably call another couple times before he actually got to her place.

What would Indie say when he saw her tonight? She'd be surprised, but would she be happy?

His mind went back to the night she'd told him it was over. He still remembered the disbelief...the pain he'd felt in every muscle of his body.

He fucking *hated* remembering that. The tears in her eyes had gutted him.

There were so many things he wished he'd done differently that night.

Well, now he was planning to make up for it.

He pulled up on the street. Not directly in front of their house, but a house back. Why, exactly, he wasn't sure. Maybe a part of him was scared that if she saw him coming, she might not answer the door.

Shit, that thought hurt. There'd once been a time she'd have run out of the house and jumped into his arms.

But that was before the strain of years of infertility combined with him being away for his job had taken its toll on them.

He scanned the exterior of the old house. Their second home. They'd bought it when Indie's best friend and cousin had gotten sick. Or at least, that was the reason Indie had given for wanting to buy it. But there was a deeper reason...a reason he'd realized too late.

Indie's mental health had been struggling with the IVF and the distance from her family...and he hadn't done a thing about it.

He should have realized earlier. He should have done something to be there for her.

He was about to climb out of his car when his phone rang, Noah's name on the screen. Even though Indie had separated from him a year ago, her brother, also a Marine, had kept in contact. Now he and Noah were ending their active service with the Marine Corps at the same time.

He pressed the phone to his ear. "Noah, hey. How's the last few weeks of transition going?"

"Strange. I can't believe this chapter of my life is coming to an end."

"I know what you mean. We spent so long giving our entire lives to something. It's hard to picture life after."

"You're not wrong." There was a small pause. "I spoke to Indie about the Wilderness Adventure Park today."

His chest tightened just at the sheer fucking mention of her name. "And?"

"She said she was okay with it…"

"But?"

"But I think she needs some time to wrap her head around it." Noah cleared his throat. "You know you're a good friend, but she's my sister—"

"Say the word, and we kill the idea."

"I don't want to kill it just yet. I just think we should move slowly, for Indie's sake. I know you're back in town tonight, but I think you should wait to see her. Give her some time to get used to the idea of you being back."

His fingers tightened around the phone. That was the last damn thing he wanted. Every part of him craved to be close to her. To hear her voice. To feel the softness of her skin.

"I know you're itching to go to her," Noah continued. "Just not tonight. Not after she just found out you're home."

He leaned his head back and closed his eyes, hating that he was going to have to wait longer. "Okay." The word was almost a growl.

"Thank you. Are you all right?"

"Yeah. I'm staying at Mom's tonight." Although, he was already regretting that decision. If he wasn't going to see Indie, he didn't really feel like talking to anyone, and all his mother *did* was talk.

"Good. Hey, I've got to go, but I'll see you soon."

"See you soon, brother." Colt hung up and looked back at her house.

It had been Colt's idea to reopen the Wilderness Adventure Park. The place had shut down ten years ago, but when it had been open, it was popular, offering zip-lining, rock climbing, mountain bike trails, and a few other activities. The owners had gone out of business, but shit, Colt had good memories of the place.

Colt had expected Noah to say no. He hadn't. And a part of Colt—probably the stupidly optimistic part—thought it was because he knew, just like Colt, that his and Indie's marriage wasn't over. When he'd married her, it had been for life. And he was going to do anything and everything to get her back.

He was about to start the engine when a familiar Subaru Crosstrek passed him before pulling into her driveway. The door opened—and Colt's breath stopped.

Indie.

The blond highlights in her hair shimmered in the light, giving her a radiant, golden glow. And when she turned her head and he got a look at her face, he was thrown back in time. To when life made sense. When he had her and they were happy and he'd thought nothing could break them.

He still loved her. He'd loved her since the day he first lay eyes on her.

They weren't over. They would *never* be over. She was his wife, and he was going to make damn sure everyone knew it.

Order book four, Colt and Indie's story, UNBROKEN, now!

ALSO BY NYSSA KATHRYN

PROJECT ARMA SERIES

Uncovering Project Arma

Luca

Eden

Asher

Mason

Wyatt

Bodie

Oliver

Kye

BLUE HALO SERIES

Logan

Jason

Blake

Flynn

Aidan

Tyler

Callum

Liam

MERCY RING

Jackson

Declan

Cole

Ryker

BEAUTIFUL PIECES

Erik's Salvation

Erik's Redemption

Erik's Refuge

SHORT CHRISTMAS STORY

Hidden Shadows

RECKLESS SERIES

Reckless Hope

Reckless Trust

Reckless Fall

Reckless Faith

Reckless Love

AMBER RIDGE SERIES

(Series ongoing)

Unafraid

Unraveled

Untouched

Unbroken

JOIN my newsletter and be the first to find out about sales and new releases! CLICK HERE

ABOUT THE AUTHOR

Nyssa Kathryn is a romantic suspense author. She lives in South Australia with hubby and two daughters and takes every chance she can to be plotting and writing. Always an avid reader of romance novels, she considers alpha males and happily-ever-afters to be her jam.

Don't forget to follow Nyssa and never miss another release.

Facebook | Instagram | Amazon | Goodreads

www.ingramcontent.com/pod-product-compliance
Lightning Source LLC
Chambersburg PA
CBHW050555190726
48283CB00007B/2148